HEALING THE MOUNTAIN MAN'S HEART

BROTHERS OF SAPPHIRE RANCH

BOOK ONE

MISTY M. BELLER

Misty M. Beller
BOOKS

Cover design by Evelyne Labelle at Carpe Librum Book Design: www.carpelibrumbookdesign.com

ISBN-13 Trade Paperback: 978-1-954810-63-1

ISBN-13 Large Print Paperback: 978-1-954810-64-8

ISBN-13 Casebound Hardback: 978-1-954810-65-5

*"Look at the nations and watch—
and be utterly amazed.
For I am going to do something in your days
that you would not believe,
even if you were told."*

Habakkuk 1:5 (NIV)

CHAPTER 1

The wildness of this mountain territory should make Dinah Wyatt turn and usher her sister right back to Fort Benton and the first steamship to the States. But something in this grandeur—the wide open blue sky, the pine-covered slopes rising on either side, the narrow creek murmuring beside the path where she and Naomi rode—brought to life a part of her she hadn't known lay dormant. This late-summer day wasn't hot and muggy like Virginia. The sun felt glorious, and a light breeze cooled any excess heat.

This would be the perfect place for Naomi to settle, if her new husband was a good man like he sounded in his advertisement.

Of course, a man could easily lie on paper, even easier than with his lips.

But his heartfelt words had encouraged them to seek God's direction about whether Naomi was the right bride for him. The two of them had done that. Dinah herself had spent many

1

hours beseeching the Lord—first begging for answers about why Naomi had let herself yield to temptation in the first place, then why God had felt it necessary for that sin to produce a child. When she prayed about whether this trip to the Montana Territory had been the right direction for them both, she'd finally felt a peace. A settling in her spirit that she could cling to when the doubts crept in.

As they did now.

She forced herself to ease out a long breath. They were so very far from home and all they'd ever known. Not that Naomi could stay in Wayneston anymore, and Dinah wasn't about to allow her to take this journey alone. They'd been born together —only three minutes apart—and the one night Dinah had abandoned her sister, the worst had happened to her. She wouldn't make that mistake again.

Now both she and Naomi would learn the true character of the man they'd both traveled nearly three months for Naomi to marry—if they ever found this Coulter Ranch he'd described.

Dinah straightened in her saddle and steeled her resolve. She would make sure Jericho Coulter would be a suitable match for her sister and a good father for the coming babe before she found her own place in this land. Hopefully, there was a quiet town nearby that wasn't consumed with gold fever, a town where she could hang out a shingle for her clinic.

A grunt from behind made her turn.

Naomi smiled from her own saddle, but the look made Dinah's chest tighten. She was more than six months into her term, and she'd swelled so much during the last part of their journey. So many hours in the saddle since they left the steamboat in Fort Benton three weeks ago had taken its toll. How much more could Naomi endure?

Dinah made sure they only rode half days, allowing Naomi plenty of time to rest with her legs propped up. Still, the bloating had increased. The puffiness in her face made it appear she'd doubled her weight. And panic had twisted in Dinah's chest when Naomi hadn't been able to squeeze her feet into boots. At least she'd felt the babe move again that morning. But surely the mother's suffering would have an effect on the unborn child. Her sister desperately needed time to rest in bed. Days, or maybe weeks, on her back with her feet raised on pillows.

If they didn't find that respite for Naomi at the ranch, what could they do? Maybe they should set up camp beside this stream and settle in until Naomi's swelling lessened.

Lord, let us reach this ranch today. Let Jericho Coulter be the man my sister needs. A man who will care for her as the treasure she is. And her baby too.

She guided her gelding as the path crossed the creek, the animal's hooves splashing in the shallow water. Behind her, Naomi's horse crashed with a heavier stride, dislodging pebbles with each step.

"Look."

The tension in her sister's voice made Dinah jerk her gaze up to the trail in front of them.

About twenty strides away, a figure stepped from the trees. He wore a leather costume similar to many they'd seen since Fort Benton. From this distance, she couldn't make out features, only broad shoulders and a bearded face.

Did he have weapons? At least he wasn't brandishing a gun that she could see.

Could this be Naomi's intended? Her pulse picked up speed. She couldn't tell his age yet, but he didn't look as respectable as she'd hoped.

He watched them approach. When they'd closed half the distance between them, he raised his chin. "You need something?"

She fought the urge to glance at her sister. Instead, she made her voice sound friendly. "We're looking for the Coulter Ranch."

Should they say who they were? Better to find Mr. Coulter first.

He studied them, his scrutinizing gaze doing its best to make her nervous, though she fought the feeling. "What do you want there?"

Before she could answer, Naomi reined her horse up beside Dinah's. "I'm here to be Mr. Jericho Coulter's wife."

Dinah tensed, cringing inside. Just because Naomi had made peace with her situation as a mail order bride didn't mean Mr. Coulter wanted his private affairs broadcast to all his neighbors.

A flash of surprise flickered in the man's dark gaze. Then he sobered, eyeing them warily. "Jericho's not looking for a wife, and this isn't the Coulter ranch."

Dinah frowned. He sounded insulted. He could at least point them in the right direction.

She opened her mouth to ask, but Naomi cut in once more. "Can you tell us where to find him? He sent for us—for me— and we've come all this way to accept his proposal."

Dinah slid a look to tell her to hold her tongue, but as Naomi met her gaze, a shout echoed in the distance.

She spun to find the source, somewhere in the trees the man had stepped from.

Again, the voice came, far enough away she had to struggle to distinguish words. "Help...hurt."

She couldn't make out the name spoken.

The man in front of them turned and charged back into the trees.

Dinah's chest thundered and she plunged her heels into her gelding's sides. If there were injuries, they would need her.

As she rode through the woods, she had to duck under branches and swerve around trunks. Her horse caught up with the man quickly, and she reined down to a trot to follow.

At last, the forest opened into a clearing, where two horses were hitched to a wagon. A man knelt beside the rig, and the stranger she'd been following sprinted to his side.

A body lay before them. Not moving, from what she could tell.

She reined her horse hard and jumped to the ground. Naomi rode up behind her, and Dinah called out as she ran to the patient. "Naomi, get my case."

The men knelt on one side, so she positioned herself on his other.

The man they'd met at the stream held out one arm. "Lady, you'd better—"

"I'm a doctor." She had no time for the fellow's opinions, so she started her assessment. The patient's chest rose and fell in a steady rhythm. Harder than a resting rate, which could happen due to pain or shock.

Dinah looked at the man who'd been here at first. "What happened to him?"

"The wagon backed over him. I think over his leg. Not sure why he won't wake up." His voice sounded frantic.

She scanned the length of the injured man for blood. None visible, his face had paled, and a sheen of sweat glimmered on his skin.

She turned her attention to his lower half. His leather trousers bulged in the middle of his left thigh. She ran her fingers over the spot, and the man flinched, even in his unconscious state. A fracture in the body of the femur most likely. Not good, but at least no damage to other limbs that she could see.

A sneaking suspicion began to creep in. She slid a look to his face again, then pressed fingers to his cheek.

Cold and clammy. She shifted those fingers to the carotid artery in his neck. Pulse light, but racing. That matched her own heart rate, but she wasn't in nearly the same condition as this man.

Naomi was out of breath as she dropped down at her side

with the medical case and began unfastening the buckles to open the pouch.

She needed to make sure her sister didn't overtax herself through this emergency, but the man before them was in far more danger at present. His body had begun to tremble. "He needs blankets."

"I'll get mine." Naomi pushed to her feet.

She glanced at the two men kneeling across from her. "I need to see this leg. Does either of you have a knife?" She could cut his pants open at the thigh with her surgical blade, but she'd rather not dirty it if there was another tool available.

Both men studied her, gazes wary, their looks so similar they had to be brothers. The man who'd found them at the creek must be the elder, unless the thick growth of beard simply made him look so. The other fellow wore his beard much shorter.

Neither man offered up a knife.

Frustration clenched inside her. "I'm not going to cut his leg open, I just need to see inside the pant leg to tell if the bone pierced the skin."

The older brother's gaze narrowed even more.

She glared. "I'm a doctor. I've served six years at the side of Richmond's finest physician. I know what I'm doing here. If I don't work quickly, this man could bleed to death. Maybe we'll be lucky enough that the bone broke through the skin and the blood is flowing out. Otherwise he's bleeding internally, and I'll need to make an incision to release the flow before his organs drown in bone marrow."

The younger looked to his brother, questioning, but Scruffy Beard never took his eyes off her face. Thankfully, he finally withdrew a hunting knife from his waistband and held it out to her.

She grabbed the handle and moved in to slice the leather encasing the injured thigh. The blade was sharp, so it cut through the leather without catching.

"Here are blankets." Naomi dropped the load of covers beside her.

Dinah didn't shift her focus from parting the buckskin. "Cover his upper body to get him warm."

When she had a full view of the bulging thigh, her insides clenched. The skin wasn't pierced, and it had turned dark purple and swollen to twice the size of her fist. She had to let out the blood pooling in there. She'd need to set the bone, too, so an incision would have to be made and soon.

She raised her head to study the landscape around them. "Is there a house? Somewhere close we can take him?" Hopefully a place that would be more sanitary than here in the dirt.

The men looked at each other again, then the older brother spoke. "We can take him in the wagon to the house. It's about a half hour up the mountain."

She eyed the conveyance beside them. Bumping in that would move the bone even more, perhaps pinching the femoral artery, which would practically ensure the man bled out if she didn't stop the problem immediately.

She searched the area for another option, and her gaze caught on a wooden structure tucked into the edge of the woods. "What about that? Is it clean inside?"

"No." For once, the bushy-beard man answered quickly. "It's dirty and full. There's no floor."

That wouldn't do then. She turned back to her patient and his swollen purple leg. "I need a blanket to put under this."

The brothers helped her lift the leg while she held the broken section, then slipped the cloth under. While they worked, she gave Naomi instructions for what to pull out of her case. Her bag held enough basic supplies that she would be able to bandage the incision and splint the legs together. That should hold until they got the man back to his house.

At last, she took out her surgical blade and pulled the cut leather farther back from the swollen area.

"Wait." The older brother spoke, and she looked up at him.

His dark eyes studied her, worry darkening them even more. "What are you going to do?"

Of course he would want the details. Back in Wayneston, she would have taken time to inform the patient's family of her plans. She lowered the blade. "See this dark area? His femur—um, thigh bone—is broken. It's a break significant enough to release blood and marrow from inside the bone, and it's pooling beneath the skin. I'm going to make an incision, release the blood so it doesn't spread into his organs and drown them, and then set the bone pieces back into place. After that, I'll suture the incision and tie his legs together as a brace until we get him to his bed." She'd need to reset the leg with traction at that point, but she could explain when the time came.

She turned to Naomi. "Can you prepare a needle and thread?"

Naomi reached for the supplies, so Dinah returned her focus to her patient. Though his eyes remained closed, he flinched and shifted around a bit. Probably the pain and blood loss kept him from being fully aware of what was happening. That would work in his benefit for this next part.

She leveled a serious look at both men. She'd need their help. "Hold his shoulders and feet so he doesn't move. One of you at each end, please."

The men positioned themselves as requested. Before she began, she lifted her eyes to the heavens.

Guide my hands, Lord. Let me do good, not harm.

CHAPTER 2

*B*ile rose in Jericho Coulter's throat as he watched the blade pierce his brother's bruised flesh. It wasn't the sight of the blood gushing through the slitted skin that made him want to cast up his accounts.

Jonah could die.

This couldn't be how his baby brother's life ended. Yet, inadequacy snaked around Jericho's neck. For nine years now, he'd done his best to keep his siblings alive. Ever since their parents succumbed to illness, he'd battled one challenge after another. He'd failed Lucy, and now this single slip-up might cost Jonah his life.

Jonah shifted beneath Jericho's grip, and Jericho tore his gaze from the flow of blood that thankfully slowed. He looked down at the boy's face. His brother was no longer a boy, though, not at twenty-two. With his skin as pale as snow, he didn't look sturdy enough to be called a man.

"It's all right now. You're gonna feel a lot better soon." He could only pray those words would be true. *If* he was a praying man. Which he hadn't been for a while.

He lifted his gaze to the doctor. A woman doctor, so she'd

claimed. Certainly, she hadn't hesitated to take charge of Jonah's injury. Only a person experienced in medicine would dive in the way she had. That confidence was the only reason he'd allowed her to do all she was doing.

Did she truly have the skills to set the leg correctly? If this was a break to the thighbone, as it looked to be, placing the bone correctly could make the difference in whether it could ever bear weight again.

Back in Fort Scott, a man in town once fell from the second story of the West Hotel and broke his thighbone. After it healed, he'd never been able to walk without a cane. Would the same thing happen to Jonah?

The thought shot a jolt of fear through Jericho's veins. Jonah would be miserable restrained like that.

But he kept a tight hold on his brother's shoulders while the doctor continued her bloody task. Her mouth set in a grim line as she adjusted the leg, her fingers disappearing inside the wound, probably moving the bone around.

How did she learn such procedures?

Jonah stopped shifting beneath his hands, maybe passed out from the pain. Jericho's own body trembled.

God, if You're looking down on this, help my brother. Don't let us lose him.

Had the doctor been right that his brother could bleed out from a broken bone? A river of crimson had run from the leg, pooling in the blanket before it soaked through the fabric.

At last, the woman straightened and blew out a breath, wiping the hair from her face with the back of her arm. "There. Now I'll stitch and bandage, then splint the legs together."

She glanced at Jonah's face, but she gave no hint of what she thought about his brother's blanched skin.

Then she lifted her gaze to Jericho, and the intensity in her blue eyes struck him just as it had every other time she'd looked at him. This woman did nothing in half measure.

"I think he's passed out, so you don't need to hold him. You can prepare transportation to take him home."

He kept his own expression from showing his surprise at the stark words. She was simply stating the facts. He should appreciate that.

Turning to Jude, he nodded to the wagon, using his eyes to silently ask if there was room to lay Jonah. They'd been in the process of loading crates when he'd heard Crowley's shrill cry that strangers were around.

Jude moved to the rear of the wagon. He would clear a spot. They had no blankets, but hopefully these women would allow them to lay Jonah on the quilts they'd covered him with.

At last, the doctor finished her bandage and, using a long strip of cloth, tied Jonah's legs together in four different places. She straightened and looked around, probably checking to make sure they'd accomplished her instructions.

He nodded toward the wagon. "We have a place to lay him."

With the doctor lady giving directions, they shifted the blanket beneath Jonah so it could act as a stretcher. Then he and Jude lifted him, hoisting him over the side of the wagon.

Crates still lined the other side of the conveyance. It would have been better if Jude had moved all the boxes back into the storage building, but that would have drawn attention to the shed. In case these women ever discovered what the Coulter family actually did on their property, he certainly didn't want them to know where the crates were kept.

He nodded to Jude. "Can you drive?" Jericho would stay in the back with Jonah. Especially since the doctor was already climbing up beside him.

Her sister held the reins of their two horses, and looked like she might need help mounting. The women certainly bore a resemblance, but this one carried a few more pounds than the doctor.

He took the animals' reins from her and received her thanks

with a nod. He'd have thought she would be able to mount on her own, given the fact that they were traveling alone out here in the mountain wilderness of the Montana Territory. But after she struggled to lift her leg up to the stirrup, then gave an unsuccessful hop that was probably intended to pull herself into the saddle, he moved in.

"Here. Put your boot in my hand."

She didn't argue, just removed her left foot from the stirrup and placed it in his cupped palms. As she pulled herself up, he lifted, and though he had to endure a face-full of skirts, they managed to get her into the saddle.

She was breathing hard as she settled. "Thank you. That's getting harder every day."

Strange thing to say. He nodded and helped her gather her reins, then handed over the leathers for the horse she would lead. A few months in this land would slim her down, no doubt. Food was too hard to come by out here to overindulge.

He turned to the wagon and climbed in as Jude started the team moving. The doctor woman—he should find out her name —sat in the only open spot beside Jonah, so Jericho settled onto the crates.

He needn't have worried about her scrutinizing the boxes in the wagon. She kept her attention locked on Jonah, glancing from his bandaged leg to his pale face. His mouth puckered in a frown, but he showed no other sign of wakefulness. Was that good?

Jericho certainly didn't want him to be in pain, but wasn't his being unconscious for this long even more concerning? Would this doctor know? If she possessed any experience in her profession, she should.

He gripped the side of the wagon as the wheels bounced over a low boulder mostly covered by dirt. "Why hasn't he woken up?"

"He's lost a lot of blood, and the pain has caused a shock to his system. Once his body rests and makes new blood, he should be more alert."

She looked up at Jericho, her expression serious. "Do you have a place he can lie without being disturbed? A clean bed. He'll need foods to rebuild his blood too. Liver, or any kind of meat, really. Greens, nuts, and beans."

He nodded, his mind scanning the few crates of supplies they had left. "We've plenty of meat. There might be some beans too." It'd been a few weeks since it was his turn to oversee the cooking, and even longer since he'd made a supply run to Missoula Mills.

The woman frowned but refocused her attention on Jonah's leg.

The half hour ride felt like it stretched two hours, but at last they rolled into the yard.

Sampson poked his head from the barn, and when he saw the women, he stepped all the way out, striding forward.

Jericho jumped to the ground as his second-to-youngest brother met them. "Go to my room and see things are straightened. Jonah's hurt, and we're going to bring him into the bed there." He glanced toward the quiet house. "Where are Sean and Lillian?"

"They went with the others to handle the foals."

Maybe that was for the best. The children didn't need to see all this blood, though Lillian would have been a help in getting Jonah settled.

As Sampson sprinted to the house to obey, Jericho turned his attention to helping Jude lift their brother's limp body from the wagon. Jude carried the blanket at Jonah's head and led the way into the house. The doctor woman followed right behind Jericho, clearly feeling it her duty to stay with her patient.

Or maybe she was using him as an excuse to invite herself into their cabin. What had she said? That one of them was coming to be his bride?

What kind of hogwash was that? A woman was the very last thing he would invite onto their ranch. Or rather...a *wife*.

He could deal with that ill-begotten notion in a bit. For now, they had to get Jonah comfortable so he could start recovering. Unfortunately, it seemed they'd be beholden to the doctor woman for help with that task.

∼

Dinah adjusted Jonah's leg, carefully straightening the femur now that he was settled in the bed. She would need to create some type of traction to extend the leg so his fractured bone could heal without any further displacement. And hopefully that would help the femur maintain its original length and minimize any permanent limp.

The bed frame was made of logs, with a rough-hewn footboard just high enough to work perfectly.

She had enough bandages in her supplies to wrap the ankle, though she might need more later when the incision had healed enough to add a splint. "What will I use for weight though?" She eyed his leg. She'd have to gauge that once everything else was in place.

As she turned to send someone for her case, Naomi's quiet presence near the door grabbed her focus.

Dinah frowned. "You need to be sitting with your feet up."

Naomi offered a weary half-smile. "I'm fine."

Dinah turned to the man who'd first found them by the creek. She still didn't know his name, and maybe that needed to be remedied before anything else. "Who are you, sir?"

He opened his mouth to speak, then paused. Something flashed across his face. Something like uncertainty.

Then he closed his mouth, and determination replaced anything else he might have displayed. "Jericho Coulter, ma'am."

She nearly choked on her breath. This was Naomi's intended? She couldn't help a quick glance down his grubby clothes. He was much younger than she'd first supposed. No more than thirty, surely.

But...he didn't appear to be what she'd call respectable. Not with his shoulder-length hair loose and a beard covering most of his face. He still wore his hat, even in the house, and though his leather clothing disguised any dirt, she had a feeling he was covered in plenty of grime.

She turned back to her patient so she could gather her thoughts. They could worry about matters of the heart later. For now, she had two patients who needed care.

"Can you please bring a chair for my sister? And my case from the wagon? I'll need the larger bundle that's tied behind my saddle too." She kept her gaze toward the bed but listened for his footsteps to signal he'd obeyed.

As he left the room, she moved to her patient's head and lifted his eyelids to check their color. Would it be better to give laudanum now to see if bringing his pain down made him more alert? But that almost seemed unkind, to wake him so he could experience the agony. Perhaps letting his body take the lead in this situation would be best. He could rest better like this.

A moment later, the scrape of the outer door sounded in the front room. All had been quiet from there, but now a host of voices sounded, some of them young.

She met her sister's gaze, but Naomi looked too exhausted to worry about who might be entering. Maybe they had another bedchamber she could rest in.

A young man poked his head through the doorway, his gaze landing on the man in the bed. Then he stepped in and nodded to Dinah. He saw Naomi tucked behind the open door and offered her a nod, too, before his gaze roamed back to Jonah.

15

"How is he?" His voice came out quiet, as though he didn't want to wake the sleeping man.

"In pain. He needs a great deal of rest and time to heal. I pray he'll make a full recovery, but time will tell if he lost too much blood."

Jericho entered, with a chair in one hand and her case in the other, her pack thrown over his shoulder.

The younger man removed his hat, as though coming to his senses. "My name's Gilead Coulter. Most folks call me Gil."

Mr. Jericho Coulter set the chair behind Naomi, so Dinah shifted her focus to Mr. Gilead Coulter. "I'm Dr. Dinah Wyatt, and this is my sister, Miss Naomi Wyatt." Naomi had already written of her condition in letters to Jericho, so there was no need to hide her unwed state.

Her gaze moved to that man before she could stop it. "You two share a common surname." She could assume they were brothers, but they might share a different relationship.

Mr. Gilead Coulter nodded. "Brothers, all of us. Jer is the oldest, then Jonah." He nodded toward the bed. "Next is Jude. I think he helped bring Jonah back. I'm fourth in line, then Sampson. You might have met him too. Miles is the baby. He'll be here in a minute."

Was he the young voice she'd heard? That high-pitched voice had sounded a great deal younger than these other brothers.

Another face peeked in the doorway, fair and feminine. "Can we come in?"

Gilead glanced back. "This is Lillian. She and her brother Sean are our sister's children." He motioned for the girl to enter.

She stepped in, revealing herself to be somewhere around nine or ten years old. The boy behind her shared the same flaxen mop of hair and appeared younger, but only by a year or two.

Dinah smiled at them both. "It's nice to meet you, Miss Lillian. Master Sean." She reached for her belongings, which

Jericho still held. "I'm going to wrap your Uncle Jonah's leg so it can heal properly. Perhaps you'd like to help."

Some physicians wouldn't welcome children in a sickroom, but Pop had invited her in when she'd come running to him at the tender age of five. She'd never have discovered this calling if not for him and his willingness to share his knowledge.

As she pulled out her supplies, she talked through the medical names of each. Then she explained her actions as she placed her stretchiest bandage around her patient's heel and wrapped another strip of cloth around and around the ankle and calf. "This needs to be tight enough that it won't slip when a little pressure is applied, but not so tight it hinders blood flow." The poor man needed all the blood flowing through him they could allow.

She glanced up to see what the others were doing. A crowd had gathered between the door and the footboard. All men. The room felt so much smaller than it had seconds before.

She swallowed down her nerves and returned her attention to her work.

She didn't speak again until Sean's little voice sounded. "Will he be able to get out of bed?"

"When his leg heals." The lad probably only meant to ask if the cloth she was wrapping around the footboard would require his uncle to stay on the mattress, but the question struck her in the larger sense. Would Jonah Coulter ever be able to rise? If he recovered from the blood loss and didn't develop a lung condition from lying abed so long, would his leg heal enough to support him?

Lord, give me wisdom. She'd successfully worked with Pop to help two other patients heal from a similar break, and both had eventually recovered enough to walk with only a slight limp—a year later. Both patients had been willing to put forth the effort to regain their strength and movement. They'd had to struggle for every skill they re-learned.

Would Jonah Coulter be willing to fight—day in and day out, battling against his flesh to build up his strength and movement? If he didn't, these men would think the fault was hers.

Her reputation in this land as a capable doctor would be tainted. Her clinic would be doomed before she could even hang her shingle.

And Naomi. Would Naomi be welcome here? If Dinah failed to bring their brother back to his former abilities, would they be so angry at her that Jericho would refuse to marry her sister?

She barely held in a snort. He'd already refused.

As soon as she finished adjusting the weight hanging over the footboard for proper traction, she would find a place for Naomi to rest.

Then, she'd have a talk with Jericho Coulter and find out the truth about the advertisement he'd placed.

CHAPTER 3

*N*ow was the time.

Dinah tucked the worn paper in her skirt pocket, then stepped from the little bed chamber and pulled the door closed.

Apparently, there were only two rooms off the main living area in this little cabin. One where Jonah rested, and the other where the two children slept. Naomi now laid on one of the narrow, lumpy cots in that chamber. The way the mattress sank in the middle, it hadn't taken much to prop her feet up high enough to be above her heart. When Dinah had a moment, she'd tighten the bed ropes beneath both mattresses.

Just now, though, she needed to have a candid conversation with Mr. Jericho Coulter.

He stood with Lillian at a work counter on the far end of the room, chopping something as the girl watched. When Dinah approached, he looked up, meeting her gaze with wary eyes.

Best be straightforward. "May I speak with you privately, Mr. Coulter?" She offered Lillian a brief smile. "I'll only take him for a moment." Hopefully they wouldn't need long to sort through his behavior by the creek and what should happen with her sister's future.

If he was a man of his word, they could simply clear up whatever caused the misunderstanding and decide how to move forward. Naomi would want to be part of any conversation that included plans for their nuptials of course, but it might be best that Dinah get things to that point without putting her sister's tender feelings in peril.

The man spoke something to his niece, his deep voice rumbling too low for her to make out the words. Then he turned and strode toward the front door.

He didn't motion for Dinah to follow but didn't tell her to stay put either. She strode after him.

When she'd descended the single log step to the barren ground in front of the cabin, he spun and braced his hands at his waist. "Well?"

This was their privacy? She glanced toward the barn. She'd left one of the brothers—Gilead—to keep watch by Jonah's bed. That meant three more must be out here somewhere, as well as the boy. If they were with the animals, could they hear the conversation taking place twenty strides away?

She squared her shoulders. It was Jericho's business whether he wanted his kin to overhear. An audience wouldn't change what she had to say.

She met his gaze squarely. "I find it interesting you didn't give your name when we met you by the creek."

He didn't answer, nor did the guarded expression on his face change. His only acknowledgement of her words was the way he tipped his head the smallest bit.

It seemed she would have to ask a direct question if she wanted a direct answer.

"Perhaps we weren't clear in our questions there. My sister and I have come from Virginia in response to the advertisement you placed. My *sister* is responding to the advertisement, that is."

She motioned toward the cabin. "You'll find she has all the qualifications you required, including the babe she'll give birth to in about three months." She worked for a smile. "We both prayed extensively and felt the Almighty's prompting that she was to make this journey. That her future lies here on the Coulter ranch."

Didn't it, Lord? Had they gotten things mixed up? Naomi's future certainly didn't lie back in Wayneston, that was for sure. Not after that one poor choice left her with a shame she'd never be able to overcome.

His defensive posture had turned even warier, if that were possible. "I know nothing of an advertisement." His words and tone asked what he didn't speak. *What in the wide open sky are you talking about?*

But they raised even more questions in her. Could he be telling the truth? Had someone else placed the advertisement on his behalf? Or...could there be another Jericho Coulter in this area? The ranch had been exactly where the advertisement said.

She eyed him. "You don't, by chance, have another family member named Jericho? An uncle or cousin?" There were certainly enough men with the surname Coulter around here.

He shook his head.

She sighed and reached into her pocket for the advertisement and held it out to him. As he took it, she wanted to grab the paper back. What if he became angry and ripped it to shreds? They would have no way to force him to honor his agreement.

But really, if he would ask a woman to come all this distance —a journey of three months from Virginia—then pretend he'd never placed the advertisement, she didn't want Naomi tied to him anyway.

As the man stared at the paper, it occurred to her to wonder if he could read. If he'd grown up in this remote mountain wilderness, he might not have had access to schooling.

But his gaze shifted from that wary look to something a bit more like shock. His eyes stayed on the paper long enough to read it through twice.

Finally, he raised his eyes to her. "I didn't place this advertisement."

She had to fight to keep from stepping backward in frustration. He sounded sincere. But someone had created that notice. "Who did then, sir? The *Richmond Gazette* didn't fabricate your name and location from the early morning fog."

He lowered his brows in a scowl. "I don't know." Then he swung around to the barn and bellowed, "Boys, get out here. Jude, Sampson, Miles. You too, Sean. Gilead and Lillian. I want everyone."

The explosion of words from the man who'd barely strung a half dozen into a sentence before made her want to shrink back. His anger couldn't be missed, but at least he was turning it on his family. For now.

She'd not thought to tuck her derringer into her skirt pocket when she came out here. She should have remembered it.

In truth, after she'd worked so hard on his brother's leg, she'd not expected to need protection from him.

At the barn, the three brothers and nephew charged out as though the house were on fire. A moment later, the door opened and Gilead stepped out. "What's wrong?" He held the door, giving Jericho a worried look.

Jericho Coulter only motioned him forward.

Gilead glanced back into the house and frowned. "Come on."

A reluctant Lillian shuffled out, her chin tipped down. Her frown made her look every bit the child she was. Poor thing, alone here with all these men. Where were the children's mother and father?

Once all had gathered except the injured brother and her own sleeping sister, Jericho held up the advertisement. "Who's responsible for this?"

The tense silence that followed made Dinah's middle clench into a knot.

"What is it, Jer?" Jude, the one who'd been with Jonah when he was injured, shuffled a step closer.

Jericho turned the paper so he could see it better. "It's an advertisement in the Personals section of the *Richmond Gazette*. I'll read it to you. 'A good man living in the Montana Territory seeks a God-fearing wife. Must be of strong character and not afraid of hard work. Even better if she is a mother, as I am eager to start a family. I am trusting that the Almighty will carry this advertisement to the wife He intends for me. If He is prompting you, travel west to Fort Benton, then follow the Mullan road past Helena. When you reach the gully at the base of the second mountain, turn left and follow the creek ten miles to the Coulter ranch. I will reimburse all travel expenses and provide a safe, comfortable home. Signed, Jericho Coulter.'"

She watched the men as he read. As far as she could tell, none of the brothers seemed to be trying to conceal a secret smile. The shock in their expressions couldn't be feigned. Except for Gil. His mouth did tip in a grin, but even that looked more like humor at something so outlandish it couldn't be real.

Jericho's voice broke the silence. "I'm not going to ask again. Who placed this advertisement?"

Dinah glanced at the boy, Sean. His face held a pinched look. Like a lad who expected to be called out by his mother for something, but wasn't sure what yet. Interesting.

A motion near the door caught her attention. Lillian still stood near the opening, holding the door in her hand. She seemed to be trying to slide behind it, maybe to escape into the house. She glanced at her brother, shifting another inch. The boy sidled toward his sister.

Something definitely wasn't right with these two.

"Lillian." Jericho's bold voice sliced through the air, and the girl jumped. Her reaction made Dinah's own heartbeat catch, and she turned to see how the man intended to ferret out the truth.

Would he hurt the children? Part of her wanted to edge forward and put herself between them. But she was close enough she could spring forward and grab him if he charged. Surely he wouldn't though. Neither child bore any sign of bruises or ill-treatment.

Though the girl's eyes, growing wide with fright as her uncle drew near, made Dinah tense.

"What do you know about this advertisement?" He barely lifted the paper.

Beside him, the boy seemed to be trying to scoot away while the focus was aimed at his sister.

Jericho never took his gaze from the girl. "Sean, stand here next to your sister."

When her brother moved beside her, Lillian finally gathered enough courage to speak. "We were tryin' to help. Mama said you weren't happy 'cause you didn't have a wife. Then a bunch of the miners were sendin' off for mail-order brides. We thought that would be perfect for you. Slops helped us write it, an' we made sure to put that she had to be God-fearin', 'cause Mama said that's what you needed more'n anythin'. And children too. Mama said she wanted you to have a whole passel of little-uns."

Lillian raised hopeful eyes to him in a look that would surely soften any person with a heart. "It'll all turn out right, Uncle Jericho. You'll see."

The girl's optimism made even Dinah want to believe her words, but the rock in her middle kept pulling her back to the truth.

Naomi wasn't wanted here.

Jericho Coulter hadn't placed that advertisement.

That left her sister still with a babe on the way and no prospects for a husband or a stable future, just as she'd been in

Wayneston. And now Naomi was also exhausted and unable to travel farther, stranded in this land, a three-month journey from their home and the grandparents, who might have been willing to support Naomi and the child, despite the ill effects to their reputation and to Pop's clinic.

Maybe these men would at least let her and Naomi stay on a week or so for her sister to rest. Dinah needed to care for Jonah's injury anyway. The incision would need care several times daily, and she'd have to adjust the amount of traction as the bone healed.

Jericho still hadn't eased the rigid line of his shoulders. His brows lowered, so his eyes were hard to see—except for the glint that must be anger. She couldn't make out the line of his mouth through the beard, but his jaw was surely locked tight. Would he strike the children?

But he used words, growling through that clamped jaw. "Do you have any idea how many lives you've affected by this stunt?" He motioned toward Dinah. "These two women traveled all the way from Virginia. Probably more than two months to get here. For nothing. They'll have to turn around and journey all that way back. Who knows if they can afford it?"

Dinah's heart pounded a little faster. They couldn't go back. Even if they had a decent prospect to return to, Naomi couldn't make the journey, not as her time became imminent.

Lillian peered up at her uncle with a half-penitent, half-hopeful expression. "You can give them the money. Or maybe they could stay instead. Uncle Jonah needs them, right?"

Dinah cleared her throat to gain the man's attention. This was her chance. When Jericho's gaze swung to her, she began. "She's right, actually. Your brother's leg will require a doctor's care for several weeks. And my sister needs a safe place to rest for at least that long. We don't have the means to travel back to Virginia, and it would be dangerous for my sister to attempt it in her condition. Perhaps we can stay on for a time. I'll care for your brother and help around the house"—she shot a meaningful glance toward the children—"in exchange for temporary room and board."

Jericho's eyes narrowed. "How long until your sister... reaches her...?" He trailed off, clearly not sure how to speak of Naomi's condition.

"The babe should come in November."

His eyes rounded. He must think she wanted to live here until then.

"We won't stay that long. Just a month or so until Naomi recovers her strength and your brother heals sufficiently to move around. I intend to open a clinic in a nearby town, so I'll be able to continue monitoring his recovery through regular appointments."

The tension hung thick in the air as she waited for Jericho's response. His expression—or what little she could see of his face —gave no sign of his decision.

At last, he spoke. "A week. We'll try it for a week. Then I'll decide if you stay longer." He raised the paper again. "But you will not be staying as mail-order brides. Is that clear?"

The man didn't have to be so heavy-handed. It wasn't as though she was asking for charity with no work in return. If she were charging for her services—for round-the-clock care of such an injury—he'd pay more than the little bit of food she and Naomi would eat.

She forced herself to nod instead of speaking her mind. "I understand." Perhaps she should say thank you, but she couldn't bring herself to.

At least they had a place where Naomi could rest, no matter how crude the dwelling. She glanced at the log walls. The outside was rustic, though not unappealing. It was the inside that needed work. A good cleaning to start with. Then some sprucing up.

She wouldn't accomplish it all in a week, not with caring for

Jonah and helping the children, but she could make a start. By then, Jericho would see how much better things looked with a woman's touch.

She turned toward the door. "Well then, I'd best tell my sister." Naomi would be crushed. Maybe Dinah had done wrong by allowing her to dream so much without injecting more warnings about all the ways this arrangement could go wrong.

Surely the two of them could manage on their own in this land. Once Dinah had her clinic set up, they would do just fine. All three of them, once the baby was born. They would live happy, independent lives. *Right, Lord? That must be what You planned all along.*

CHAPTER 4

*J*ericho waited until Miss Wyatt retreated into the house and closed the door behind her before he turned back to Lillian and Sean. What was he going to do with these two?

He gave them his sternest look. "Are there any other women we can expect to show up on our doorstep hoping for a husband?"

Lillian shrugged, still trying to play the innocent child. She clearly wasn't as naive as she pretended. "We don't know. We didn't want there to be a lot of letter-writing back an' forth, since that would take too long. So we just told 'em to come if they thought the Almighty was nudgin' em."

That was another thing. The advertisement made him sound like a white-robed saint who sat around all day listening for the voice of God. He and the Lord hadn't talked since Lucy ran off. What these children had fabricated was nothing but lies. Every word of it.

He crumbled the paper in his hand and spun. He needed to release this anger somewhere it wouldn't hurt anyone. But he had to deal with the children first.

He turned back to them. "You two need to understand what you've done. You've wasted these women's time and resources. That one is apparently in the family way, and the trip was too much for her. What if the baby dies? What if the woman dies?" He stepped closer to them, making sure they felt the weight of his words. "And what if they learn about the strawberries?" He used their code word for the real purpose of this ranch, the sapphires they secretly mined. "We don't allow other people onto the ranch for a reason. Do you understand the consequences of your actions?"

The children nodded, their faces pale and scared.

He softened his tone slightly. "I know you thought you were helping. But this is serious business. You can't go around playing matchmaker like it's a game. And you can't invite strangers onto the property."

Lillian's eyes filled with tears. "We didn't mean to cause trouble, Uncle Jericho. We just wanted you to be happy again."

His chest ached at the sight of her tears, but he couldn't let her or Sean think this was all just a game. "You two need to apologize to Miss Wyatt and her sister. Then you're going to work."

He looked to Sampson. "Have them scoop out the barn and the corrals. Then oil all the leather."

His brother nodded in his usual quiet way.

Jericho turned and started toward the barn while Sampson herded the children inside. He'd grab Pinto and ride down to check the stock in the west pasture. But maybe he should stay around the house to make sure the women didn't cause trouble. His brothers were here though. And he desperately needed to clear his head.

He glanced back at Jude. "Keep an eye on things. Send Miles for me in the west pasture if you need anything."

Jude nodded. His expression looked a little too close to

amused for Jericho's liking, but he ignored it. Jude would be careful. He always was.

Which was why it seemed so strange Jonah had been hurt as badly as he was with Jude in charge.

After slipping a halter on Pinto and swinging aboard, he urged the horse from the barn. The trail to the west pasture hadn't been traveled as much since they'd moved the mares and foals down to the valley, and he allowed Pinto his head over the familiar terrain.

Those children... They'd placed the advertisement back when they lived with Lucy, so this didn't necessarily show they'd grown worse since coming to the ranch. But though they sometimes needed a stronger hand to remind them of the rules here, he'd not thought they were capable of such trickery.

Their joke had uprooted two women's lives and brought them thousands of miles. What should he do with these Wyatt women now? He owed them far more than a week's room and board after they'd tended Jonah—maybe saved his life—but at least setting that parameter gave him an out in case things turned bad with them on the property.

He'd have to help them get back to their home, but when would the one in the family way be able to travel again? Heat swept up his neck at the reminder of how he'd simply thought her plump. That just went to show how bad he was at anything related to women. He'd messed things up in the worst way with his sister. Who knew what he'd do to muddle things with these two strangers?

But Miss...er, Dr. Wyatt was right that Jonah needed someone who knew what they were doing with an injury like that broken bone. He'd never heard of a female doctor, but she did seem to know how to tend Jonah's leg. Maybe she'd spent time as a doctor's assistant.

This coming week would allow him to learn more about her

and her sister. He could only hope he wouldn't regret letting them stay even that long.

~

*D*inah slipped into Naomi's room quietly in case she slept. Her sister lay without moving on the bed, but as Dinah approached, her eyelids lifted.

A knot twisted in Dinah's belly as she sat on the edge of the mattress. It sagged even more with her weight. If there was a chair in here, she would pull it over, but the room only held a single chest of drawers and the two narrow beds. If this was the children's room. Why were there not dresses and clothing lying around? And toys and books?

"What is it, D?"

She turned to her sister's weary face, concern adding wrinkles to the puffiness there, and tried for a smile. "I've had a talk with Mr. Coulter, and I'm afraid things aren't what we hoped."

As she shared the sordid details, Naomi took her hand. Her expression turned sad, but not devastated as Dinah had worried.

"I see," Naomi said softly. "I suppose we should have been more cautious. But I had hoped this was the answer to our prayers."

Dinah squeezed her fingers. "We'll figure something out. Hopefully I can scout out the local towns and find a place for us before we have to move on."

Naomi nodded, her weariness showing as her head sank deeper into the pillow. "We'll make it work. We always do."

Despite all she'd been through, Naomi's optimism never wavered. That was why Dinah had to stay practical. Her sister needed her now more than ever.

She patted Naomi's hand. "Rest now. I just wanted to let you know what I learned so you wouldn't—"

"Doc?" A voice called from the other room.

Dinah rose. "Jonah must be waking up. Call if you need me."

Hopefully Jonah hadn't slipped into fitfulness—or worse, a fever. The call hadn't sounded frantic, but why else would one of the men shout through a house where two patients rested?

She slipped out of Naomi's room and closed the door, then stepped through the open doorway beside it. Two of the brothers, Jude and Gilead, stood beside Jonah's bed.

The patient still lay with his eyes closed but muttered something under his breath.

Not a fever. *Please, Lord, no fever.* She approached and touched his forehead. The skin felt clammy, but no excess heat.

"Jonah, can you hear me?" she asked softly.

He groaned, and his eyes opened to slits. They stared ahead, unfocused.

She brushed the hair from his brow. "How are you feeling?"

He squeezed his eyes shut, maybe trying to decide how to answer. She should probably offer laudanum.

Gilead moved down to the foot of the bed so Jonah could look straight at him. "You awake there, big brother? Bet that leg's got a powerful hurt."

She moved to his thigh and lifted the quilt to examine the bandages. A tinge of red seeped through the fabric. The dressing had to be changed and the wound cleaned. Better to give him something for the pain first.

She glanced at his face. "I need to change your bandage, but I can give you laudanum first."

He squinted at her. "Who...are you?" His voice came out so raspy it was hard to decipher.

She offered a professional smile. "Dr. Dinah Wyatt. My sister and I came along just in time to help you."

Jonah's brow furrowed. "A doctor?"

She smiled. "I know, it's not common for a woman to be a doctor. But I assure you, I've been trained by the best."

Gilead leaned forward. "We're glad to have her. Jude said you nearly died out there. A bucketful of blood leaked out of yer leg."

She glanced at Jonah's face to see how he responded to such crassness, but his eyes had drifted shut.

She turned to her case and prepared a small dose of laudanum, then helped Jonah drink it. Within minutes, his breathing evened out, and he fell asleep.

She turned to Jude, who'd been watching her work. "I'll need warm water to change the dressing and clean the wound."

Jude headed out, and Dinah took a deep breath, trying to calm her nerves. The sight of blood never bothered her, but so much had happened this day. This past hour, actually.

Standing against the wall, Gilead met her look with a grin. "You should see how Jericho put the young-uns to work for that prank they pulled."

Her middle tightened. It was far more than a prank. She and her sister had set their dreams on what they thought was clear direction from the Lord. She did want the children to see the error of their ways, but not to be treated cruelly. "I hope they're not being overworked."

Gilead waved away her concern. "A little sweat's good for the soul. That's what Dat used to say. Said it points a body to the straight 'n narrow."

At least some of these people were God-fearing. Whether they truly knew and trusted the Father was another question, but at least they spoke of Him in a somewhat-respectful way.

Voices sounded from the other room, and a moment later Jude returned with a basin of warm water, his older brother trailing behind him.

Jericho met her gaze as he entered, and it was probably the forcefulness of it that made her breath catch. He shifted his focus to his brother on the bed, releasing her from the hold of those eyes.

"Jonah, you awake?" His voice came out strong and commanding, a leader telling one of his men to rally.

"Mmm-hmm." Jonah managed a murmur, but the laudanum had already taken hold.

She offered, "I've given him something for the pain."

Jude placed the pan of water on the floor next to the bed, and she turned her focus to the leg. Removing the soiled bandages, she worked not to grimace at the mass of crimson and flesh. She cleaned the area around the wound, gently wiping away the crusted blood and debris. Heat radiated from the incision area, but that was to be expected with as much trauma as this limb had endured. His body had to work hard to heal itself.

Though she didn't look up, the intensity of Jericho's gaze never wavered from her, his focus making her itch. She wouldn't let him see her nerves though.

At last, she secured the clean bandage around the leg and pulled the blanket back over. "There now. We'll do that once more tonight, then see how things look in the morning."

Jonah didn't answer, and any color that might have returned to his face before had now fled once more.

She touched his arm. "I'll see what we can do about a liver broth and some warm mashed vegetables to restore your blood. Sleep until I have it ready."

After scooping up the soiled cloths and the pot of water, she headed toward the door. The men scooted over to allow her to pass, then filed behind her into the main room. She marched the pot to the front door, then tossed the dirty liquid out to the side of the stoop. There were no flowers to water, but maybe she could teach Lillian how to do that next spring. Dinah wouldn't still live here, of course, but hopefully she and Naomi could find a place close enough to visit the girl occasionally. Living among all these men, she needed female influences in her life.

Back in the cabin, she turned toward the corner of this wide open room where the cookstove sat. All three men still stood by the door to Jonah's room, watching her. She ignored their scrutiny and moved toward her new workspace.

"I need to prepare foods for Jonah's healing. I don't mind making enough for everyone if you have no plans for the evening meal." Jericho and Lillian had been cutting something at the work counter, but the girl was still working. Surely they wouldn't mind Dinah cooking a large enough portion to feed the entire group.

"By all means," Gilead answered. "Cook as much as you want."

Dinah turned to the stacks of crates and burlap sacks piled in the corner, trying to locate the ingredients she needed. One of the bags held potatoes, and there was a whole crate full of smoked meat, but not a single vegetable.

She turned back to the men who stood rooted to the floor, watching her. "Is there a root cellar or garden where I can find greens?"

Jericho shook his head. "We've not planted a garden in years." He didn't look the least ashamed of that fact.

She glanced toward the front door. "What do you eat then? Surely you don't buy everything." Even if there was a town at the base of the mountain to make it convenient, such an arrangement would be expensive.

He shrugged. "I suppose we don't eat as many greens as we should, but we buy staples from Missoula Mills and hunt for meat. There's plenty of deer, elk, and bear stored in the barn if you don't find a cut you like there."

These men lived a shade above barbaric.

She sighed and turned back to the food stuffs. "I suppose I'll make a meat and potato stew. Is it too much to hope you have butter and cornmeal?"

"Cornmeal's in that barrel on the end. The larger tin on that shelf is full of bear fat. It cooks better than butter or pig lard."

She pulled the container he'd specified down and began measuring out ingredients for cornbread to go with the stew. She would have a lot to get used to in this wild land. Bear fat would likely be the least of her challenges.

CHAPTER 5

$\mathcal{T}$he men couldn't sleep in the same house as the women.

That was for certain. Not only because it was indecent, but Jericho also wouldn't give any female the chance to say she'd been wronged by a Coulter man. The Wyatt sisters didn't seem like the type to pretend they'd been mistreated, but they *had* come all this way to find a husband. The sister closed away in the children's bed chamber was in the family way, and he'd not heard anything about her being a widow.

He couldn't be too careful.

As he stood in the main room next to Jude, watching Miss Wyatt scurry around the kitchen area, his mind worked through all the details.

If the men slept in the barn, that would leave Jonah in the house alone with these two strangers. He sure couldn't move to the barn any time soon.

Maybe Jericho and the others should take turns sitting at Jonah's bedside through the night. Would he need that? It'd be nice to just bed down on the floor in his room, but then they'd be back to the situation of an able-bodied man sleeping in the same house as unmarried women.

Would the children be the best solution? Lillian and Sean could sleep on bed pallets in the room Jonah had taken over—Jericho's room, but he'd been doing his best not to think of it. His brother sure needed the bed more than he did right now.

That could work. It wasn't right to ask Lillian to sleep in the barn, anyway, but he didn't cotton to her staying in the house alone with women he didn't know. With her brother there, one could come running for Jericho if they needed to. He likely wouldn't sleep much anyway.

In the kitchen, Dinah bent over to stoke the fire in the cook-stove, and Jericho couldn't help but watch her. Something about her got under his skin. Maybe it was how she carried herself, like she wasn't afraid of anything.

Or perhaps the way she spoke, with a quiet confidence he rarely saw in women. Not that he met many women, mostly those who entertained the miners in Helena or Missoula Mills. But each summer when he took a load of sapphires to New York City, he had ample opportunity to study other females.

No one had snagged his notice like Miss Wyatt did, but probably only because he wasn't used to seeing a lady here in their cabin. Her presence made the place feel smaller than usual.

He had to pull himself out of this stupor and get things organized for the night. The boys would be done with the day's work soon, and he had to have his plan in place.

He glanced at Jude. "We're all sleeping in the barn tonight. Lillian and Sean can bed down in Jonah's room."

Jude nodded as though he'd expected as much. "I'll tell Sampson to have the young-uns clear a place in the loft for us."

Jericho nodded, and his brother headed toward the door. Best he do something with himself now too, instead of standing here gawking at a pretty female.

He moved to the back corner of the room where their

supplies were kept and opened the top crate. He needed to take inventory and plan his next trip to Missoula Mills. They were running low on gunpowder and ammunition and to restock basic supplies. Time in town was his least favorite task, but he'd rather go himself than risk one of his brothers talking too much or being lured by something they saw.

The way Lucy had.

As he dug through the crates, he heard a soft thud and a small gasp from behind him. Dinah had dropped a pot on the floor, and now she was on her hands and knees, frantically trying to salvage the contents.

He strode over to her and knelt down.

"I'm sorry." She was scooping the gloppy mess—maybe corn-bread batter—back into the dish. Surely she didn't plan to cook the stuff still.

He didn't mind a pinch of dirt mixed in with his food, but he couldn't say when this floor had been swept last. Probably not since the children came and he'd ordered Gil and Miles to clean the entire house. That had been nearly ten months ago. There was no telling what kind of dead bugs and dirt now mixed in with the batter.

"I know food supplies are precious here. I didn't mean to squander..." She scraped the last of the mess from the floor with her hand and plopped it into the container.

He eased the dish out of her hand. "I'll go dump this for you and clean out the pot. I'll bring in another bucket of clean water too." He stood and reached out to help her up.

She didn't take his hand, just pushed to her feet, holding her messy hands in front of her.

He glanced over at the clean water pot. "Sean is in charge of refilling the cook water each evening before he and Lillian help with the food." He sent her a rueful look. "He's otherwise occupied this afternoon. Working off his punishment for an adver-tisement the two of them shouldn't have placed."

She offered a weak smile, grimy hands still splayed in front of her.

He turned toward the door. "I'll show you the water wagon so you can get what you need any time."

As he strode outside and to the left of the house, sounds of hammering drifted from the barn. Miss Wyatt had to scurry to keep up with his long steps. *Slow down, Coulter.* Mum would have expected better of him when walking with a lady.

Matching her stride felt ridiculously slow, but he forced himself to relax. She'd been traveling for weeks and was likely exhausted.

He stole a sideways glance. She didn't *look* tired. Most of her blond hair was pulled back in a knot, but loose strands had escaped to frame her face. A face that looked far too delicate to withstand the hard life in this territory. Her skin wasn't weathered or lined. The line of her jaw looked strong, but her nose dainty. Maybe that was why he had trouble seeing her as a doctor. She seemed too feminine to think clearly in the middle of blood and crisis.

Yet, she'd proved herself capable.

She glanced his way, catching him looking.

He turned his attention to the water wagon ahead. "When this is empty, one of the boys will hitch the horses to it and refill the barrel at the creek. Usually about every five days." A smile tugged at his mouth. "Miles wants to build another so we can fill them both each time, then not have to worry about water as often. For now, though, we just have the one."

She studied the rig, and he tried to see it through her eyes. Dat had used an old four-wheeled wagon axle, then attached a large barrel that was about three feet wide across the center.

Miles had studied the barrel enough that he planned to make the second one himself. He would likely try to form the axle frame too, but they didn't have a full-sized forge, just an open fire and an anvil. The boy loved his tools though. He might attempt it anyway, if Jericho could find enough time to let him work on the project. Maybe once the first snow came and they weren't spending as many hours training the two-year-old horses.

Miles was right that having a second wagon would make the chore easier.

He reached for the spigot on the side of the barrel. "Put your hands under here, and the water will flow out to wash them."

She did as he said, moving far too close to him, as he had to keep twisting the handle for the water to flow. His arm brushed hers, but thankfully his shirt sleeves kept him from feeling her warmth.

When her hands were clean, he released the spigot. Then he dumped the dirty batter into the grass and turned the spigot so he could wash the pot.

"Is it better to bring the used dishes here to wash them then?" Miss Wyatt nudged his hand aside and turned the spigot so he could focus on the dish.

"If you like. That's what Sean and Lillian do, but before they came, whoever had kitchen duty usually brought in a bucket of water for the washing."

He could feel her interest sharpen, even without looking sideways at her.

"How long have they been here?"

She probably wanted to ask whose they were too. Every woman he'd ever met had been nosy. It wouldn't hurt for her to know these details. Might keep her from saying something that would hurt the children.

With the pot clean, he filled it with fresh water, then stepped away from the barrel. "Since last October. Our sister Lucy is— was—their ma. She, um, died, so I brought the children here to the ranch." He would never forget knocking at that shanty where she'd stayed in Virginia City. Little Sean had opened the door, and when the boy saw Jericho, he'd burst into tears.

It took a few minutes to quiet him enough to find out that Lucy's no-account husband had died of a fever, and the lad thought his mama was about to end the same way.

He'd pushed down the fear that gripped him, telling himself the boy's emotions made him exaggerate. But when he stepped into the bedroom, one look at Lucy on the blanket pallet on the floor made fear squeeze his throat with its clawing fingers. She barely lifted her covers, and the place stunk of vomit.

He'd tried to save her. He'd done everything he could. The doctor wouldn't come to that part of town, no matter how much Jericho offered to pay him. Said the epidemic was so bad in the shanties, there was nothing he could do. It simply had to run its course.

Jericho understood his meaning clearly—once everyone died who was going to anyway, the disease would clear up.

He'd not allowed his anger rein, though. Lucy and the children needed him. He'd spent the rest of that day and part of the night trying to get water and thin soup into his sister. But she'd passed away just before sunrise.

The children had cried, of course, but when he told them they were coming to live at the ranch—and that he'd bring their mother's body to be buried there—the first sign of hope touched their expressions.

They didn't deserve the life they'd been forced to live in that mining-town slum. Nor did Lucy. The difference was, she chose to stay with the lout she married, to allow that varmint to take away every dollar or bit of supplies Jericho brought her.

At least now the children were finally away from that hovel. Back on the ranch, where they could breathe freely and have plenty of food and a warm place to sleep.

"I'm sorry for your loss." Miss Wyatt spoke the words gently, not in that rote way that people often spoke condolences, but like she really felt them. Almost as though she could see his memories.

He nodded, then opened the front door. "It's good for Sean and Lillian to be here. Good for us all." He might have failed Lucy, but he wouldn't fail her children. He'd make sure they stayed here where they would be safe and happy and never want for anything.

After placing the pot of water on the stove for Miss Wyatt, he gathered up the other two buckets. "Use as many supplies as you need. I'll be making a run to Missoula Mills soon to restock."

He turned toward the door, a pail in each hand. "I'll fill these." It was about time he made himself useful around here. He had a house full of people depending on him, and he couldn't make a mistake.

CHAPTER 6

*S*ome of the potatoes had turned bad, so the stew would be more meat than anything, but this was the best Dinah could do. Naomi could have put together a much heartier meal, but the Coulter family would have to appreciate what Dinah could offer them.

That wouldn't go far in proving her worth to Mr. Jericho Coulter though.

She stirred the watery mixture in the pot, then laid the spoon aside and wiped her hands on her skirt. She'd found no aprons, of course. Nor hand towels. Once she unpacked some of her clothing, she would have her own apron, but for now, she had patients to see.

A peek through Jonah's open doorway showed his eyes closed. He would likely sleep quietly for a few hours under the effects of the laudanum.

At her sister's room, she quietly pulled the latch string and eased the door open. Inside, the bed was empty, and Naomi stood by the pile of their belongings.

Dinah stepped into the room and closed the door again. "What are you doing up?"

Naomi was opening the pack where she kept her clothing and personal belongings. "I feel much better. I thought I'd clean up a little before the evening meal." She gave a tired smile. "Surely at least one of these men is looking for a wife."

Dinah's throat squeezed. "Naomi." Her sister deserved far more than any man who would take her.

Naomi sighed and pulled a brush from the pack. "I know it's not the best way to think, but I don't have another choice." She sent a look toward the closed door as she brushed hard strokes through her thick, blonde hair. Hair identical to Dinah's except with more loose curl. "These men all seem to be decent and hard-working. Surely any of them would make an acceptable husband. And father." Her brushing slowed as her free hand cradled her belly. The motion seemed more reflex than anything these days, as her abdomen grew larger.

Dinah took the brush from her and turned Naomi to face away. She used long gentle strokes to work out the tangles from the trail. "You and my little niece or nephew deserve far more than *acceptable*. You need a man who will treasure you for the remarkable woman you are."

She made one final swipe, then set the brush aside and gathered Naomi's hair for a braid. "And until we find that man, we're going to stick together. Mr. Coulter said he needs to make a supply run to Missoula Mills soon, so perhaps I can ride with him and explore a little. He can help me locate a place we can afford to live in and house the clinic."

By *afford*, she meant a place that would allow them to wait to pay the first month's rent after she'd seen a few patients and been compensated for her work. Maybe she could barter free services with the owner in exchange for such leeway.

Naomi sighed, a long breath that showed how much she worried about their future. It wasn't Naomi's job to worry though. Dinah did enough for them both.

Dinah tied off the braid with a ribbon, then took her sister's shoulders and turned her so they faced each other. "But until then, your doctor is ordering you to bed rest." She pointed to the cot with the mussed blankets. "Stay there with your feet propped above your heart, please. We have to get the swelling down. Do you need more water?" She glanced at the cup on the floor, where liquid glimmered halfway up the side. "You have to drink, Na. If you don't take in enough water, we could have serious problems."

She waited until Naomi met her gaze, then gave a pointed look. "I'm serious. If you don't obey on your own, I will sit on you and force you. You know I will."

Naomi grinned, surely remembering the time Dinah had wrestled her to the ground and forced her to eat peppermint leaves because she had a cough and Pop said that would help. They'd been ten at the time, and Naomi had looked green for the next hour. But her cough had gone away. Eventually.

Dinah released her, and Naomi turned to the bed and slumped down to sit on it, then took up the cup and drank. She sent a begrudging glare over the rim of the mug, but Dinah only returned a smile.

"Good girl."

Once Naomi was settled in bed with her still very swollen feet propped on blankets, Dinah turned to do some unpacking of her own. Cleaning up might be a good idea. There was no telling how trailworn she looked...and smelled.

Would there be any way to get a bath in the next few days? Something other than the creek? With so many men on the property, she wasn't sure she trusted them to give her complete privacy without a door she could lock. Maybe she could ask Lillian.

"So what's your plan?" Naomi asked from the bed.

Dinah turned, raising her brows. "Plan?"

"I'm sure you have things mapped out for tonight and

tomorrow at least. What you plan to accomplish. What you need to learn to undertake those things."

Dinah couldn't help a smile, but she turned to her pack to hide it. She did like a good challenge, but she hadn't anticipated this situation. "My main goal tonight is to check Jonah's bandage again and make sure he eats some and drinks plenty of water." She turned and gave a pointed look to the cup in Naomi's hands. "The same for you."

She turned back to find a ribbon in her bag. "Then I want him to rest well and keep his pain under control. Tomorrow, he needs to eat a number of small meals throughout the day, and I'll check his bandage thrice at least."

She ran the brush through her own hair, cringing at the knots that snagged. "I also plan to do some cleaning in the cabin tomorrow. I'm hoping Lillian will help me with that, if they don't have her working in the barn again." A tight snarl fought the bristles, and she sucked in a breath as she worked through it. "I'd like to get to know her. Jericho said the children's mother was his sister. That she died last year."

Naomi gave her a strange look, and she replayed her words in her mind. Had she spoken too casually about the woman's death? But then the real reason settled in. She'd not meant to call Jericho by his Christian name. That was something Naomi had done all along the journey, but Dinah had made sure to always speak of him as Mr. Coulter.

Dinah cleared her throat and tried to cover her mistake. "It must have been difficult for the children to transition to living so remotely. And to having only men—all those uncles—as caretakers."

Naomi nodded slowly, her eyes searching Dinah's face. "I'm sure Mr. Coulter will be thankful for anything you can do to help his niece and nephew settle in. I would imagine they're still grieving."

Dinah laid the brush down as she re-braided her hair. Had

Naomi used his surname to prove she was resigning herself to not marrying Jericho? Or did she think Dinah had set her sights on the man?

That wasn't the case. Not at all. *Naomi* needed the husband.

But she didn't really. Her history wasn't known in this place, and she didn't have to say anything more about the child's father than she wanted too. Dinah had a profession that could provide for them both.

Neither of them had to marry unless they chose to.

After securing her braid, she looked down at her shirtwaist and skirt. They were hopelessly dirty from days on the trail, but she needed a bath before she dared change into her only clean dress. Hopefully washing could be added to tomorrow's list too. Somewhere near the top.

⁓

*D*inah forced herself out of the sagging cot as the first faint streak of gray lightened the horizon through the only small window in this room. She had so much to do today. She couldn't waste a minute.

Naomi continued a light snore as Dinah refastened her hair and straightened her clothing in the darkness. Snoring was another thing that had begun these past weeks, the more Naomi's body swelled.

After slipping into the main room and closing the door behind her, she peered into the darkness of the chamber where Jonah and the children slept. Steady breathing sounded from inside. Her patient had slept better than she'd expected. She'd given him laudanum just before retiring for the night, then had awakened only once to his moans. Another dose eased his pain, and he seemed to still feel the effects now.

The men outside must not have fared as well, for she'd heard someone come into the house three different times. The soft boot thuds always went into Jonah's room, stayed a few minutes, then thumped back across the main room and outside.

She'd moved the chest of drawers in front of the door in their chamber, just in case. But thankfully, its strength had never been tested.

They'd made it through the first night.

To celebrate, the men might enjoy a hearty breakfast. Johnnycakes would be possible given the supplies she'd found last night. There might not be syrup, but maybe she could find a jar of jam, or mix a sweet topping from the sugar she'd spotted.

The coals she'd stoked in the stove still looked warm, and with some poking, she nurtured a small flame. Naomi or Nana usually handled most of the cooking and related chores back in Virginia. Dinah was always working in the clinic or visiting patients.

But she knew her way around a cookstove well enough. When she added kindling from the crate beside the stove, the chunks of bark and small wood lit easily. There were only two logs left inside, which meant she'd need to bring in more for cooking.

Did these men drink coffee? Or maybe tea. She preferred a good warm chocolate herself, but that might be a luxury she had to forego in the Montana Territory.

After adding the two logs, she closed the door to the firebox and filled the kettle with water, then moved it to what would be the hottest part of the stove. Best find coffee or tea and start it brewing before she went for wood. Had there been a stack of split logs outside? Not that she could remember.

Lord, don't let me have to split wood to make this breakfast too. Surely with all these strapping men around, they would have a supply somewhere.

She'd already gone through all the tins on the shelf, which was where she'd found the sugar and salt and two other powders she couldn't identify. Saleratus maybe, a staple Nana used often to make her cakes rise. So now she waded through the crates and burlap bags stacked in the corner. Even if she didn't find coffee or tea, she needed to know what food items were on hand to plan for meals.

"What are you doing?"

She jumped at the voice, nearly losing her grip on the crate she was lifting off the stack. When she turned to find the source of the voice, her heart skipped a beat at the sight of Jericho Coulter standing in the middle of the room, arms full of firewood. The only dim light came through the open door behind him, silhouetting the line of his broad shoulders. The outline of his hair looked especially wild this morning. Did he always keep it hanging to his shoulders?

Dinah cleared her throat and straightened her back, keeping her voice steady. "Good morning. I'm just looking for supplies to make the morning meal. Do you have coffee or tea?"

He stepped forward, dropping his load into the box they used for firewood. "We did have coffee. Not sure if there's any left." As he moved beside her and reached for the next crate on the stack, his nearness overwhelmed every other thought. He smelled rich and woodsy, and maybe a bit like hay. He was so tall, at least a handbreadth taller than Pop.

She tried to step back. To allow him more space and her mind to clear, but with her first attempt, her feet tangled in her skirts. She scrambled to grab something to keep from falling flat on her rear.

Her fingers caught cloth, and she grabbed hold, stopping her backward momentum and allowing her feet to find solid ground.

"Easy there." Jericho grabbed her wrist, securing her firmly.

The cloth she gripped was covering a strong arm—Jericho's arm—and the muscle rippling beneath was sturdy enough to keep a horse upright if need be.

"I'm sorry." She released him, but he still gripped her wrist with his other hand. She tugged to pull away—to get far from this man she'd just embarrassed herself in front of.

"Those skirts can be a nuisance on a homestead." He finally let go of her arm, and she took two steps back—without tripping this time. "My sister wore trousers like the rest of us. The only time she put on a dress was when we went to town."

She dared a glance at his face. Did he think she should wear pants too? Not likely around so many men. Her ears burned just thinking about it. Nana would be mortified. An image slipped in of how shocked her grandmother's face would be if Dinah paraded in trousers across the parlor during one of her weekly teas. All those high-collared women with even higher opinions of themselves would need smelling salts for sure.

"Something funny?" Jericho eyed her, a hint of amusement glimmering in his coffee eyes.

She shook her head. "Just imagining how that would go over back in Wayneston. I think I'd better stick with skirts." That was all she owned anyway.

She turned to the cookstove and grabbed a log to add to the firebox. "If you find coffee, the water's ready for it." Best refocus his attention where it should be. "I thought I'd make Johnny-cakes this morning. Do you have maple syrup or jam?"

"There's syrup in this jug. We harvest it ourselves in the winter."

She glanced over to see the container he meant. "Excellent."

He straightened. "Better slice bear steak to go with those cakes. The boys need full bellies to work all day."

She frowned. "They don't come in for the noon meal?"

He pulled out a nearly-empty sack. "Not if they're out with the stock. Most of us take a little something to eat if we get hungry, but it'd waste too much daylight to ride back and forth."

She took the bag he handed her and peered inside. A handful of black grounds. Enough for one round of coffee, maybe two if she stretched it. Better than nothing.

As she poured the grounds into the top of the kettle, Jericho heaped the supplies into a tidy stack in the corner. Should she recommend items he was missing? Maybe that would be presumptuous.

Better to focus on today's tasks. "If you don't need Lillian's help, I was hoping she could assist me with cleaning here in the house."

He set the last box in place and turned, brushing off his hands. "If you like." Without a backward glance, he sauntered to his brother's bed chamber and slipped inside.

She shouldn't have expected any kind of thanks for the work she was putting in around here, but his casualness stung a little. She turned back to the stove and scooped enough batter for a Johnnycake. When the men came in, they would be hungry.

Best she was prepared.

CHAPTER 7

$\mathcal{T}$he brothers filed in one and two at a time, coming and going for the next hour or so. They brought more firewood, and some climbed the ladder nailed to the wall up to the loft above the bedrooms. That must have been where they usually slept and where their belongings still stayed.

The first time one of the men grabbed two Johnnycakes off the plate where she was stacking them beside the stove, she stopped herself from slapping his hand. Could they not wait to sit down at the table like a normal family?

She settled for a glare behind the man's back. "I have maple syrup if you'd like to sit down with a plate."

He turned, and his name finally came back to her. Sampson. The...second to youngest brother? He was the one who'd been assigned to keep the children working yesterday afternoon.

His eyes brightened. "I forgot about the syrup." Then he stepped around her to the work counter and scooped up the jug. Holding the container in the crook of one arm, he poured syrup onto the Johnnycakes in his other hand, cupping them like a bowl to receive the sweet liquid without spilling a drop.

Once finished, he plopped the jug on the floor beside the

stove. "I'll leave this here for the others." He flashed her a grin. "I sure am glad you ladies came. Stay as long as you like, no matter what Jericho says."

He turned and strolled out of the house, eating a third of the double-roll of Johnnycakes in a single bite.

She could only watch the door close. Did they all have such abominable manners? Maybe they never used the table and chairs pushed up against the opposite wall. She'd thought they must pull them out for each meal.

Last night, the men had straggled in a few at a time and scooped bowls full of soup, then taken them in to eat with Jonah or carried them back outside. She'd assumed their rhythm had simply been disrupted because of their brother's injury. That they would return to normal meal patterns this morning.

Perhaps *this* was normal.

Should she say something to Jericho? The children needed regular family meals so they could learn proper manners and receive consistent nutrition. She could still remember the times Nana made her and Naomi stay at the table until they'd eaten whatever food they disliked. *Children need good quality foods to grow properly*, she would say.

Maybe she wouldn't speak to Jericho about it yet. Better not to list all her complaints on the first day. But she could start a new routine with Sean and Lillian herself. This very morning.

When Sean came in with his Uncle Jude and tried to swipe a handful of Johnnycakes in one hand and a chunk of meat in the other, she placed her own hands on top of the boy's, stilling him.

She met his surprised gaze. "You, Lillian, and I are going to sit at the table for our meals. If you'll take a seat, I'll bring you a plate."

He scowled, releasing the food as he backed away, sending a questioning look to his uncle.

Jude, thankfully, didn't belittle her suggestion. Though he'd already taken a bite of meat, he nodded. He even waited to swallow before speaking. "Sounds like a good idea. I'll join you."

Maybe there was hope for them yet.

She handed Jude a plate and loaded the food Sean had handled onto a second dish. She'd cooked enough that she should be able to sit for a minute to eat. She had a feeling if she didn't herd these two to the table right now, she would lose them to their day's work.

Lillian came in with the water Dinah had sent her for, and she smiled at the girl. "Good timing. We're going to sit at the table for meals from now on. Will you join us?"

Lillian's eyes widened, and she nodded.

As Dinah carried the plates of food to the table, she caught a look pass between the children.

Just get ready. There are going to be more changes around here. But she kept that thought to herself for now.

Once they all settled into seats—with Jude at one end and the children and her on one of the long sides—the others dove in with gusto. Maybe she should have suggested they offer thanks before eating, but Sean had already inhaled half his food. She'd have to jump in sooner for the next meal.

As she used her best table manners, she tried not to be too open as she observed the children. Sean didn't seem to know what manners were, but Lillian appeared to be giving an effort. She kept her elbows off the table, but her bites were too large and she chewed with her mouth open.

Challenges to tackle later.

"Well, lookee here." Miles stepped through the open doorway and surveyed them, then headed toward the cookstove.

"We're sitting at the table like civilized folk," Jude called out. "Join us."

Miles chuckled as he filled a plate. "Guess I could use some sophistication." He ambled toward the table and took a place at the end opposite Jude. Beside her.

Dinah shifted her legs so they didn't brush against his. Not easy since he sprawled them out beneath the table. All the brothers were tall, but Miles seemed the shortest. Maybe he wasn't finished growing yet. He looked to be about seventeen or eighteen.

He sent her a grin before biting into his Johnnycakes, and she turned her focus to her own food. The last thing she wanted was to encourage any sort of infatuation from this young man. Not that he would have reason to be interested in her except for the scarcity of women in their little corner of the world. A lack of people in general, for that matter.

Only the rather-loud sounds of eating filled the room. They should have some conversation.

She glanced up at Jude with a pleasant smile. "I understand you have livestock you men care for each day?"

He nodded, then swallowed his bite. "Horses mostly. A few cattle. We're just starting that herd."

"I see." She glanced toward Miles to include him in the conversation, though she was careful not to make eye contact. "We saw mostly tree-covered mountains as we traveled along the creek. Are there pastures for the animals to graze, or do you have some other way of feeding them?" Hopefully they wouldn't think her questions impertinent. She knew so little about these men, this land, and ranching in general, she could barely make conversation without it sounding like an inquisition.

Miles spoke around a mouthful of meat. "Three main pastures. One to the west." He pointed that direction. "The east." A jab opposite. "Then one down near the base of the mountain in a little valley. That's where the mares and foals are now. The cattle too."

He'd swallowed his bite by the time he finished speaking, then took another, so she turned her next question to the children. "Do you help with the animals too?"

Sean grinned around his own mouthful of meat. "I'm taming

one of the colts myself. Uncle Sampson's helpin'. I've got 'im leadin', and he plays games with me."

She raised her brows. "Really? How old is the colt?"

The boy looked to Jude, who responded for him. "Most of the foals were born in May." He nudged Sean's arm. "You got to see Spirit born, didn't you?"

Sean grinned again, this time without the food in his mouth. The look revealed a missing tooth she'd not noticed before. "That's why he's mine. I was there from the very first."

She couldn't help but return his proud smile. Then she turned to Lillian. "Do you have a foal you're raising?"

The girl shrugged, not looking up. " I don't really like horses."

Jude frowned at the girl, and her words threatened to cast a pall over the room as everyone refocused on their food.

Dinah worked for a light tone. "Well. There are many other things to enjoy in this beautiful territory. I hope you'll stay at the house today with me, Lillian. I've concocted a plan that I'll need your help with."

Dinah sent a *don't worry* look to the brothers' startled expressions, then focused on the interest she'd piqued in Lillian. "Did your Uncle Jericho tell you my idea? If so, he might not have shared the interesting parts." That way the men would know she'd already spoken to their big brother about her intentions.

Lillian looked up, her eyes brightening. "He only said I'm to work with you here in the house."

Dinah grinned. But before she could answer, the girl's attention moved to something behind Dinah. Sean and Jude looked up too.

She turned, and for the second time that day, Jericho stood in the middle of the room watching her.

This time, instead of carrying firewood, his hands were propped at his waist. How had she not heard him enter? Her stomach tightened. There was something about Jericho Coulter that made her uneasy, something she couldn't quite put her finger on. He seemed like a decent man, but he was...mysterious.

"Morning, big brother." Jude broke the awkward silence. "You're just in time to eat. Fill a plate and come sit down."

Jericho flicked his gaze toward the cookstove. "Need to head out." His focus moved back to the table, scanning from one end to the other.

Then without another word, he turned and strode to the cookstove. He scooped up food in both hands, then turned and headed to the door. "Sean, you're riding with me to the cattle today. Get a move on."

As he disappeared outside, the boy shoveled in the last of his Johnnycake and scooted his chair back. "Thank you." Except with his mouth full, it sounded like "Ain u."

Jude and Miles also rose, and she accepted their thanks with a nod. Both men carried their plates to the work counter, leaving her and Lillian alone with the remainder of their meals.

She worked up a smile for the girl.

Expectations. She needed to adjust her expectations for how much she could civilize these men. Especially in one week. Now that she knew what they were accustomed to, she could work on one thing at a time.

As soon as she fed Naomi and Jonah and changed his bandage, she and Lillian would set to cleaning. That one thing would make a significant difference in the place.

Surely.

~

*T*his was a sight he would never tire of.

As Pinto picked his way down the slope, Jericho stared out at the cattle grazing in the valley below. Peaks rose up beyond the animals, and the morning sun cast pink and orange hues across the sky. His chest swelled, and he breathed in a crisp breath.

The mares and foals must have moved to the other end of the valley where he couldn't see them yet. He scanned the cattle, doing his mental count of cows and calves. Twelve mamas and ten babies, plus the bull. They'd had thirteen calves born that spring, but the set of twins didn't make it, and another calf was brought down by wolves.

He glanced at the trees beyond the clearing. Thankfully, they'd not heard any howling recently.

He'd rest easier, though, once they added a donkey to the herd. He'd asked Two Stones to find one for him. Surely a trapper or miner would have an animal he'd be eager to sell for the amount of gold Jericho had sent with Two Stones.

But his Salish friend hadn't returned yet. Maybe Jericho should head to Missoula Mills this week and find a donkey himself.

Except he couldn't leave the ranch with women here. And Jonah was injured. The trip would take a solid two days. Longer if he couldn't find a donkey the first night he arrived.

He'd have to rely on Two Stones.

When they reached the valley floor, Sean pushed his horse into a lope, leaving Jericho behind. Thankfully, he remembered to give the cattle a wide berth so he didn't spook and scatter them. The lad was eager to reach his colt, no doubt. Assigning that boy a foal had been the best thing for him. If only Jericho could find a way to reach Lillian too.

He'd tried to get her to pick one of the horses to work with. Or even a calf. But she didn't seem to care about the animals at all. Nor did she do work around the house like cooking or sewing. She did what she was told and nothing more.

This mail-order bride advertisement was a whole new debacle. Would more women come riding up the creek, thinking God had told them they were *the one*?

His belly tightened. What a preposterous way to request a response. The whole thing was an infuriating mess. Lucy clearly hadn't been as involved with the children's activities as she should have been. The stories they'd told of the miners they considered friends...

Yet he couldn't be angry with his dead sister. She'd made a string of poor choices, but she must have been doing the best she could by the end.

If only she had let him help more.

An angry screech sounded from the sky, somewhere in the distance.

Jericho jerked his focus upward, searching for the bird. He couldn't see Crowley yet, but that was definitely their unique guardian sounding his warning call. And probably coming from the creek that led to the Mullan Road. That was the way everyone approached the ranch. Unfortunately, it was far too close to the mine.

He spun back to where his nephew had disappeared around the curve in the valley. "Sean."

"Yeah?" the boy called back.

"Stay here while I see what Crowley's found. Don't work with the horses until I come back. All right?"

"Aw." The disappointment came clearly in his tone, even over the distance.

But Jericho didn't have time to soothe him. He turned Pinto as he called again. "I mean it. Don't touch the horses until I'm with you. I won't be long."

Hopefully.

CHAPTER 8

*J*ericho pushed his gelding into a lope and followed the creekside trail. Surely more women hadn't come already. These, he wouldn't allow to stay. He'd turn them around at the creek and send them back to wherever they came from. If he had to pay their fare—or double it—he would gladly do so, just to be rid of them.

He didn't have any money with him now, though. Maybe he could call for one of the boys and have them bring gold down while Jericho held the newcomers in place.

The last thing he needed was anyone else coming up the mountain. Not just because letting strangers get friendly with his family always brought disaster, but because he had to protect their mine and livelihood.

As he neared the place where Crowley, the Raven who always signaled newcomers, circled overhead, he slowed Pinto to a walk. Voices sounded through the trees. Men's voices.

As if he hadn't been hard enough. He pushed the gelding into a faster walk. Had one of his brothers already come down to meet the stranger? They knew better than to make their presence known unless they recognized the person.

Or maybe this mail-order bride had brought a father or brother. He groaned inside. The last thing he needed was an angry family member claiming Jericho had wronged his daughter and demanding recompense.

But as he rode closer, he picked out Gil's voice. He and Jude were working at the mine, trying to finish moving the full crates of sapphires—the work Jude and Jonah had been doing yesterday when the accident happened.

When he rounded the bend and saw who Gil spoke to, relief swept through him. Two Stones sat on his spotted horse—and even better, he held a rope attached to a long-eared donkey.

Jericho couldn't help but grin as he closed the distance between them. Finally, something was going right.

He pulled up beside Two Stones and dismounted. "You found one."

The Salish brave nodded and grinned back. "I did. Took much riding to find, then I had to give all the gold and another horse with it."

Jericho moved to the donkey and ran his hand down its scruffy gray coat. It was a sturdy female with a head too large for its body. But its eyes were kind and calm, and it brayed softly as Jericho rubbed its nose. "Thank you, my friend. She'll be a big help."

Two Stones shrugged. "I am glad to help."

Jericho eyed the man. "For the horse you had to give, do you want to pick from our stock, or would you rather have gold coin?" Two Stones interacted with whites enough that he could trade the coin for whatever he needed.

A twinkle touched the man's eye. "I get my own horses."

Jericho nodded. "Ride up to the house with me then so I can get you money." They'd talked many times about the superior qualities of the spotted horses Two Stones bought from the Nez Perce. Jericho wouldn't mind purchasing a mare himself and adding her to his breeding program. Maybe he'd give Two

Stones enough money to obtain goods to trade for such a horse.

Most of the Salish lived quietly in the villages of their ancestors, growing cammas on plots of land handed down from one generation to the next. But Two Stones had restless feet, staying on the trail as often as he could. He'd stopped in to introduce himself when Mum and Dat first came to this mountain and had helped hoist some of the logs to build their cabin.

He'd been a good friend since then, one of the few the Coulter family possessed. And the only man Jericho trusted on the ranch. Two Stones had answered their questions about the colored stones they first found in the creek and had only shrugged when Dat told him they were sapphires and worth a great deal of money to the white men in the east.

After swinging back up on Pinto, Jericho took the rope from his friend. "Follow me to the house. Are you hungry? Jonah was injured yesterday and is laid up in bed. He'll be glad if you come speak to him."

"I guess I'd better get back to help Jude." Gil sounded reluctant, but Jericho gave him a nod.

They certainly didn't need another accident. Loading the wagon wasn't usually dangerous, only hard, heavy work. Jude had said Jonah slipped as the horses were already backing, and by the time he called out, the animals couldn't stop the heavy load in time on the slope.

He met his brother's gaze. "Be careful."

Gil returned a cheeky grin. "That wouldn't be any fun."

While Jericho tightened his grip on his reins to keep from throwing something at his little brother, Gil turned his mount and trotted off, disappearing into the trees.

Two Stones chuckled, and Jericho nudged his gelding up the slope toward the house. "We have other visitors too."

As he told about the advertisement and the two women now lodged in Lucy's old room, Two Stones's chuckle turned to a belly laugh. Jericho sent him a dark look, but the man only shook his head, barely able to catch his breath.

"You only think it's funny because they didn't come to marry you." But he could see how the situation might be a little humorous if it wasn't a fellow's reality.

Two Stones had finally settled down to a grin by the time they entered the clearing where the house and barn sat.

Jericho slid to the ground and reached for the spotted horse's reins. "I'll feed your horse while you go in and see Jonah." After Two Stones left, he needed to get back to the meadow where Sean worked with the horses.

Two Stones moved toward the house, and Jericho led the three animals to the barn where hammering sounded. He'd left Sampson near the house today with a list of work that needed to be caught up on. He must be repairing the loose boards in the stalls now.

As he entered the dim building and started to call out for his brother, a scream ripped through the air—coming from the house.

∼

*D*inah's mind raced as she gripped the broom. An Indian. Not ten steps away from her.

He'd simply walked in.

Not crept in or even knocked. Just...strode inside. As if he lived here.

But he didn't. No one had said anything about Indians in the area.

He had no weapons drawn. With the light from the open door behind him, she couldn't tell if anything hung from his waist.

Maybe he spoke English. Perhaps he was friendly. She worked to draw breath to speak. "Who are you?"

"Two Stones?" Lillian's voice came through the open doorway to Jonah's room.

Dinah's heart hammered. He must be known to them. Part of her wanted to step forward and slam the door to Jonah's chamber shut. To protect Lillian and her patient from this intruder.

But Lillian strode out, slowing when she reached the main room. She dipped her chin shyly.

Dinah stepped forward to distract the man's attention from the girl. "Hello." Her voice cracked, and she cleared her throat.

Behind the newcomer, Jericho stepped into the house. For once, his presence brought relief, not that strange tension in her chest. Yet he didn't wear his usual studied expression. He was frowning.

At her.

She swallowed. He must have come running at her scream. If this man was a friend, her behavior would be considered quite rude. Yet, how could she have known?

"Miss Wyatt, I'd like you to meet Two Stones. A very good friend of ours." He accentuated those last words, and she swallowed again. She'd certainly blundered, though no one had warned her. Surely her response was natural for any woman.

Jericho turned to his guest. "This is one of the women I told you about."

A smile touched Two Stone's mouth. "Any friend of Jericho is a good friend to me." He spoke with an accent, but the words were clear and flowed easily.

Heat flooded up her neck, but she summoned a smile. "It's a pleasure to meet you. I'm sorry about my...outburst. I didn't realize..." She cleared her throat to give more strength to her voice. "I didn't realize Mr. Coulter was expecting company." Especially since he'd said they never had visitors on the ranch.

Jericho's frown deepened at her words, if that were possible. "Two Stones is welcome any time."

She nodded. "Of course."

The native man peered through the door to Jonah's chamber. "I come to see my wounded brother."

Lillian stepped to the side. "He's sleeping, I think."

Perhaps not after her scream.

Two Stones moved quietly to the door, then into the room. He approached the side of Jonah's bed and stood for a long moment. She'd given Jonah more laudanum after the men left for the day's work, so he likely wouldn't wake now. What did this native man think of the traction she'd set up? Did his people have a method like this to help a broken femur heal without shortening the leg?

He stepped forward and placed one hand on Jonah's forehead. His lips moved, as though he were speaking quietly to himself. Some kind of incantation? She'd heard Indians had their own religion and sometimes made gods of the sun and other natural objects.

Lord, should I say something? Have You brought me here to tell them of You?

Of course the Lord had. Maybe this was only part of His purpose in guiding her and Naomi to this land, but Scripture said to *Go into all the world and preach the Gospel.* She should share of Him with everyone, using every opportunity.

As Two Stones turned from Jonah and left the bed chamber, Dinah stayed out of his way and took a deep breath. She kept her voice kind and curious. "Can I ask what you were saying just now, when you touched him?"

He dipped his chin. "I pray for my brother."

"Praying...to who?" Or perhaps she should have said *to what.* Best she understand what she was dealing with before telling him of the Truth.

The corners of his mouth curved the smallest bit. "To God."

She hesitated. To the sun god? Or the moon? How could she

ask what kind of god without sounding silly—or worse, insulting him? Again.

But Two Stones seemed to understand her hesitation. "The one God. The Creator of all things."

Dinah's heart skipped a beat. Was he saying he believed in the God of the Bible?

Before she could ask him more, Jericho cleared his throat. "Two Stones is a Christian, if that's what you're wondering."

Two Stones nodded, his grin no longer hiding. But it held kindness, not like he was laughing at her. "Jericho's father told me of Him many years ago. My life is not the same since I believe."

She returned his grin, breathing out her relief. "That's wonderful." Once more, things in this territory were not at all what she expected.

But this time, she could be more than thankful.

CHAPTER 9

*W*eariness tugged at Jericho as he rode into the ranch yard with Miles and Sean. This wasn't simply the exhaustion of a hard day's work.

The churning in his mind had consumed far more energy than the animals had worked in his body. He'd not realized how many of their family's traditions he'd let fall by the wayside after Mum and Dat's death. Sitting at the table for meals was the most obvious, and Miss Wyatt's reminder that morning had stung.

But then Two Stones speaking of how Dat had so freely shared his faith. Jericho had stopped trying to please God years ago, but that didn't mean his brothers should lose their faith too. Dat read a chapter from the Bible each night, and he'd prayed before every meal.

Meals they ate around Mum's table.

Mum was always singing hymns as she worked and insisted her boys spend an hour each Sunday singing with her. *Raising praise to the Father,* she'd called it.

Jericho couldn't carry a tune, but some of the other boys weren't half bad. Maybe they could sing a hymn or two on

Sundays. And reading a chapter at nights would give them all time to settle in the evenings. Jericho only had to make it happen. He didn't have to be the one to read. The same with a prayer before meals.

As they dismounted and began unsaddling the horses, Sampson came over to help.

Jericho kept his voice even. "We're going to start eating meals at the table again, beginning tonight. Sampson, you can say the blessing before we dig in. Miles, help me move the table out so we can all fit. Sean, go tell Jude and Gil to come in and eat." He'd seen them unhitching the wagon team as they rode in.

All the boys eyed him, but Miles raised his brows more boldly. Best put a stop to what that look insinuated.

He met his youngest brother's gaze. "I'm not doing this because of our female visitors. It's something Two Stones said today about how Dat taught him to pray. I realized we've stopped doing some of the things that were important to them."

All three of the boys sobered, and Miles nodded. "It's a good idea."

Once they finished settling the horses for the night, Jericho followed his youngest brother to the house. The main room was empty as they stepped inside, but a rich aroma filled the air. Not just fried meat either. Something sweeter.

He glanced through Jonah's open doorway but couldn't see anyone in there with his brother. The other bed chamber door was closed, as usual. Was Lillian in there with both sisters? He'd barely seen the one who was in the family way. Her name was Naomi, he was pretty sure. Once she'd gone to bed that first hour, the door had stayed closed.

Which was the way things should be with her in bed and so many men around, but...

He turned away from the closed door and his unending questions. Miles had already pulled the chairs back from one side of the table and positioned himself at the short end.

As Jericho took up the opposite side, a sound drifted from the closed bedroom door. A sound he'd not heard in years. Not in this house at least.

Women giggling.

He turned to look, but the door was still closed. What were they talking about in there? Did Lillian like being around females again? He couldn't tell if she was one of those laughing or not. Had he *ever* heard her laugh? Not in several years.

His chest squeezed, and he forced himself to turn back to the table. Miles was staring at the closed door too, a look of curious awe on his face. The boy needed to guard himself. He was far too young for the likes of these. Too young to be thinking about women at all.

Jericho lifted his end of the table, and Miles snapped to attention. As they shifted the heavy piece of furniture, Jericho had to strain more than he'd expected. "Dat build this for Mum." It was hard to carry and speak at the same time, but Miles might not remember the details. And it was important he know them. "It was the first thing he made after the cabin was finished."

They set the table down, then went back for the chairs. Did Miles remember all the hard work they'd put into the homestead in those early years? He'd only been six when they first came to the haven of this land. Hopefully too young to remember the bloody chaos they'd left in Kansas.

A movement to the side caught his eye. The bed chamber door opened, and Dinah stepped through the doorway. Something was different about her, something that drew his glance in for a longer gaze.

She wore a different dress, for one. A pretty blue color that curved more than the brown she'd worn before. And her hair... Instead of the braid, she had it pinned up with loose curls falling around her face. Both the dress and the curls brought out the clear blue of her eyes.

He swallowed, trying to rein in his gaze. His mind and body, too, if he could manage it.

"You sure do look pretty, ma'am." Miles's voice broke the haze around Jericho's mind.

Miss Wyatt turned a pretty smile on him. "Thank you." Then her gaze swept over their work. "You're moving the table?"

She looked to Jericho for an answer, and he nodded like he'd been struck dumb-witted.

He scrambled for words. "We're, um, going to eat in here tonight. All of us."

Her smile brightened enough to make him wish he'd done more. What else could he do to bring out that sunshine?

She started toward the stove. "Lillian and I have been busy today. We hope you like what we've prepared." Her voice hesitated, like she was shy or worried.

He raised his brows. "I'm sure it'll be good." The smells were making him hungrier by the minute.

As she took the lid from the pot and stirred its contents, she sent him a glance. "Are you planning to…restock…supplies any time soon?" She sounded like she was trying to make a suggestion without stepping on his toes.

He dipped his chin. "We're low on things, I know." He glanced toward the door, where Missoula Mills sat a day's ride away. "I need to get to town. Soon." But he couldn't leave now. Not with Jonah's injury and these women…

"Would you mind if I go with you? If you're going to town I mean. I'd like to look around for the best place to open a medical clinic."

He swung his focus back to her and barely kept his thoughts from spilling out before he could sift through them. She was going to run a clinic?

In Missoula Mills?

That den of heathens—otherwise known as miners—was no place for a respectable woman. And to run a business on her own? Doing work that required close physical contact with her customers...? Not if he had anything to say in the matter.

Which he didn't. Not really.

He could give his opinion of course, but she wouldn't likely abide by his wishes unless she asked his advice. He eased out a breath, doing his best to quell his racing thoughts with the action.

"I also need to purchase additional supplies for my sister and me." She gave him a smile that seemed to be trying to ease his worries.

It didn't work.

He nodded and turned back to the chairs lined against the wall. "We'll see how Jonah is tomorrow. Maybe I can go the next day. Make a list of what you need. Here in our cabin, and for yourselves. I'll bring them back for you." He certainly wasn't taking her along on a two-day journey.

Footsteps sounded outside, and the rest of the boys filed in.

Jericho motioned them toward the table, but before anyone could sit, Miss Wyatt spoke up. "I've set a washbasin and towel here for you to use before meals."

Ah, yes. That was one other bit of civility he'd lost these last years. He required baths at least once a week, or whenever the boys got too rank to stand near, but Mum had kept a basin of water in just about the exact spot Miss Wyatt placed it now.

While his brothers and nephew availed themselves of the water and cloth, Jericho poked his head into Jonah's room. His brother opened his eyes partway and offered a tired curve of his mouth.

"You up to coming for the meal?" Of course Jericho new better, but it might help Jonah to think about doing normal things. Remind him what he could look forward to.

Jonah's smile became a little more real. "Already had mine. Broth and mashed potatoes." His voice sounded drowsy, and his eyelids lowered again.

"Sounds good." Did that mean they would be eating something similar? He hadn't had a good plate of mashed potatoes streaming with gravy in a while. A long while. "I'll leave you to sleep then. Work hard on getting better."

When he closed Jonah's door and turned back to the others, most of the boys were seated, and Miss Wyatt and Lillian carried bowls of food to the table.

The water in the wash basin had turned a brownish color, but he used it anyway, then moved to his seat. His brothers had taken the seats each of them used to occupy, and Sean sat in the one Jericho had always used back when their parents were alive. That left Lucy's old chair, Jonah's, and both ends, where Mum and Dat used to sit.

He swallowed. He was the head of the family now, but taking Dat's seat—that felt like trying to fill his shoes. He was doing his best, but Dat had excelled in so much. Not the least of which was his faith.

Jericho couldn't even bring himself to try in that area. There were too many walls between him and the Almighty to break down.

But the boys would expect him to take Dat's seat.

He eased into the spindle-backed arm chair. He was taller than Dat had been, but the frame fit well.

Lillian and Miss Wyatt set the last of the dishes on the table, then his niece sat in the chair her mother had once occupied. The girl patted the seat beside her for Miss Wyatt.

Mum's old chair. Lillian wouldn't know that. She probably only wanted her new friend close. The two of them seemed to be getting along well after working together all day.

Miss Wyatt settled into the chair and looked around at the rest of them. Of course all the boys were watching her. He needed to have a talk with them. Needed to tell them not to let themselves get attached. These women would be leaving soon.

As soon as the sister felt better and Jonah healed enough not to need such constant care.

Her gaze met Jericho's as though she could hear his thoughts. Those blue eyes had the power to lock a man's focus and keep him from turning away. That dress sure brought out the depth of their color.

"Bow for grace, boys." Sampson's voice broke through the hold of Miss Wyatt's eyes, and Jericho ducked his head while his brother's voice rose again. "Thank you, Lord, for these thy gifts, and for the gift of the people here to share them with."

It was the prayer Dat often said. He should be glad Sampson still remembered it. But thinking of the Miss Wyatts as *gifts* would get him into trouble.

He opened his eyes at the "Amen," then focused on loading his plate with food as the others did. No one spoke while the sounds of eating filled the room. The mashed potatoes were even better than he remembered, especially with gravy drizzled on top. Why hadn't he thought to make this instead of simply cutting potatoes into stew?

"I tell ya, Miss Wyatt, this food's better'n any of us've had in years." Gil raised a fork full of meat and potatoes.

She offered a smile that leaned toward sheepish. "I'm glad you like it. And, um, most people call me Dr. Wyatt. My sister is Miss Wyatt." She sent a glance around. "Although, I suppose you could call us Dinah and Naomi." She licked her lips. Was she nervous?

She'd looked so confident every other time he saw her—even when faced with a strange Salish brave entering the house. But correcting a room full of men, and offering to let them use her Christian name...he could imagine that would be unnerving.

"Those are both right nice names, Miss Dinah." Gil nodded, then poked another bite of meat into his mouth. Maybe that'd keep him quiet for a while.

Sampson looked at Lillian. "You haven't come to see the new

74

donkey yet." He shot a look to Sean. "Someone should give him a name."

Sean turned a gap-tooth grin to his sister. "You should see him, Lil. He's got the longest ears. And when he brays, it sounds like he's crying."

Miss Wyatt—or rather, Miss Dinah—raised her gaze to Sampson. "A new donkey?"

Sampson shot a look at Jericho that showed he wondered why he'd not shared the news. In all the fuss about Two Stones, he'd forgotten to give that detail.

"That's why Two Stones was here," he explained, "bringing the donkey."

She nodded. "I see." Then she turned to Sampson. "A jenny or a jack?"

"A jenny." He sounded impressed by her knowledge of the male and female names.

"Well then." She looked from Sean to Lillian. "My pop has a jack donkey who pulls his cart when he needs to make sick visits. We named him Adam, and I always thought it would be fun to have a female named Eve."

Lillian's eyes lit. "Oh, that's good." She turned to Sampson. "Can we go see her now?"

Lillian wanted to visit an animal? She'd never seemed this excited about anything on the ranch. He couldn't help looking at Dinah, who was smiling at his niece with an expression that seemed almost motherly. Like she was proud of her.

He was still trying to get an accurate read on these visitors, and he needed to see a great deal more of Miss Naomi before he could make a judgement there. But he was more and more hard-pressed to find things he didn't like about Miss Dinah Wyatt.

CHAPTER 10

$\mathcal{T}$he wound was healing exactly the way she'd hoped.

Dinah adjusted the clean cloth over the stitches on Jonah's leg and secured the bandage again. Two days since the injury, and the bleeding had nearly stopped. No sign of festering either.

When she finished with the bandage, she pulled the blanket back and turned to her patient. He'd been awake and watching the last two times she'd changed the dressing, and she was always careful not to meet his gaze until she'd covered him up again. She had no qualms about tending injuries in any area of a patient's body. But she didn't want Jonah to feel uncomfortable.

She offered a smile. "It's healing nicely. How's your pain? Do you need more laudanum?"

He gave a slight shake of his head. "Tired of sleeping."

She nodded. "That's a good sign."

A rustle sounded at the open door, and she glanced up to see her sister peering in.

Dinah moved the extra cloth from her lap into her case, then stood. "What are you doing up?" She'd even put a chamber pot beside Naomi's bed so she didn't have to leave the room.

Her sister wrinkled her nose and stepped into the bed chamber. "I can't lay there another minute." She turned a smile on Jonah. "Thought I'd come a-visting."

"Naomi." Dinah moved to her sister's side and took her elbow to lead her back.

Naomi pulled from her grasp with a frown. "You're being overbearing, Di. I feel worlds better. A few minutes out of bed won't make me puff up again."

Dinah scrutinized Naomi's cheeks. Most of the swelling had diminished. Her hands looked much better too. "Just for a minute."

From the bed, Jonah lifted a hand, drawing their attention as he pointed to the chair Dinah had just occupied. "Come sit." His voice still sounded exhausted, but that could be from the laudanum.

Naomi moved forward. "Thank you." Though she didn't look at Dinah as she settled into the seat, the air of triumph was hard to miss. She smiled at Jonah as she settled back and laced her hands in her lap. "How are you faring now? Is my sister treating you well?"

Dinah turned with a groan toward the door. "Five minutes, Naomi. Then it's back to bed if I have to carry you myself."

It might have been the swish of her skirts, but it sure sounded like Jonah chuckled as Dinah left the room.

She rejoined Lillian, who knelt beside one of the chairs lining the dining table, rubbing oil into the wood with a rag. "How's it coming?"

Lillian used the back of her wrist to swipe loose hairs from her face. "I can't believe how dirty these are. There's food caked between the spindles that must have been there for years."

Maybe since the last time the table was used for a family meal, judging by the layers of dust they'd wiped off yesterday from the chairs tucked between the wall and the table. She and Lillian had done basic cleaning most of the day yesterday, then stopped in time for the two of them and Naomi to take a bath in the large tub Lillian had shown her.

All that dusting and sweeping and mopping had helped the place look far more respectable, but not one of the men had commented on it. Had they noticed the difference? It seemed impossible they couldn't have, but they'd not said a word.

Today she and Lillian were moving a bit deeper with their cleaning, scraping away years of dirt and grime from the cookstove, the dining table, and now the chairs, polishing each piece until it shone with the luster of newness. Surely the men would notice these improvements.

If not, tomorrow would be the baseboards and walls. Unless she could talk Jericho into taking her to town.

"Uncle Jericho said he's going to Missoula Mills in the morning. I'm going to ask if I can ride with him."

Dinah stared at the girl. Had Dinah spoken her thoughts aloud? Strange that Lillian would make that comment when she'd just been thinking about the journey.

But why hadn't Jericho told Dinah? She'd asked if she could accompany him. She eyed Lillian. "When did he say that?" He'd been gone all day, riding off with Jude that morning as all the brothers left in different directions.

The girl shrugged. "When I was petting Eve. I heard him tell Uncle Gil and Uncle Sampson."

Dinah forced herself to return to her polishing. "Does he usually take you with him?"

"Nah. He won't let me go to town. He takes Sean hunting sometimes, and a few times we've gone to trade with Two Stones and his family in their village. But Uncle Jericho says Missoula Mills is no place for children." She rolled her eyes with those words. "Can't be worse than Virginia City, nohow. An' we got along just fine there. Mama taught us how to know who's all right to talk to an' who's just tryin' to rob you blind."

Dinah's middle tightened at all the girl might have been exposed to. She'd heard Virginia City was even larger and more decadent than Helena, which she and Naomi had ridden through on their way here. Surely the children's mother hadn't allowed them to fraternize with all the unsavory characters they'd seen on that single ride through town.

"I've heard Missoula Mills is a much quieter town than Virginia City. That there hasn't been gold discovered there. At least, that's what we were told in Fort Benton." She watched the girl to gauge her reaction.

Lillian shrugged. "I don't know why he won't let us go."

"Quieter than Virginia City isn't very high praise." A deep voice sounded from the open doorway behind them.

Dinah turned to greet the newcomer—Jericho, of course. He might have been standing there listening a while, but she had nothing to hide. "Hello, Mr. Coulter. Your timing is perfect." She offered her most winning smile. "Are you still planning a trip to town tomorrow?"

He eyed her. "I am. But I'm going alone."

"I have business there and hoped to follow you so I don't miss the direction. But I can ride there later if you'd rather go by yourself."

He frowned, annoyance clear in his expression. "I said to make a list of what you need and I'll bring it back."

She shook her head. "I also need to see the town. That requires my physical presence." She gave a shrug and turned back to her chair. "I'll go a different day."

"Miss Wyatt." It sounded like he was speaking through gritted teeth. "Missoula Mills is not a safe place for you to venture alone. Nor is it a respectable town for two women to abide. You'd be wasting your time coming with me. Besides, what about my brother? Is he recovered enough he won't need you for two or three days?"

She glanced up at him. "Why three days?" According to the man they'd asked in Helena, they should be a half day's ride or less from the Missoula valley.

"It's a full day's ride to get there. That's leaving here at first light and reaching town after dark. If you're lucky enough to purchase all you need that night, you can sometimes make it back by midnight the second day. The animals have to pull uphill most of the way, so the trip back takes longer."

The knot in her middle tightened. She'd not accounted for that. Could Jonah do without her for two full days? As long as Lillian followed her instructions to the letter, and one of the men agreed to stay near the house to oversee things.

And Naomi. Would she stay in bed without Dinah here? The two of them needed a serious conversation about the dangers to the babe. Surely then Naomi would take more care.

But perhaps Dinah should wait to go to Missoula Mills. Another week or two would see Jonah faring better and his pain greatly lessened so he might not need laudanum anymore.

Yet she and Naomi might not have another week or two.

She had to be prepared for Jericho to send them away in five more days, and that meant finding a place they could go.

She met his gaze. "I need to see Missoula Mills. If you don't want me to accompany you tomorrow, I'll go on my own when you return."

His scowl made her want to look away, but she stood her ground. At last he grumbled, "I'm leaving at first light."

He turned and stomped back out of the house, leaving her a little uncertain about whether he'd conceded or not.

❧

*M*aybe Jericho should have allowed her to ride her own horse.

He eyed Dinah on the bench beside him. When she'd stepped into the barn carrying full saddle packs and looking for her mount, he'd thought it silly to make the horse ride all that way when she could just as well sit in the wagon.

But he'd not accounted for what it would be like having her beside him for two solid days. At least twenty-four hours, so close it would be rude not to converse at least occasionally. If she'd been mounted and trailing behind, small talk would have been a challenge. He'd get to enjoy the ride in silence.

Not that she talked overmuch. Most of the morning she'd stared out at the landscape they passed, occasionally remarking on the beauty of the sunrise or the abundance of chipmunks.

It was just having her so near.

He couldn't clear his mind with her pretty face smiling at him every time he glanced her way.

He kept his gaze locked in front of them. Probably a good idea since they were traversing down one of the steeper slopes on the Mullan road.

When they reached the bottom, Dinah spoke up. "Mr. Coulter, may I ask you something?"

He sighed inwardly but kept his eyes trained straight ahead. "What?"

"How long have you lived in these mountains? Did you grow up here?"

He shook his head. "We came from Kansas back in '58." He wasn't sure how far word had spread of the chaos in that state, but she likely had an idea why they'd left it.

She nodded. "Why the Montana Territory? Did you come for gold?"

Once more, he shook his head. "Dat wanted to come west, away from all the politics and fighting. My parents decided to load up the wagon and ride until they found a place they wanted to stay."

81

She was looking at him, but he didn't look back. "That must have taken a lot of courage."

Though the softness in her voice pulled at him, he shrugged. "Anything would have been better than staying in Kansas."

She didn't answer, just turned back to watch the scenery. Maybe they'd done enough small talk for a while.

A few moments later, she turned back to him. "You know what you need?"

He nearly snorted. "What's that?" He couldn't imagine what she was thinking.

"A dog."

His chest tightened. They'd had a dog. A puppy Two Stones brought them during their first winter on the mountain. They'd all loved Skipper, and when Lucy asked to take him with her when she left with that lazy, scoundrel of a husband, Jericho couldn't tell her no.

Skipper might have been the only part of home Lucy would take.

He'd loved seeing the dog every time he went to visit her. To try to help her. But that last time, the dog hadn't been there. And Jericho hadn't had the strength to ask what happened to him. Not with all the loss the children were already suffering.

"Why would I need a dog?"

She gestured to the woods around them. "For safety. Protection. Companionship."

He shook his head. "I don't need a dog for protection." A rifle worked much better against a grizzly.

She tilted her head, those bright blue eyes catching his. "I didn't mean it like that. I just thought it would be nice to have a friend to keep you company on these long rides."

He shrugged. "Maybe someday." Skipper used to ride along on trips to Missoula Mills. The memory stung a little.

"Lillian misses her dog."

Jericho's chest clenched, and he looked back at her, trying to sort through the jumble of thoughts and emotions and pain those words brought.

She met his look squarely. Earnestly.

He swallowed, working to summon his voice. His words came out in a hoarse rasp. "What did she say?"

Her eyes turned glassy. "That Skipper was her best friend. That he went everywhere with her and Sean. He kept them safe."

Something in her voice with those last words made him sit straighter. "Safe from what? What happened?"

Her mouth pressed in a sad smile. "I didn't ask. I thought it might be better if she didn't relive it."

Probably so.

He turned back to the horses with a sigh. "I'm glad Skipper went with Lucy. I'm glad he helped make things a little better for them." It had certainly been more than Jericho managed. He guided the team around a boulder the size of the wagon, their harness squeaking in a steady rhythm.

"You missed him here on the ranch though, didn't you?" Her soft voice reached in where he'd been trying not to go. But instead of raising up pain, it soothed the ache somehow.

He swallowed again. "Skipper was a good friend."

She didn't answer, and the quiet helped. Relieved some of the pressure in his chest. One by one memories of the pup slipped in. "He used to sit on my feet under the table during meals. Jude always complained that I fed him scraps, but I didn't. Sometimes I'd reach my hand down and he'd lick it, then I'd scratch behind his ears."

Jericho couldn't help the smile that tugged at his lips. "He loved chore time in the mornings. He'd come bounding out with the first person, and run full-out from one brother to the next. Getting in the way, scaring the new foals. But he really just loved the mornings. The babies would get used to him after a few days, and he'd play tag with them."

Dinah chuckled. "Sounds like a great dog."

Her smile stayed as she turned forward again, the breeze brushing the loose hairs back from her pretty face. Maybe it wasn't so bad to have another person on this trip. A friend to keep him company on this long, winding road.

CHAPTER 11

"*T*here it is."

Dinah sat up at Jericho's voice and peered into the darkness before them. The sun had long since set, and she'd nearly nodded off several times. Now she blinked to focus her gaze.

Lights shone ahead, outlining the forms of buildings. A little town along the river. Not at all the size Helena had been.

And not the same level of noise either. She and Naomi had ridden through that raucous town at dusk, and every building seemed to be a saloon, hosting drunken miners and the occasional flamboyantly dressed woman. As much as they'd been hoping for a night in a hotel with a bathing tub and a warm meal, they kept riding and found a quiet place to camp farther down the road.

Missoula Mills had more the look of a peaceful town. Figures walked the dark streets but—at least from this distance—they didn't appear drunken or disorderly.

Dinah let out a relieved breath. "Looks like a nice place."

Jericho grunted. "I wouldn't say that."

The horses' hooves clopped against rocks as they

approached. To the right ran the Blackfoot River, and a building at its edge must be the sawmill she'd heard about. The sounds of the town drowned out the waterwheel though.

Most of the structures were dark, but a few had open doors with light and people spilling out. Those looked more like the saloons from Helena.

They passed one such place, and she peered inside at the men surrounding several tables. Jericho kept the team moving, so she couldn't see more than that.

He reined in before a quiet building marked with the words "Trading Post." "I'll see if anyone's here. We might have to track down Higgins or Worden to get supplies tonight." He jumped to the ground and strode to the door.

She'd been counting on getting loaded tonight so they could be on the road at first light. She'd left Jude and Lillian careful instructions about how to care for Jonah, along with plenty of medicine and clean bandages in case their trip went an extra day or two. But in her mind, she'd been planning to be back tomorrow night.

If they had to spend a second night away, sleeping on the trail... It was already indecent enough her traveling alone with this man. But spending a night with him? Away from town or the ranch, and any possible chaperone...

She didn't fear that he'd take advantage. He'd had plenty of opportunity and never gave her a moment's concern. The opposite actually. He seemed to go out of his way to keep distance between them.

But her reputation. It was all a woman had sometimes.

Really though. Who in this land except his brothers and her sister would know or care that they were alone? And they would all know well that the overnight together was innocent.

But what of the children? The last thing she wanted was for Lillian or Sean to think it acceptable for a man and woman to spend a night alone together. It simply couldn't happen.

If supplies couldn't be purchased and loaded tonight, she'd have to insist she and Jericho stay in Missoula all day tomorrow, then leave before first light on the third day.

No one had answered Jericho's knock, so he returned to the wagon, stepping up to the bench in an effortless motion. "There's a hotel down a ways where I usually stay. I'll get you settled there, then look for them." He released the brake and signaled the team to walk.

"Where will you look?" Surely he wouldn't have to enter the saloons. If he did, would he stay on for a drink while he was there?

A knot tightened inside her. Pop and Nana had warned so often against alcohol and how it affected people. She and Naomi had so rarely seen anyone who over-imbibed—before leaving Wayneston anyway. They'd seen plenty since then, and that experience certainly hadn't made her think better of the stuff.

She'd been relieved to find no fermented drinks in the supplies at the Coulter cabin. But he might avail himself readily enough when in town. If he did, at least she could stay clear of him here. That might delay their trip a day, but so be it. Maybe she should have brought her gelding after all. She could ride back tomorrow and let Jericho sleep off his headache.

They passed three more saloons filled with men before Jericho reined in at a building at the far end of town. The front rose up two stories, and a light shone through the window. But it looked far more like a respectable hotel than a saloon.

Jericho jumped to the ground and turned to help her down, as he had the other times they'd stopped to rest the horses. She took his hand, ignoring the warm strength of his grip. Certainly far sturdier than Pop's hands had been. Pop had the touch of a physician, the careful and sensitive hold of a man used to feeling for fever and crafting tiny stitches to mend torn flesh.

Jericho's calluses seemed natural for this man, an expected

part of someone so large and virile, tanned from working every day under the expanse of the Montana sky.

When she reached the ground, he released her hand, turning to stride toward the door. She couldn't move as quickly though. Her body needed a moment to adjust to the sudden loss of his touch.

He was knocking by the time she summoned a breath and followed.

The door opened, and a man stood in the frame. "Yes?"

Jericho cleared his throat. "Need two rooms. The nicest you have for Miss Wyatt."

The man looked at her, his gaze scanning up and down quickly. What did he see in her? Hopefully, he didn't think her the kind of woman who'd been in Helena.

He turned back to Jericho. "Only have one open. Surely that will suit." The corners of his mouth curved, and he stepped back. "It's two dollars. Up the stairs, last door on the right."

After a nod, Jericho turned to speak to her. "I'll sleep with the wagon at the livery."

A spurt of panic clutched her chest. "Is it safe here?" The proprietor already thought her a loose woman and seemed fine with that scenario playing out in his establishment. Jericho hadn't set him straight either. Maybe he thought the man wouldn't believe him. Truly, she didn't care what this stranger thought of her.

But she did care about whether a drunken man would barge into her room during the night, thinking she'd welcome him.

Jericho paused, his gaze meeting hers. In the shadows, she couldn't read his expression. "This is the most respectable lodging in town. I wouldn't let you in the door of the others. Let's get you settled, then maybe I can bunk double with someone else here."

The weight inside her eased. Maybe he could stay close enough to hear if she screamed. Surely that wouldn't be necessary, but still, it made her feel better. "That won't be comfortable for you."

His mouth curved a little. "Wouldn't be the first time."

He returned to the wagon to grab her pack, and she followed him into the building, up the narrow stairs, and down an even narrower hallway. Their footsteps echoed in the silence. If the rooms were all taken, where were the occupants? In the saloons, maybe.

The door at the end on the right was open, and a light glowed from inside. Jericho stopped in front of it and motioned her in. A lantern sat on a small table, illuminating the closet-like space. A cot barely wide enough for a single person sat in one corner, a three-drawer bureau with washbasin and pitcher in another, and the table and a single chair filled a third, leaving barely enough space to walk between them.

She turned back to Jericho, who waited in the hall. "Will you come get me when it's time to purchase supplies?" As late as it was, it didn't seem a businessman would want to open his shop tonight, but Jericho would know, surely.

"I can. Wouldn't you rather just give me a list? That way you can settle in for the night."

Would she? She'd expected to peruse shop shelves, walking along aisles and examining goods. Maybe even find some cloth so Naomi could begin stitching baby clothes while she lay in bed.

But Dinah couldn't do that tonight. Not well after ten o'clock, or maybe even pushing midnight. Those niceties would have to wait until she and her sister were more settled.

For now, Jericho could load the things they couldn't do without. In the morning, she could inquire from the hotel owner and any other shopkeeper she saw about whether an open building existed that she could rent for a medical clinic.

After seeing Missoula Mills, she wasn't as certain there would be a vacant space. But if she had to, she could set up a tent at the edge of town until a more permanent structure became available. There had been hundreds of medical tents during the war, which had proven a viable means of providing care, especially in a frontier setting like this.

For now, she gave Jericho a grateful smile. "I'll write a few things down for you."

~

*A*t least the saloons were closed this early in the morning.

Jericho strode to the livery before the sun turned the edge of eastern sky gray. After loading the supplies, he'd only slept four or five hours. And for those, he'd been stretched out with a blanket in front of Dinah's door. It was the only way he could truly keep her safe. He would be relieved to shake the dust of Missoula Mills off his wagon wheels.

Maybe this place wasn't as decadent and rough-shod as Helena, but since the Mullan Road opened, that lot had been trickling this direction, searching for the next big strike. All those rows of tents along the river proved it.

When the first strike happened, this place would become every bit as bad as Helena or Virginia City. He could only hope no one spotted any pretty colored stones and realized what they were.

When he stepped into the open livery, Clip was already hitching the team. "Morning."

The livery owner nodded. "Thought you'd be heading out early. These boys've had their breakfast and are raring to go."

Though Jericho only came to Missoula Mills a few times a year, somehow the man remembered him. Or maybe the pair of matched chestnuts stood out to him. Either way, he was a good fellow. Kind to the animals.

Jericho moved to the horses and worked with Clip to finish

hitching the wagon. Somewhere back in the barn, a whine sounded. An animal of some kind. Or several of them.

Clip must have seen him glance that way. "Got some pups I'm weanin' from their mama. They're not fond of the process."

Something inside him raised its head in interest. "Pups?"

"Two boys an' two girls. Cutest little things. Their daddy's a good herding dog, owned by a rancher who comes to town every week. Their mama's been a good friend to me for years now. You couldn't ask for a better companion."

Part ranch dog, part friend. Sounded like Skipper. But did he dare bring a young pup home? If it brought a smile to Lillian, it would be worth the trouble.

Of course, Dinah would know he was following her suggestion. She might start making other requests. He was his own man though. He could tell her no if he wanted. Nor did he think so highly of himself that he couldn't recognize good advice when he heard it.

"You think one of those would make a good friend for a lonely little girl?"

Clip grinned. "I've got just the one."

That one turned out to be the runt. A female who wriggled all over Jericho's lap as he drove to the hotel to pick up Dinah. It had taken him longer than he'd expected at the livery, so she stood in front of the building waiting as he approached.

The grin on her face showed she'd seen his little passenger. When he reined the team in beside her, she stepped close, her smile widening. "She's perfect."

The way her eyes lit made her look so pretty he couldn't quite peel his gaze away. It wasn't fair, her gazing up at him like that. Even if she was really just looking at the dog.

He scooped up the pup and held it out to her. "Clip was weaning the litter, so I thought this might be a good one for Lilly."

She took the runt in gentle hands, holding her up at eye level as she spoke to her. "Wait until you meet Lillian. She's going to be your best friend, no doubt about it."

She drew the pup into her chest and raised that beaming gaze up to him. For a moment, she didn't speak, just grinned at him, that smile stretching her pretty mouth and making her blue eyes sparkle.

Tying his belly in knots.

He fumbled for something to say. "You'll have to hold her all day. She doesn't seem fond of sitting still."

Dinah stroked the pup, dipping her chin to look at the animal—who'd stopped squirming in her arms, of course. "I think we can handle her."

She might be able to manage the pup, but when Dinah turned that pretty smile back on him, he wasn't altogether sure he could stand a day of being so near her without doing something he would very much regret.

CHAPTER 12

*D*inah had her hands full keeping the pup entertained during the long hours on the wagon bench. The animal slept much of the morning, made a mess on the wagon floor once, then yapped at a passing freighter until Dinah worried Jericho might turn and swat her.

He'd proven he wasn't given to temper. But even Dinah could admit the incessant high-pitched bark was annoying. Once they reached the cabin, Lillian's pleasure would make every frustration worth it. And the girl could take over responsibility for all this wiggling energy.

Dinah finally settled the bundle of fur quietly on her lap while she stroked, but then the pup lifted her head at something in the distance. A squirrel no doubt. She'd barked at every one they'd seen so far, and a few that were probably her imagination.

The pup jumped to her feet, straining toward whatever she'd spotted.

"Easy." Dinah kept her voice soft and her strokes steady.

"I think someone's coming. Try not to let her bark if you can." To his credit, Jericho's voice held only a hint of frustration.

His stern manner was definitely a cover for the reasonable—even kind—man beneath.

She held the pup to her chest. "No barking. We don't bark at friends."

The oncoming riders were clearer now. A group of five or six. Something looked different about them though.

As they drew closer, the truth jolted through her. These weren't miners or mountain men. They were Indians. Dressed in cloth shirts and leather trousers, just like Two Stones had been. But also like so many other men she'd met since leaving the steamer in Fort Benton. What set these natives apart was their black hair and something in the way they rode their horses.

She glanced at Jericho. She was learning not to make assumptions about a man's character by the way he looked or his occupation. "Do you know them?"

He was eyeing the riders, but he hadn't stopped the wagon. Just kept driving down the road as if they were passing a group of miners. "I think so. That looks like Two Stones's cousin. They're probably Salish. A hunting party, from the look of the pack horses."

When the group reached them, the road was wide enough for them to come alongside, and Jericho reined in the team. The men halted their horses beside the wagon, one of them raising his hand in greeting.

Jericho spoke first, but not in English. She couldn't help studying him. She'd had no idea he spoke a native language, though with Two Stones such a good friend of their family, it made sense.

The man who'd greeted them answered Jericho, and they carried on a brief conversation. At one point, the man looked over at the pup in her lap and grinned, his smile infectious as he glanced at Dinah.

Did he know Lillian and Sean? Maybe he'd even met the first Skipper.

At last, the group turned their horses aside, and Jericho waved farewell as he signaled the team to walk on.

When the newcomers moved down the trail, she finally asked, "What did they say?"

"They were just passing through on a hunting trip." Jericho kept his focus on the road ahead. "But they asked about the pup."

"Did you see how he smiled at her?"

He spared the dog a look. "That was Two Stones's cousin from a different village. He's the chief's son there. In line to take his place."

"I didn't know you spoke their language." She tried to sound casual.

A small smile quirked his lips. "I picked up a few things from Two Stones."

"It's a good skill to have." And how many other unexpected talents did Jericho possess? Every time she thought she understood this man, something more surprised her.

*D*inah woke to a squeal somewhere in another part of the cabin.

She sat up, doing her best to force her scratchy eyes open in the early morning dimness of the chamber.

"Who is that?" Naomi raised up on her elbows in the other cot.

Dinah pushed her blanket aside and sat up, slipping her feet into her boots before standing. She could fasten them later. "Sounds like Lillian." Had she found the puppy already?

Dinah and Jericho had arrived at the ranch around midnight, and Jericho offered to keep the dog in the barn with him until morning. Dinah had peeked in to check Jonah, and thankfully his breathing and color looked good, the bandage was clean, and the traction still set correctly. Then she'd barely taken time to remove her shoes before collapsing into bed.

As she opened the door and stepped into the main room, the source of the squeal came clear. Lillian sat on the floor, the puppy bouncing on her lap. Sean knelt beside her, trying to tease the dog onto the floor to play with him, but the animal seemed intent on jumping up to lick Lillian's chin.

With every puppy kiss, Lillian giggled, which seemed to spur the dog on for more. Jericho stood back against the wall, leaning with his arms crossed and one leg propped. A small smile played at his mouth, and his eyes drank in the scene of his niece so happy.

Then Jericho's gaze lifted to hers, and something in his eyes held her. They'd done this together. A team, bringing joy to this girl who'd had so little pleasure in her hard life.

His chin dipped in a tiny nod, as if he understood her thoughts. She smiled, then turned her focus to the children.

As she approached Lillian, the pup bounded up to Dinah, wagging her tail so hard her whole body shook. "Well, good morning to you too." Dinah scratched behind the dog's ears. "I knew you'd love the children."

"Uncle Jericho said I can name her." Lillian beamed, then glanced at the man as though to make sure she'd heard right.

He nodded. "Any ideas?"

"Aren't you going to let the poor invalid see her?" Jonah called from his chamber.

"I agree." From the other room, Naomi grumbled. "It's not fair to those of us chained to our beds."

Dinah chuckled. "I guess you'd better take her visiting."

As Lillian scooped up the puppy and Sean followed her into Jonah's room, the front door opened. Jude and Gilead carried in full armloads of firewood.

"I'd better start the morning meal." She headed toward the

cookstove. Hopefully someone had banked the coals last night so she could nurse a flame back to life.

Excitement flowed around her as the brothers tromped in and out of the cabin, playing with the children and the pup. Lillian christened the dog Apple, since her coat was the rusty color of the apples that should be ripening on the fruit trees in the valley soon.

As Dinah stared at the small stack of supplies in the corner, her mind scrambled for what she could make. The boxes hadn't been unloaded from the wagon yet. Maybe the men would be content with Johnnycakes and fried meat again. She would do better once she had more to cook with. And a full night's sleep.

While she fried the first heaping plate of Johnnycakes, the men started carrying in the crates from the wagon. Each man's load stacked two or three boxes high, showing just how much strength ran in the Coulter family. The crates must weigh fifty pounds each, at least.

She didn't know everything Jericho had purchased for the house, but she motioned to open places around the kitchen where they could stack each load. She'd have to sort through the contents later and find places for it all. More permanent places than the way the men currently stored their supplies—in haphazard stacks around the edges of the room.

"Jericho said these belong to you two ladies." Gilead looked at her as he held two crates near the door to the room she shared with Naomi.

Dinah nodded. "Thank you. Just set them inside the door and I'll go through everything later."

She'd not expected her short list to fill two crates, but maybe the milk had been packed well. Naomi needed to drink as much as they could find to help the baby grow strong. Too bad Jericho didn't have a milk cow on the ranch.

He *did* own cows though. Could any be tamed for milking?

Maybe she could ask him when they had a quiet moment. Had he thought about it when he'd purchased the milk from her list?

When she'd piled three plates high with Johnnycakes and two more with fried meat, she caught Lillian's attention as the girl exited Jonah's chamber, the pup in her arms. "Lillian, can you wash your hands and set the table? Then we'll be ready to eat."

No one had said whether the men planned to sit around the table for this meal like they had the others, but if she prepared everything, surely they would come, despite the increased chaos of the pup and unloading the wagon.

As she'd hoped, Gilead saw Lillian setting out plates and called his brothers in to eat. Jude headed to the washbasin first, and the others followed him. Sampson and Sean even rose from their chairs to wait their turn in line to wash. She tried not to smile so broadly she embarrassed them.

These mountain men weren't so hard to train.

Jericho didn't meet her gaze as he waited for Miles to finish with the water. Maybe the camaraderie they'd developed over the last two days wouldn't last now that they were back among the others.

But after he dried his hands on the cloth, he turned to the plates of food beside the stove. "These go to the table?"

She nodded as she pushed the frying pan to a cooler surface. "They do."

He scooped two plates of Johnnycakes, then turned to Sampson and Sean. "You boys get the rest."

That made her work easier. She used a leather pad to pick up the full pot of coffee she'd just brewed from the grounds in one of the crates the men carried in, then headed to the table to fill cups.

When they were all seated, Gilead spoke the same prayer one or other of the brothers had said before every meal they'd eaten at the table so far. There was never discussion about who would pray, they all just bowed and one of the men began speaking. Was Jericho or someone else arranging who would pray ahead of time? They had to be, unless there was a system already set up she didn't know about. That seemed unlikely.

As they ate, conversation flowed easily, with Sean chattering on about Apple and some of the brothers teasing him and his sister about the pup. Lillian responded with shy answers that showed how protective she would be of her new friend.

For her part, the pup sat at Lillian's feet. Dinah kept an eye on the girl to make sure she didn't try to feed her from the table, but Lillian didn't attempt it.

When a moment of quiet settled, Jude turned to Jericho. "I'm planning to look for new...um, strawberries today. If you don't need Sampson, thought he could work with me."

Something in his voice seemed strained. Was it her imagination, or did Jericho glance her way for half a heartbeat before eyeing his brother. Maybe he thought picking berries would be a better job for the women and children. Perhaps that was already Lillian's task, but he didn't want to pull her away from helping Dinah.

She spoke quickly before Jericho could answer. "Lillian and I can do that. Sean too, if you don't need him elsewhere.

Jude turned to her with a startled look, then his brows lowered. "I, um. No. Picking strawberries is usually what I do."

What in the wide blue sky? She studied him, trying to find a reason he would cling to this work. Did he love the taste of strawberries so much? Did the berries grow on some rocky cliffside that only he had the courage to maneuver? If that were the case, she might let him do it. Heights unnerved her more than anything else.

But he hadn't said that was the case. Maybe he was just trying to be chivalrous and take the work himself.

She tried once more. "We could at least help you. Many hands make the work lighter."

"Sampson will help him." Jericho spoke up, his tone sounding final. "Jonah needs you here, since you've been gone two days."

She nodded. He was probably right, but something about the conversation felt off.

"Miles and I are headed to work with the two-year-olds today." Gilead eyed his oldest brother as though waiting for approval.

Jericho nodded. "Sean and I will ride down to the valley. He can halter the foals while I tar the cattle." He swept his gaze around his brothers. "We should wean the calves on Monday."

The men nodded, though nobody seemed pleased with the news. Miles dropped his gaze to his food and mumbled something she couldn't understand before stuffing a bite of meat into his mouth.

Nana and Pop had never owned cows, but she'd heard many a milk cow bawling for the calf that had been separated from it at the farms outside of town. This might be the time to raise her question.

She tried to make her voice as cheery as she could as she addressed Jericho. "What would you think about bringing one of the mama cows up to the barn so we can milk her after the calf is weaned?"

Every eye swung to her, most widening. But the corners of Miles's crinkled as he flashed a grin. "That sounds like a fun time."

Dinah offered a rueful smile. "I know teaching her to milk might not be easy, but once we accomplished it, we'd have milk for the household, and we could even make butter and cheese."

She turned her gaze back to Jericho. He would be the one to decide, no doubt.

His expression was hard to read. At last, he said, "We'll see."

Maybe he needed to think on how such a feat could be undertaken. Or debate the risk to him and his brothers in trying to tame a wild cow. At least he was considering it.

She nodded. "Thank you."

He turned his gaze to his niece and nephew. "Did you look in your crates?"

Sean straightened. "You mean the dog wasn't all you brought us?"

"Nope." A smile played at the corners of his mouth.

Sean leaped from his chair and skidded toward the front door, jerking it open and leaving it wide as he disappeared outside.

Lillian started to rise, but paused, looking from Dinah to Jericho as though for permission. Jericho gave her a nod, and the girl scrambled after her brother. "C'mon, Apple."

Dinah tried to meet Jericho's gaze as the rest of the men piled food in their mouths, but he'd already finished his meal and pushed back from the table. "Get a move on."

As the brothers rose and headed to the door, she stacked used dishes from the table and carried a load to the wash pot. She and Lillian could finish cleaning soon, but first, she needed to spend some time with her patient.

CHAPTER 13

*J*onah was awake when she entered his room, lying with his eyes open. She carried a cup of meat broth in one hand and a plate of Johnnycakes in the other. "You look like you're feeling better this morning."

He nodded, his eyes on the food. "Hungry."

"I'll have to start feeding you before the others then." She made sure Naomi received the first helping of each meal so she didn't have to lie in bed hungry, listening to the others eat. If Jonah's appetite had returned, he could have the same privilege.

While she fed Jonah, the sound of the outside door opening drifted in, and Lillian's voice called through the cabin. "Look, Dinah."

Dinah straightened. "In here."

The girl skipped in. "Look what Uncle Jericho brought." She held up a thickly-folded fabric, a cheery blue pinstripe.

"Oh my." Dinah rose and set the plate in her chair so she could examine the fabric. "This is lovely." Cloth this luxurious would be expensive, even back in Virginia. She could only imagine how much it cost after being hauled all the way out here to the Montana Territory.

"Do you think there's enough to make a dress?" Lillian sounded hopeful.

Dinah lifted one edge. "At least. Maybe an extra skirt too."

"Oh." The word came out nearly breathless, and the girl hugged the material to her chest.

Dinah couldn't help but smile. "Maybe you can start washing the morning dishes while I help your Uncle Jonah. After that, we'll ask Naomi to help us cut out the dress."

Lillian surely didn't know how to cut and sew a dress herself. Dinah could manage it if she had to, but Naomi had always been a much better seamstress. Much better at most household work. Dinah had spent every free hour with Pop in the clinic when she didn't have to focus on schoolwork.

The girls eyes lit and she spun. "I will. Thank you."

When Dinah took up her seat again, Jonah was watching her with a faint grin. "Jericho always brings a crate full of things for each of them. I think he must be ordering goods in now. What he brought these last few trips is a lot nicer than at first."

Jericho's kindness didn't surprise her anymore. She'd seen the soft side Jericho Coulter worked so hard to hide. "He seems like a good uncle." But that sounded like she didn't think the rest of the men were as capable. So she added, "All of you are. The children are blessed to be here with you."

As Jonah took another bite and her own words replayed through her mind, she realized they were true. This place might not be as clean and charmingly decorated as Nana kept the little white house in Wayneston, but Sean and Lillian were surrounded by family who loved them, doted on them even, if you could see through the manly facades. And they always had plenty of food and secure shelter. That was probably more than the two'd had while their mother lived, from the bits and pieces she'd gathered.

After Jonah finished eating and she changed the bandage on

his leg, she carried his used dishes out. At Naomi's door, she tapped a light knock, then pulled the latch string.

Naomi wasn't in the bed.

"Dinah, this is perfect." Naomi's voice drew Dinah's gaze to the floor, where her sister sat in front of an open crate. She held up a folded piece of pale yellow fabric. "There's enough here to make several gowns. And the blue too. It's beautiful." Naomi lifted a length of the same blue striped material Lillian had. She beamed a smile free of the weariness that marked her these past weeks.

Dinah's middle tightened. "Naomi, I don't think that's ours." Oh how she hated to steal her sister's pleasure. To layer another disappointment on top of so many others.

She dropped to her knees and touched the blue cloth. "I think this might be something Jericho brought back for Lillian." Naomi's mouth stayed curved, but her eyes lost their sparkle.

Dinah pressed on. "It was late when we arrived in Missoula Mills, so Jericho had to track down the trading post owner. I gave him a list of what we needed. I thought about adding fabric to it so you could begin making gowns for the baby, but I didn't want to put the burden on him of choosing colors and patterns. I didn't even know if a post all the way out here would sell cloth suitable for a baby." If she'd known he was already purchasing for his niece, she would have asked differently.

Naomi smoothed her hand over the yellow, her gaze on the material. "This *will* make a nice shirt for Sean." When she looked up, she seemed to have recovered her poise. "They do need new clothes. Shall I help sew?"

Dinah's chest ached for her sister, but there was nothing she could do to make this better. Not yet. She wrapped an arm around Naomi's shoulders. "You know I couldn't do it myself." Then she pushed to her feet and took up the used dishes, adding Naomi's to the stack. "I'll finish cleaning up the kitchen while you and Lillian start."

As she strode toward the work counter next to the stove, the front door opened. Probably Lillian coming in with more wash water.

But it wasn't Lillian.

Two Stones paused in the doorway, and once more, his appearance made her heart hammer. But she forced herself to exhale. "Two Stones. Welcome." Maybe he'd never been told of the English custom of knocking.

He strode forward. "Jude said come to you."

Her stomach lurched, and she fought to keep from stepping backward. "He did?"

He stopped in the middle of the room, probably realizing he'd frightened her. "There is sickness in my camp. My father and mother, they are laid low."

Her pulse leapt forward for a very different reason. She covered the last two steps to drop the dishes on the counter. "Let me gather a few things, and I'll come with you."

~

"Why would you do that?" Jericho slid from his horse and fought the urge to pull Jude down from his own mount and wallop him.

"He said half the camp is sick. White Bear and Running Woman too. We have a doctor here. We should see what she can do to help them." Jude dismounted, but Jericho didn't stop to respond, just strode into the house.

Lillian was speaking to Two Stones in the main room, but they turned when he entered.

Two Stones met his gaze, and he couldn't miss the worry in the man's eyes. Fear even. No wonder Jude had sent him for Dinah.

"How bad is it?" At least Jericho could go and see what he could do to help. Maybe Dinah would send medicine.

"The spotting sickness. Running Woman does not rise from her bed."

Bad then. Two Stones's mother never stopped moving when they visited her, always working.

Jericho scanned the room for Dinah. "I'll come with you. Let me gather a few things to bring them."

"I'm ready." Dinah emerged from her room, a saddle pack slung over her shoulder and a bundle of blankets in the other arm. "Can you carry that pack?" She pointed to the floor, where her medical case sat by the door to Jonah's room.

Jericho shook his head. "I'll go with him. Can you send medicine or something with us?"

Dinah bent to the case. But instead of opening it to pull out supplies to send, she hoisted the container and tucked it under her free arm. "I'm coming too."

Two Stones stepped quickly to take it from her.

Jericho reached for the bundle of blankets. "No, Dinah. Stay with Jonah and the children. There might be nothing we can do in the village. Two Stones said it's the spotting sickness."

She paused, her brows drawing together. "Smallpox?"

She was familiar with it then. "I can't risk you or anyone else getting it," Jericho said. "Do you have medicine I can take to them?"

She straightened, inhaling a breath. "There's much I can do for them." She started for the door, not looking back to see if Two Stones was following. "I was inoculated as a child, so I can't contract it again."

Jericho wanted to stride forward and grab her arms, drag her back into the cabin, and make her stay put. But he couldn't do that. Not without looking like a cad.

Two Stones was already following her. If the woman wanted to put herself and her sister—and that unborn baby—at risk, maybe he couldn't stop her. But he'd be there to help too.

Jude already had Dinah's horse saddled and stood holding all three animals as Jericho exited the cabin. Within minutes they were riding down the slope, Two Stones in the lead.

Jericho shot a look at Dinah. She was focused on guiding her horse around the stones scattered along the trail. In a couple of hours, she'd be faced with a challenge far greater than navigating a rocky path.

~

*T*he conditions at the camp were worse than Dinah had imagined.

Two Stones's village was nestled in a valley, surrounded by pine-covered slopes. A picturesque scene, with the homes a combination of bark huts and animal-skin tipis. But she could smell the stench of sickness before they dismounted at the edge of the trees. Moans and crying drifted through the air.

Her heart ached as she untied the bundle of blankets and her saddle pack from behind her saddle. Two Stones had her case of medical supplies.

"I will take the horses." Two Stones handed her bag to Jericho, then reached for both their reins.

Jericho motioned for her to follow him as he walked between a bark hut and a leather lodge. Two children sat at the base of one hut, staring up at them as they passed. She forced a smile for them. The younger had a half-dozen postules dotting her sweet face. They looked to be scabbing over, one of the final healing stages. *Thank You, Lord.*

Dinah had spent half the ride here praying and the other half trying to remember all the phases smallpox went through from the moment a patient contracted it through the final scarring.

They passed more people—mostly children—sitting outside as Jericho led her through the maze of homes. At last, he paused in front of a bark hut, looking back at her with his brows raised, sadness marking his eyes.

She nodded to show she was ready.

He pushed aside the leather curtain hanging in the doorway, and she peered in as she followed him into the dim interior. The smell stung her nose, pressing on her chest.

Jericho shifted to the right, and her eyes made out two bed pallets.

She stepped closer, crouching beside the nearest one. A gnarled face stared at her, crowned by white hair that looked greasy. Even in the dimness, she could see the dozens of pustules peppering the wrinkled skin.

"This is White Bear, Two Stones's father." Jericho's voice sounded grim as he stood beside her. Then he spoke something in the man's language.

The man stared up at Jericho while he spoke, and when he finished, the Salish father dropped his gaze to Dinah. The weariness in his eyes squeezed her insides.

He opened his mouth, and she leaned in. His voice came out with a wheeze. "My Running Woman. Two Stones say you help."

His English was clearer than she'd expected, but the pain in his voice drew her gaze past him to the form lying on the furs beside him.

The woman was as wrinkled as her husband, with large postules all over her face, some scabbed and some oozing. Her eyes stayed closed, but her chest rose and fell.

Dinah's own breath wouldn't come as she studied the signs of a case that might be too far gone for help. She rose and moved around to the woman's side. The sores continued even onto her scalp, visible between strands of white hair.

Dinah knelt and ran her fingers over an unblemished section of skin. Feverish. Her lips were chapped and bright red. Time to do what little she could.

She reached out for her case, and Jericho brought it to her. "I'm going to need clean water. Both for drinking and cleaning." From the smell of things, she would need to wash both of her patients well from the effects of how smallpox always irritated the digestive system.

While Jericho left to carry out her request, she pulled a salve from her case and applied it to Running Woman's lips, then reached over to do the same for White Bear. She had to get them both drinking and make a broth for nourishment. She could offer something for the pain, but that might do more harm than good. Pop had always felt most patients who died of the disease succumbed to weakness from not eating while the body fought so hard. She needed Running Woman to be awake enough to fight if she could.

Two Stones arrived as she was inspecting his mother's legs and feet, and she set him to work preparing meat for the broth. Jericho returned with water, and she used some of it to clean Running Woman and change her bedding.

While she worked, she should find out the extent of the epidemic. "How long has it been since the first person here showed signs of sickness?"

Two Stones looked at his father. "It was after I left to find the donkey. A moon maybe? Or not quite that."

The older man grunted. A yes, perhaps.

So not quite a month. "And how many in the camp are ill?" She would check the others once she'd done what she could for these two.

Two Stones tore chunks of meat into the pot of water. "I did not count. When I returned from taking donkey to Jericho, I find the sickness here."

She pulled the clean blankets over Running Woman and moved to her head to help her drink. "When you finish that, I need to know how many in the village are healthy and how many have felt any sign of the sickness." She met his gaze. "Not just sores. Fever, upset in the belly. Anything. Once you know that, gather every person not sick and bring them to me. We have to do what we can so they don't get the worst of the disease."

She hated exposing healthy people to puss from those who were sick, but that was the only way to keep them from succumbing to Smallpox in earnest. They would feel sick after she placed the infected liquid in their nose, but the nausea and fever would fade quickly, and they wouldn't contract the full disease. She could stop this epidemic.

She refocused on the frail woman before her. Running Woman had groaned as Dinah cleaned her, and now her eyes were open in slits.

Dinah offered a smile. "Hello. I have water for you to drink. I'm going to lift your head a little to help you." She slipped her hand behind the woman's head, keeping her touch as light as she could in case there were more sores back there.

She poured a small amount through her open lips, then paused as Running Woman tried to swallow. Her face squeezed with pain, probably from postules down her throat. *Lord, grant her peace. Heal this woman and ease her pain.*

When Running Woman drank everything she could manage, Dinah eased her head down again and adjusted the covers. "I'm going to help your husband now. I'll be back when the broth is ready. You'll both feel better soon." *Please, Lord.*

Only God could keep these precious lives from being lost.

CHAPTER 14

Thirty-one in the village were in some stage of sickness. Twelve healthy that she'd exposed to puss so they could develop immunity to the disease.

And two dead. One of them only a child.

Dinah stared at the family lying in the dim lodge before her. The young girl who'd passed had been their daughter, and the mother now curled around herself, grieving even as she slept. Both parents would recover, she was fairly certain. Their postules had already scabbed over, and their strength hadn't waned enough to worry her. As long as grief didn't drain them too much more.

The remaining child, a boy about Sean's age named Kicks the Stone, was the one she worried about. He was weak from vomiting for days and just now entering the hardest part of the disease. But his mother said he'd been strong before taking ill, so that would help him.

If he died though...she could well imagine his mother's grief. It would be her undoing.

Dinah simply couldn't let him die.

She turned to the opening in the hide wall and stepped out

into the cooling dusk.

Jericho was walking toward her. He'd been helping some of the other healthy men bury the dead.

When he reached her, the sad weariness that lined his face made her want to step into his arms. To take the pain of what he'd just had to bear.

"We need to get home." His voice rasped with exhaustion.

"I'll stay the night here. Go make sure all is well there." Poor Lillian would have to continue as woman of the house, but with her uncles helping, they would manage.

Much better than the hurting people here.

He shook his head. "You need to come too. You need rest. We can return tomorrow."

She raised her brows. "Ride two hours in the dark tonight, just to turn around and ride two more hours back in the morning?" She shook her head. "I'll stay, thank you. Besides, I'm needed here." There were some who might reach a turning point tonight, and her help could make the difference.

"Dinah." He stepped closer. He didn't touch her, but she had the strong sense that he wanted to. His words came out in a growl. "I'm not leaving without you."

She squared her shoulders and met his gaze. "Then I guess we're both staying, because I'm not leaving my patients until I'm sure they'll be alive when I return."

The hardness in his eyes dimmed. The pain of what he'd just done slipped back into his gaze, and part of her wished she'd not been the one to put it there.

She reached out and laid her hand on his arm. "Tonight will be hard for Running Woman. I want her to pull through, but I need to be here."

He nodded, his Adam's apple bobbing. He didn't speak for a moment, then said, "I'll let Two Stones know we'll be staying."

She let the air ease from her lungs as weariness threaded back through her. "Thank you."

Then she turned and started toward the only lodge she hadn't yet visited. So much still to do, and nowhere near enough time to accomplish it all.

～

*A*s weary as Jericho was, the woman walking beside him must be nearly dead on her feet.

He glanced sideways at Dinah as they made their way to another sick lodge. "After we finish here, you're going to lie down and sleep."

She gave him an exhausted attempt at a smile. "We'll see how Kicks the Stone is doing." Deep shadows lined her eyes.

Except for the few minutes when he'd found her slumped beside Running Woman, Dinah hadn't slept in the two days they'd been at Two Stones's village. Unfortunately, as he'd tried to back out of that hut without waking her, he'd tripped on a stick, and she'd jerked upright.

"Why don't you let me see to him? You've shown me everything that can be done." He'd stayed at her side as often as he could, doing whatever possible to ease her load and help those suffering around them.

She didn't answer right away. Probably too tired to form words. He was close to that point himself, though he'd slept a couple hours in the night.

But when she spoke, her voice came softly. "I'm concerned about him."

"Kicks the Stone?"

She nodded, her brow creased as she stared at the ground. "He's not gaining strength like I'd hoped."

But surely she could find a way to work the same magic with that boy that she had with Two Stones's mother and so many others. As weak as Running Woman had been when they first arrived yesterday morning, he'd thought he would be helping to bury her now. Instead, she was already starting to sit up and talking again.

Dinah had worked a miracle. Surely she could do the same with Kicks the Stones.

Maybe she needed encouragement. "What do you think should be done to help him?"

They'd nearly reached that family's lodge, though they were probably still far enough away not to be heard. Dinah stopped and turned to him, her gaze still troubled. "His mother. She's so deep in grieving the daughter she lost that she's not helping the son she still has. He needs his mother. I don't think anyone else can help him until he feels her love."

Jericho nodded, but the idea didn't fit clearly with the rest of his thoughts. "What...can you do?" Dinah had seemed so invincible these past days. Proving herself to be an excellent doctor, not just with knowledge, but she possessed a caring that infused hope in her patients. Just having her there seemed to give them strength.

She squared her shoulders, maybe trying to summon the determination she needed. "I'm going to talk to her." She met his gaze. "A mother is the heart of a family. If she loses hope, so does everyone else. I have to help her find that hope again."

Dinah must have also found the hope she needed, for she strode toward the lodge of Kicks the Stone's family.

As he started after her, a voice called his name. He turned as Two Stones walked toward him. He didn't look upset, so maybe nothing was amiss.

When he met him, Two Stones raised his brows. "You are faring well?"

Jericho nodded. It was Dinah he worried about, but he'd rather know what Two Stones had to tell him before he could offer small talk.

His friend likely realized that. "The boy has returned from your ranch."

The tension in his chest coiled tighter. With all the chaos and pain here, he'd forgotten Two Stones had sent one of the healthy boys with a note Jericho wrote to his brothers. He'd let them know what was happening here in the village, and instructed them to send word if they were urgently needed at the ranch. He hated being gone so long, leaving the family to manage without him. But he needed to be here.

To help his friends. And Dinah. He couldn't abandon her.

Two Stones held out a paper. Jericho's own note.

Jericho grabbed it and flipped the missive over. Jude's careful handwriting stared up at him.

We are well. Should we come help you there? Send for us.

Of course Jude would offer that. But they didn't need anyone from the ranch infected with the disease. He was pretty sure Mum had said he'd had smallpox when he was a lad. But he couldn't remember if any of the others had. Lucy, Jonah, and Jude would have been the only ones born at that time.

He eased out his breath. If he didn't send for them, surely his brothers would stay put.

He raised his gaze to Two Stones, who was studying him with those eyes that saw everything.

"Now tell me how you are."

Jericho gave a half shrug. "Holding up." He looked to the lodge where Dinah was working. "I'm worried about her, though. She's pushing too hard."

"She's a wonder." Two Stones's voice held enough respect that it bordered on awe.

Jericho jerked his gaze to him.

Two Stones met the look with one corner of his mouth twitching. "Do you disagree?"

Jericho worked to relax his clenched jaw. He looked back at the lodge so he didn't have to meet that gaze. Two Stones saw too much sometimes. "Of course not. She's a good doctor." That felt like an insult, it so understated Dinah's abilities.

Two Stones's voice dropped, all humor disappearing. "She is more than that. My mother still lives because of her. She has changed every one of our people. Keeping alive those who would be buried by now." The chastisement in his words came through clearly, forming a knot in Jericho's throat.

When Two Stones spoke again, his voice softened a little. "I think you know this. It is time you say it also."

Jericho forced himself to meet Two Stones's eyes. "You're right. I'm glad she was here."

Was he really? Glad she was there to save the village, certainly. But glad she'd come to the ranch? *His ranch*, the refuge for his family? He was thankful she'd been there when Jonah was hurt. She might well have saved his life. The memory of Lillian's laughter slipped back in. That never would have happened if Dinah hadn't suggested he get her a dog. Just being around Dinah seemed to have given his niece a new hope.

A mother is the heart of a family. If she loses hope, so does everyone else.

Dinah's words from a moment before sounded in his mind. She *wasn't* the children's mother. Lucy would never be there for Lillian and Sean again. But could another woman fill that place for them? Could someone like Dinah Wyatt inspire them the same way a mother could?

The answer was obvious. She already had.

Two Stones tapped his arm. "You should make her your wife, my friend."

Then he turned and walked back toward his parents' lodge. As though he hadn't just spoken the word that Jericho had avoided at all cost for years now.

Two Stones spun, walking backward. "What I came to tell you is that the wife of my cousin has returned. She will come to Dinah to learn what should be done for the sick. Then the two of you can go home."

~

*D*inah leaned so close to the creek water, she nearly pressed her face into the flow. As she splashed the cool liquid on her cheeks, then her neck, slowly but surely, her body came back to life.

"Feels good, doesn't it?" Jericho's voice sounded as weary as she felt as he knelt beside her at the creek on their way back to the ranch.

She raised up, water dripping down her neck into her dress. "Really good."

Now that they'd washed, she had to find the energy to stand again. Then remount her horse.

Her entire body ached. Her legs didn't have enough strength to hold her. But she'd have to force them to.

Jericho must have overheard her thoughts, for he pushed to his feet, then reached for her elbow. She allowed him to help her stand, staggering a step before she found her balance.

"Well, would you look what washed up in the creek."

She spun at the voice. Gilead sat on horseback on the opposite bank, grinning.

When she turned, Jericho's hand dropped away from her elbow. But Gil had surely seen it. Would he think something had happened between the two of them? Heat flushed up her neck, no matter that she tried to stop it. Of course nothing had. They'd simply spent a great deal of time together, working side by side to bring relief to those who were miserable.

And Jericho had been extending that same offering to her.

Like any gentleman would.

"How are things?" Jericho stepped to his gelding and mounted.

She attempted to do the same. She had to struggle more than he did, but she managed to land in the seat.

"All right, I guess." Gilead propped his wrist on the front of his saddle. "We wondered if we'd have to come after you two."

Jericho sent him a scowl as they joined him on that side of the creek. The two brothers' mounts fell in beside each other, with hers bringing up the rear as they climbed the mountainside up toward the cabin.

Gilead asked about Two Stones's village, and Jericho filled him in on the details of their stay in a few short sentences, including how Sweet Medicine arrived and worked at Dinah's side until Dinah felt she was leaving her patients in capable hands.

Gil turned and flashed her a smile. "I'll bet they were glad you came."

Again, heat flushed up her neck, though for a different reason this time. "I'm thankful I could help." And that God had saved so many.

Including Kicks the Stone. A candid conversation with his mother had helped pull her from her grief. She might need more encouragement later when the sadness tried to envelop her again, but for now, she was focused on helping her son regain his strength.

"How's Jonah?" Jericho turned the conversation in the direction she'd rather hear too.

"Seems about the same. Tired of lyin' on his backside."

If Jonah truly felt that way, he was progressing. His pain must be diminished.

She raised her voice. "How are my sister and the children?"

Gil flashed her another grin. "Miss Naomi's as good a cook as you. We sure have been thankful for ya both."

She stiffened. "She's out of bed?"

He shrugged. "She insisted. Lillian's been helpin' her, and she only gets up to cook." He turned to Jericho. "We had more visitors."

Jericho jerked his head to study his brother. "Who?"

"Three trappers. Rode up the creek trail."

"Not miners?"

Gil shook his head. "All three had packhorses. Said they were starting out for the winter season."

She couldn't help but ask, "Are trappers better than miners?"

Jericho's tone had made it sound so. Maybe he disliked miners because of how rough they'd turned Helena and Virginia City.

And Lucy's husband. Jericho had said he was a miner. And a gambler.

Jericho didn't respond to her question, so Gilead gave her a shrug and a smile that didn't flash quite as bright as before. "I suppose it depends on the man."

They rode in silence the rest of the way, but when they arrived in the ranch yard, Sean's voice sounded through the open barn door. "They're here!"

Apple sprinted from the building, yipping as she ran. Sean jogged after the pup.

Dinah slid down from her horse, clutching the saddle to help her stay upright on her weary legs. Apple jumped up on her skirts, and she reached down to stroke the pup's head. "Missed me, huh?"

"We all have."

She looked up to meet Sean's grin. "Well I sure missed you." She stepped toward him and intended to ruffle his hair. But at the last minute she slipped her hand around his shoulders. How often did he get a real hug?

Children needed to know they were loved, and sometimes actions spoke louder than words. He leaned into her, and she tucked him against her side as they walked toward the house. Jericho and Gil were taking the horses to the barn, so she needed to see how things were going inside.

She pressed a cheek on top of his head. "Tell me. What all did you do while we were gone?"

CHAPTER 15

*J*ericho paused inside the barn door, staring at the pair walking toward the house. Dinah looked more like a doting mother than Lucy had most times he'd seen her with the children, especially those last few years.

Sean was telling her something, his hands waving in wild gestures. The boy hadn't seemed as sad since coming to the ranch as his sister had, but Dinah had still managed to bring him to life in a way none of the rest of them could.

As the two disappeared into the house, he turned back to the barn's interior. Gil had already removed the saddle from Dinah's horse and was brushing down the gelding's sweaty coat.

Jericho set to work doing the same for Pinto, doing his best to ignore the way Gil watched him.

Did he think Jericho had been staring at Dinah? Not *just* her. And not for the reason Gil probably thought. She was pretty, no man could deny that. But it was the person within he couldn't stop thinking about.

Best start a conversation before Gil asked about her. Jericho lifted the saddle from Pinto's back and turned to hang it on the bar. "I think it's time to build the fence." That should send his brother's thoughts in a different direction.

"No." Gil shook his head.

They'd had this argument so many times. "A fence is the only way to show people this land isn't free to roam."

"It'll only keep decent people out. The ones we really want to stay away will just find a path around it."

Jericho sent him a glare. "We don't want anyone coming on our land, decent people or not."

Gil turned to him, folding his arms to lean over the gelding's back. "You know, Miles had a thought that might be worth ponderin'. He said we should cut a trail starting at the base of the next mountain over. A path that'll lead people up the hill to the house without bringing them up from the creek."

Jericho eyed him. "What good would that do?"

"It'll keep people from comin' up through the strawberries where we don't want 'em."

He frowned. "We don't want 'em at the house either." Maybe that was better than people finding sapphires in the creek, but only by a little. "And that will be an open invitation."

Gil's nose twitched like he was fighting for patience, but his hint of a grin never slipped. "Who says we don't? Not all of us are as ornery and unfriendly as you."

Jericho turned back to Pinto, putting his back to his brother. "You're not making me want to say yes, Gil." Not that he would agree to invite people here, even if his brothers promised to do his chores for a year.

"Jericho."

Something in his brother's voice made him turn.

His brother's expression had lost its usual pleasantness. His eyes glinted in a way that made him look like a stranger. "It's not fully your decision. The boys and I want to take a vote."

His insides twisted, a fear tightening in his chest that he'd not felt since Lucy told him she was carrying Derek's child.

He swallowed hard, trying to keep his voice steady. "A vote?"

His tone softened but his eyes remained hard. "You can't always be the one who decides things. We're a family. Families should make decisions together."

Jericho clenched his jaw. "I'm not trying to decide everything. I just want to protect you all."

Gil's voice gentled more. "I know that. But sometimes you have to take a chance. Trust each other."

"I don't want to take a chance." He turned his back to his brother again. "We've already learned what can happen when you trust the wrong people."

"I'm not suggesting we trust everyone who comes through here. But we can't completely shut ourselves off from the world either."

Jericho didn't respond. Lucy would never have gone wrong if he'd made her stay on the ranch instead of going with him to Helena. Even then, she would have been safe if they hadn't allowed Derek to ride with them.

It had all started with trust.

Gil gripped his shoulder, and he flinched at the touch. " I'm not trying to argue with you. It's just that we should all have a say in this. We'll make the decision together."

He took a deep breath, trying to calm his racing heart. "Fine. We'll vote."

Gil glanced toward the door. "Good. You want to go inside, or should I call the guys out here?"

Now? He'd not even had a chance to recover from the exhausting days in Two Stones's village. But maybe it was better to get this over with. He had to convince his brothers not to encourage strangers to come on their ranch...by leading them straight to the house, of all things.

"Have them come out here," he grumbled. "Only Jude, Sampson, and Miles though. Not the women or children."

"What about Jonah?"

Ugh. He didn't want to draw attention to the conversation by having it out inside. "I'll talk to him after."

"We've already mentioned it to him."

Jericho couldn't help but glare at Gil. "What is this? The moment I leave the ranch, you start a mutiny?" After he'd worked so hard to keep them safe. To keep the family together like Dat asked. Maybe that was the argument he should make.

Dat's wishes. And the sapphires.

Gil chuckled as he started out of the barn. "Not a mutiny. It's for your good."

Jericho finished with the horses while he waited for his brothers. He would stay calm. He would show them there was nothing selfish in his desire to keep strangers out. It was a sacrifice *he* made as well as the others so the family would stay together and safe.

As his brothers gathered around him, Jericho took a deep breath and spoke. "I don't know if I've told all of you this or not." He let his gaze move from one brother to the next. "When Dat realized he might not make it, he gave me some final instructions. He said to keep the family together."

When he spoke the words aloud, they seemed to fall flat in the air. Each face waited expectantly for more.

He swallowed. "Lucy never would have met Derek if I hadn't taken her with me to Helena. We wouldn't have lost her if she'd stayed on the ranch."

Jude straightened, and part of Jericho clenched tighter. Jude was the most level-headed of the younger group. Surely he would speak sensibly.

"What happened to Lucy was hard. She made a decision she regretted for the rest of her life." He kept his voice steady. "But that doesn't mean the rest of us will do the same. You have to let us choose for ourselves, Jer. Trust us."

Sampson piped up. "If we build the trail to lead people away from the creek, we'll still be protecting the strawberries."

He had no other rebuttal. If they wouldn't see the wisdom in what he'd already said—and the lessons they should have learned from the past—there was nothing else he could offer.

He would just have to find a way to protect them from the danger this new trail would bring.

"We should vote then." Gil spoke quietly. "Who says we build the trail?"

Four hands rose, all but Jericho's.

Jude stepped in. "*And* is willing to help cut it?"

Miles looked like he wanted to lower his arm, but after a look around the group, he kept his hand up.

They would be building the trail then. That didn't change the fact he was head of the family and had to maintain both safety and peace.

So he nodded. "All right then. Just make sure work on the ranch doesn't suffer. We still have to gather in the last of the hay and keep working the two-year-olds. The calves will need to be weaned soon too."

"Understood," Jude said. "And don't worry, big brother. This will be good for all of us."

That wouldn't be true. It just meant his work would be harder than ever.

~

"Jer, didn't you say we're singing today?"

Jericho squinted in the dim light of the barn, trying to pull himself from sleep's hold. Sampson nudged him with the toe of his boot.

Singing. Sunday. How could it be Sunday already?

He and Dinah had only come back from the Salish village late yesterday. He'd been thankful for a day of rest today. But he'd also made the mistake of telling his brothers he planned to start Mum's hymn tradition again.

He pushed Sam's foot away and scrubbed a hand over his face, then combed hay from his beard.

"You need a shave." Sampson still stood there, watching him. "A haircut too."

Jericho eyed him. "Speak for yourself."

"Actually, I did get a cut." Sampson stroked a hand through his much-shorter hair. "The beard's trimmed too."

Jericho forced himself up to sitting. He did need to clean up.

"Naomi gave us all cuts."

Jericho choked on his breath, coughing as he struggled to clear his airways. As soon as he could breathe again, he opened his eyes wide enough to really see his little brother. "She gave you all haircuts?"

An unmarried woman with no chaperone. Lillian and Sean didn't count. Why had he thought it all right to leave them all here? That hadn't occurred to him with everything happening at the village.

He pushed up to his feet, stretching out his back as he stood. His neck ached. His whole body ached, actually. They couldn't continue sleeping in the barn forever. Winter would creep in soon.

What was he going to do with Dinah and Naomi? They needed to go back home to Virginia, but by the time they got to Fort Benton, the Missouri would likely be frozen over. They wouldn't be able to get back to the States until spring.

He'd planned to take them back days ago. They might have had a chance to catch the last boat down the Missouri before the river froze. But after the delay in Two Stones's village, they'd never make it in time. The sisters would have to wait out the winter in Fort Benton.

That meant Naomi would give birth there. Would it be a suitable environment to bring a babe into? Would the men respect Dinah? His gut tightened.

He'd not cared before, not much. But now that he knew her better...

But they couldn't stay on the ranch all winter. Could they?

No. Two unmarried women around all his brothers for that long? That would only spell trouble.

They had to leave. And he'd have to find a safe place for them until spring.

An idea slipped in. One he might never have thought of before the smallpox epidemic. Perhaps Two Stones's parents would allow the sisters to stay with them through the winter. It would certainly be a safe place to live.

Would it be suitable for the baby? He could make sure they had all the supplies they needed. White Bear's hut was one of the nicer in the village, but it might not be as warm as a cabin during the hard winters in this area. Could he build them a cabin? Surely something could be done.

As he dragged himself from the barn, the chill in the air seeped into his bones. He scrubbed his arms to warm himself. It was time to pull out his heavy coat to sleep in.

When he stepped into the cabin, the smell of food made his belly churn. Maybe he'd eaten too much last night. After all those days grabbing what he could find in Two Stones's lodge, he'd been famished, and he'd eaten more than he should have of the shepherd's pie Naomi and Lillian served. Dinah had been none too happy to find her sister up and cooking, but hopefully it hadn't hurt her or the babe for those few days.

He headed to Jonah's room first and collapsed into the chair to visit with his brother.

With one hand, Jonah spooned oats from the bowl resting on his chest. His other held a slice of fried ham. Neither item looked particularly appetizing. In fact, the ham smelled down-right sour. Jericho had checked it when he loaded the meat in Missoula Mills. Had they let it get too warm on the journey back?

"You look weary." Jonah studied him as he chewed.

Jericho raised his brows instead of shrugging. His body ached too much to put forth the energy. "Worn out keeping up with Dinah."

Jonah's eyes smiled. "She's a force."

He scanned the length of his brother. "Heard you're lookin' to break out of here."

"Wanna help me?" Jonah looked like he might be ready to try it.

Too bad he couldn't come sit in the main room while they ate and sang, but this contraption Dinah had attached to his leg didn't look easy to arrange. "Tell you what. After we eat, we'll all pile up in here to sing hymns with you."

His mouth curved. "You do that."

A few minutes later, Jericho sat at the head of the long table. Instead of Dinah at the other end, her sister Naomi sat there. But it was almost like looking at Dinah, now that Naomi wasn't as swollen as when she'd first arrived. After Naomi had the baby, it might be hard to tell these two apart.

He would probably always know Dinah though. She had a spark in her gaze that Naomi didn't. That determination that showed even when she was exhausted from doctoring an entire village for three days straight.

As the others ate, he glanced at the closed door to the chamber the women shared. He'd not seen Dinah at all that morning. Hopefully she was sleeping. But was it more than that?

"She's just tired." Naomi must have read his thoughts. "She tried to get up at dawn, but I made her lie back down. She hasn't stirred since."

"She should be tired enough to sleep for two days." He'd like to do so himself.

The others were scarfing down the ham and cooked oats, but he didn't take any meat. Not with the way his belly roiled.

He took a bite of oats. They went down with a sour taste, then his belly threatened to send them back up. He had to get a few bites down. Then maybe he could climb up into the loft and sneak a few minutes' rest before they all gathered in Jonah's room to sing.

Two bites later, he'd had enough. He pushed his chair back and stood. Several faces looked up at him, so he motioned toward the dishes. "You boys help clean up. When you're done, we'll sing."

He didn't wait for responses, just started toward the ladder nailed to the wall. But halfway there, the oats surged back up into his throat. He spun and started toward the door. He didn't have long...

The moment he stumbled down the step, he lost his hold on the contents of his stomach. He heaved and retched, emptying the oats and whatever else was in his belly onto the dry grass outside. He doubled over, panting and gasping for air as the nausea rolled through him.

"You all right, Jer?"

He managed a weak wave in Sampson's direction as he wiped his mouth with the back of his hand. "Fine," he rasped out. "I guess the oats didn't sit right."

"You don't look good." Naomi stood behind him in the doorway. "I'll get Dinah."

Jericho shook his head. "Let her sleep."

He started toward the barn. "I'll lay down a minute, then be fine." If only it weren't so cold out here.

CHAPTER 16

*D*inah's chest tightened as she rested her fingers on Jericho's burning brow. "You're coming inside." She couldn't help brushing the hair back from his face. He needed a haircut, but she had more important things to help him with just now.

She pushed to her feet in the hay as Sampson helped his brother sit up. "I'll get a place ready for him."

But where? She couldn't let him be near Jonah. Naomi had been exposed to smallpox when she was a girl, as Dinah had, so she shouldn't be able to catch it. But could the disease somehow hurt the unborn babe? Not to her knowledge, but should she chance it?

Perhaps one of the smaller beds could be brought into the main room for Jonah, and Jericho could take over his chamber. That way she could shut the door and keep the others from being exposed—more than they already had been.

Jude met her in the yard, his expression concerned.

Before he could ask, she motioned him to follow her. "Come help me. We're moving Jericho to the house."

Miles and Gil were helping Lillian clear the table, but they all turned to look at her when she stepped inside. Sean stood in Jonah's room talking to his uncle.

"Gilead and Sean, please move the bed I've been sleeping on out here against that wall. Miles, move those crates to that corner." She still hadn't had a chance to find a place for it all.

"Your bed?" Naomi stepped from their chamber, shock marking her expression.

Dinah started toward Jonah's room. "It's for Jonah. Jericho needs a separate room."

The men jumped to work, and by the time Jericho trudged in with Sampson at his side, she was supervising Jude and Miles carrying Jonah on a blanket stretcher into the main room.

Jonah waved like a king riding in a chariot as he passed, but she couldn't find the humor in it.

Jericho had contracted smallpox.

How had she let this happen? He'd said he thought he had the disease as a boy, so she hadn't made him take the antidote when she gave it to the other healthy people in Two Stones's village. Why, oh, why hadn't she insisted? She hadn't wanted him to feel even the discomfort of those minor symptoms.

Some doctor she was.

She straightened the remaining blanket on the bed Jonah had just vacated. It was a large double bed, probably once belonging to his parents. Jericho would need many more covers than this one.

Once he entered the room, she pointed Sampson back out. "Go get every blanket or fur you can find and put them right here in the doorway." She raised her voice so all could hear. "No one is allowed in this room except me. I'll not risk any one of you." She pinned her sister with a narrow gaze. "Nor the baby."

Naomi blanched, but she nodded.

Dinah started toward the front door. She would gather the blankets he'd used in the barn herself so they didn't infect one of the others. Then she'd inoculate the family so they didn't succumb to the full force of the disease.

She couldn't let this illness spread to even one more person.

~

*D*inah sank into the chair across from where her sister sat at Jonah's bedside and stared at Naomi's hands weaving the needle in and out of the luxurious blue fabric. She worked so quickly, it was like watching a lovely minuet, with dancers sliding in and out of the line in perfect flow.

"Once I finish the ruffles and attach them, this dress will be complete." Naomi paused her choreography and straightened the length of fabric in her hand. She squared her shoulders, probably to stretch out the tightness from hunching for so long.

Dinah managed a tired smile. "What will you make then?" Maybe a gown for the baby.

Naomi's mouth twitched. "There's enough of this fabric to make another skirt for Lillian, as well as a shirt for Sean."

A chortling noise sounded from Jonah's bed, and Dinah glanced at him. He shook his head. "Not sure he's gonna appreciate having clothes to match his sister."

"Of course he will." Naomi spoke as though the two of them had had this conversation before. "This material is so soft, and the blue pinstripe will make a handsome shirt."

He just shook his head. They seemed to be getting along quite well, as though they'd been friends for months...or years. She needed to warn her sister to be careful not to form an attachment with anyone here. Even if the man reciprocated, she had a feeling Jericho wouldn't allow it. The last thing they wanted was to come between these brothers, or make things harder for Jericho.

Speaking of Jericho, she should check on him again. The last time she'd been in to offer him ginger tea and broth, his fever was higher than any other point these past days. Now, she waited for his stomach to settle from those liquids before she gave him willow tea to bring the heat in his body down.

She pushed to her feet and turned toward the kitchen area first. Lillian worked at the cookstove, and Dinah peeked into the pot she was stirring. "That looks wonderful."

The girl flashed a smile. "I put in a cinnamon stick. It makes the whole room smell better."

Dinah raised her brows. "That sounds like Naomi's trick."

Lillian gave a sheepish nod. "She showed me."

"You're learning from the best then." Dinah touched her shoulder as she turned toward Jericho's room. "I'm going to see if your uncle will drink a tea for his fever."

After pouring a fresh cup from the kettle she'd left steeping, she headed toward the bed chamber. She stepped into the room, staying quiet to see if he was asleep.

She'd taken all the blankets off him, revealing his bare feet. His eyes were closed, the wet cloth still lying across his brow where she'd left it. Sweat glistened on his temples, just below the rag and above his beard. The sound of his breathing became distinct as she approached.

She sat on the side of his bed, an easier position to reach him than the chair, and placed a hand on his forehead. Heat still emanated from his body. "Jericho, can you hear me?"

He groaned in response, his eyes still closed.

"I need you to drink this willow tea. It will help bring your fever down." She held the cup near his lips, but he turned his head away.

"I can't." His voice was barely a whisper.

"Why not?"

"It hurts to swallow."

Dinah winced. The rash must have reached his mouth. "We need to bring your fever down, and this will help." She set the cup down and took the bowl of water and cloth she'd been using before. "I'll put more wet cloths on you." She'd been doing this for days though, and his temperature was only rising.

She removed the rag from his brow and used it to wipe the sweat from the rest of his face. That thick beard probably held in heat. Should she consider shaving it? Pop had done that occasionally when caring for a man with a high fever. She could at least ask him. Recommend it.

"Jericho, I think we should shave your beard. It might lower your fever and will help when the rash develops."

He didn't open his eyes, but his voice came out in a rasp. "Do it."

Did that mean he wanted *her* to? As miserable as he probably felt, it might be dangerous for him to use a razor near his throat.

She pulled a pair of scissors, her surgical razor, and soap from her bag, then settled in to start the task.

After draping a damp cloth over his chest, she trimmed his beard with the scissors, cutting the hairs as short as she could. She'd been near him these past days, wiping the sweat from his face, helping him drink tea and broth. She still felt his presence when she came that close, her fingers more aware than they should be every time they brushed his skin.

But she had to lean in closer for this work, her hands practically stroking his face as she gathered the coarse hair. He kept his eyes closed, which helped her nerves.

Once she'd trimmed all she could, she made a lather with the soap and water and smoothed it over the short beard remaining. She didn't let herself linger on the way her hands formed to the strong line of his jaw.

Now the razor. She started by his right ear first, scraping down his face and clearing away the dark stubble. Between the lather and the hair, she could barely see the man himself, and she let herself focus on the details of her work, smoothing the razor slowly so it captured every hair the first time. Wiping away what gathered on the blade, then moving in for the next stroke.

The skin beneath the beard was pinkish, not yet tinted by long days in the sun. He would need to protect this area when he went out again. *Lord, let him rise to work again soon.* It seemed impossible to think that this virile man could possibly succumb to anything, even a disease as fierce as smallpox.

Once she'd finished with the jaw all the way around, she focused on the area above his lips.

Those lips.

A little red from the fever, but fuller than she would have expected. Not that she'd spent a lot of time thinking about the plumpness of this man's lips.

She moistened her own mouth, which had become far too dry. She needed to do a better job of thinking of him as a patient.

This was a medical procedure, no different than if she were splinting a broken arm on a child.

With his face completed, she had only his neck left. She tipped his chin up a little as she started again on the right side.

Just like splinting an arm.

That thinking worked for a while—until he swallowed.

The sudden dip of his laryngeal prominence—what some might call his Adam's apple—made her own belly swoop. The flexing of the muscles in his neck brought back the memory of the strength he'd showed so many times. In carrying crates, stacked three high as if they weighed nothing. In hoisting his injured brother into and out of the wagon.

In lifting the two bodies he'd helped bury in the Salish camp.

Bile churned in her belly, and she focused her thoughts in a better direction as she finished her task. *Lord, heal this man. Give him strength to fight the disease. Make it move rapidly through each stage and leave him, not linger to tear down his body's ability to recover.*

With the shaving done, she pulled the cloth from his brow and used it to wipe away the last of the hair and soap from his face. "There. Now you should feel a little better."

As she reached for the cup of willow tea again, his eyes opened partway, finding her. "Thank you."

She managed to meet his gaze with a smile, though she steeled herself to keep a professional distance. She couldn't let him know how intimate that task had felt.

She was a doctor. He was her patient.

No matter how she wanted to give in to these womanly feelings, she couldn't allow herself. She needed to focus all her attention on helping him recover.

CHAPTER 17

"$\mathcal{D}$inah, honey. You have to get some rest."

Dinah jerked upright and blinked, scrambling to recognize where she was and what her sister was talking about.

Her gaze landed on Jericho's pox-covered face, and the past week flooded back in an exhausting wave, pressing her back in the chair, weighing on her chest.

He was so sick. She'd been by his side nearly every moment these past few days. But nothing she'd done seemed to help a jot.

He lay there now, his breaths wheezing in and out. The postules must still be raw down his throat. In fact, none had begun to scab anywhere on his body.

The fever still raged, and he'd not been able to keep anything she gave him down more than an hour. *Heal him, Lord. Why haven't You done it yet?*

The Bible said to be like the widow in the book of John who pestered the judge until he gave in, and she'd been begging God every hour for this man's healing.

"You need to rest, Di. And those blankets you've been using to sleep on the floor are clearly not giving you enough sleep.

Come to my bed. I'll watch Jericho, and I'll wake you if anything changes with him."

She blinked and tried to focus on her sister, but her eyes burned. "I can't contaminate your bed." When she had her own single bed moved to the main room for Jonah, she'd thought to make up a bed pallet in the other chamber where the bed had been. But with Jericho so ill, she'd simply brought two wool blankets into this room and slept on the floor.

Naomi threw her hands up. "Then lie in his bed." She pointed to the wide space on the other side of Jericho. "It's not as if he has the strength to do anything to you. And we all know the situation. None here would judge. In fact, we'd all be relieved."

Dinah shook her head and swallowed to moisten her dry throat. "I can't do that." Though Jericho might never know she'd lain beside him, these emotional days caring for him had stripped away all her pretending that she didn't care about him.

He'd shown the strength of his character, the depth of his heart, since that day they first met him by the creek. He might not care for her at all, but he'd won her heart little by little. And lying beside him would mean giving away another piece.

If he recovered and didn't feel the same for her—or worse, if he succumbed to this sickness—she would have to heal from the damage already done to her heart. She had no desire to add more to that pain.

She pushed to her feet. "You shouldn't be in here." She'd done her best to keep Naomi and all the others away, though she'd needed Jude's help at times to assist Jericho with personal matters.

Naomi shouldn't risk herself and the baby though.

As she ushered her sister out, she paused at the doorway and glanced around the main room.

"Lillian is cleaning up from the morning meal. She's such a help." Naomi sent the girl a smile, which Lillian returned as she stood by the work counter, her hands deep in the pail of wash water.

Dinah leaned against the door frame. "I'm sorry I've left you both to do everything out here." She'd been hesitant to leave Jericho's chamber, both because he might need her and because she didn't want to spread the infection to anyone else in the household.

Naomi waved her apology away. "It's been a breath of fresh air. Lillian's done all the work really, I just supervise."

Dinah managed a smile for the girl. "Lillian, I don't know what we would do without you. Your new dress looks lovely on you. So grown up."

She smiled shyly, her gaze dipping. "Thank you."

Dinah breathed out a long breath as she scanned the room again. Her gaze caught on the door. "I think I'll walk for a minute. Get some air." Her muddled mind needed clearing.

As she stepped out into the sunshine, she had to squint against the brightness. The air possessed a cold nip though. A hint of the coming autumn.

No sounds drifted from the barn. She must have dozed off while the men came in for the morning meal, so she'd not heard where each would be working today. The last several days, a few of the brothers would ride out to train the two-year-olds who were learning to ride while the rest worked on a new path they were building from the house down the north slope. She still hadn't pieced together why they were building that trail, but they seemed intent on finishing it as quickly as possible.

She started that direction, but instead of taking the newly cleared path the men had made, with all its low stumps and freshly churned ground, she took the steeper route down the mountain. This way looked like it possessed a much richer history, with years of steady travel.

As she strolled, the hill hurried her steps. The movement

freed her body, awakening her tense muscles and stretching them out.

The cluster of trees on her left looked familiar, a stand of three pines that had grown so close, their bases converged into one. She'd not seen pines grow that way before, though certainly oak and other varieties did.

A familiarity pricked in her mind. She'd passed these trees before, but from a different vantage point. In the wagon with Jericho when they traveled to Missoula Mills? No.

In the wagon, yes, but she'd been sitting beside Jonah's pain-riddled body, praying he didn't bleed out before she could stabilize his leg.

This must be the path to that clearing where he'd been injured. She wouldn't go as far as the accident site. It had taken them nearly a half hour to ride in the wagon from there to the house, and she couldn't leave Jericho for that long.

But she was moving downhill now. Maybe she could cover the ground faster than the wagon had.

Before long, an opening in the trees appeared ahead. She lengthened her stride. Why did she want to return to this place anyway? It had been the scene of so much pain.

But she did. That had been her first real exposure to the brothers. To Jericho.

If Jude hadn't called for help, Jericho would have likely sent her and Naomi away at the creek, and they'd never have come to know this family. This remarkable ranch tucked on the side of the mountain.

She would never have fallen for the man she'd once thought would be her sister's husband. God had other plans though.

Right, Lord? Are these feelings from You? She hadn't been able to determine that yet. She only knew they'd swelled to a point that she could no longer pretend they were nothing.

As she stepped into the clearing, her gaze landed on the

place where the wagon had sat. The ground where Jonah's body had lain.

She walked toward it, reliving the scene in her mind. She'd been so worried about Naomi, but the Lord had given her sister a place to rest. Now she seemed to be thriving, and the babe within her too.

Dinah's gaze caught on the shed down the hill at the edge of the clearing. It was mostly tucked into the woods, as though its builder was trying to hide it.

Was that what Jude and Jonah had been doing that day? Storing things in that structure?

Perhaps she should leave it alone, yet curiosity tugged her feet downhill, toward the leaning door.

The weathered wood of the building was marred with cracks and knotholes, though someone had taken the time to fill each with chinking. They wanted this shed to keep out rain and snow, which meant whatever they stored in here needed to stay dry.

A root cellar perhaps? Or a corncrib? Maybe where they kept their supply of meat? But Jericho had said he stored it in a cool corner of the barn.

A wooden latch held the door shut, but it moved aside easily when she lifted it.

Her pulse pounded as she pulled the door open. She should mind her own business. Just because she felt like a significant part of the daily running of this home and ranch didn't mean she could wander anywhere she pleased and poke through hidden buildings.

As she pulled the door open, the sunlight lit the front section, illuminating rows and rows of crates stacked nearly to the top of the small building. Were these supplies? Maybe extra they stored away for the winter?

She stepped in and moved to the nearest box. The lid wasn't nailed shut, so she could easily lift it and see what they were storing. Hopefully dry foodstuffs like flour and cornmeal. That would make sense with the efforts made to keep the inside of this shed dry.

But neither flour nor cornmeal stared up at her.

Small colored stones. Many of them rounded like they'd come from the creek. And so many colors. Pink and blue and green and yellow...they twinkled in the sunlight.

She reached in to touch them. Had the brothers found them in the creek? They must be special stones to be saved in a crate out here.

She lifted her focus to the other boxes. Did they hold colored stones too? Surely not. There couldn't be so many as to fill all of these.

After carefully lowering the lid back on the first crate, she moved to the end of a row to check another. She had to lift on her tiptoes to see the top of this one, since it was the fourth on a stack. The lid was nailed securely in place.

She moved down the line, checking each cover for looseness. Only one other crate hadn't been secured shut. This one also sat on the ground, as though the brothers weren't finished filling it.

Inside this crate, too, were dozens of colored stones. Most seemed to be blue, though not all. The dim light in the shed made them look a deep midnight color, but when she lifted a few into the rays of sunlight, the richness of their coloring seemed to vary.

What were these?

A movement outside the doorway caught her gaze, and she spun to see.

Jude stepped into the opening, a rifle in his hand, aimed directly at her.

Her heart stopped, and a squeal slipped out before she could stop it.

His eyes flared with surprise. "Dinah. What are you doing in there?" He seemed as shocked to see her as she was to have a gun pointed her direction.

He didn't lower the barrel though.

She swallowed, trying to quell the nerves swirling in her middle. "I...was just..." *...combing through your private collections.* She scrambled for something better to say. "I mean. I needed to walk, and I saw this shed. I just..."

He stepped back but didn't drop the muzzle. "Why don't you come out of there?"

He didn't sound angry, just stern. But that didn't stop the dread curling inside her.

As she stepped out of the shed, she tried to avoid looking at the gun. Surely he didn't mean to point it at her. He just hadn't realized what he was doing.

She worked for a smile. Though he was nearly as tall as Jericho, he'd always seemed kind. Gentle. Not foreboding as he looked now. "I'm sorry, Jude. I didn't mean to intrude. I just saw the shed and was curious. I thought those crates held supplies you were keeping for the winter."

His gaze softened and, finally, he lowered the gun. "It's just. Well...a place we store things."

She considered the answer—and how vague it was. He motioned for her to walk up the slope, then fell into step beside her.

It seemed he wouldn't offer more details about the colored stones unless she asked. If she didn't say something now, the fact that she knew would always stand between the two of them.

She had to ask. "What are those rocks that were in the crates?" Even as she spoke, she wanted to curl into herself. Would he be furious that she'd snooped?

"That's something you'll need to ask Jericho." His tone sounded curt, and he said nothing else.

Hiking up the steep slope was taking her breath, which

might be a good thing. She should drop the topic with Jude. Maybe she'd have a quiet moment when she could ask his elder brother.

Jude seemed intent on escorting her back to the house, for as they stepped into the woods, he strode purposefully beside her along the narrow wagon road. For several minutes, they walked in silence.

Then he finally spoke. "How is he?"

She couldn't help a sigh as the weight she'd been trying to escape pressed back over her. Should she tell Jude her true fears? It seemed cruel to lay on him the burdens she carried, but she also needed to be candid. She'd never struggled in the past when speaking of a patient's condition with family members. With this family, she'd become too personally invested.

Her eyes burned. She had to warn him what could happen. She swallowed the lump in her throat. "I'm worried."

He slid her a sideways look, then turned his focus forward again. After another minute, he let out his own sigh. "I'm afraid to ask if you think...he might not..."

Tears sprang to her eyes again. She did her best to fight them back. "I don't know. His case is severe. He was strong at the start but... I don't know." She looked at him. "We need to pray."

An idea pressed through her, filling her chest with certainty. "All of us. We need to pray."

She lengthened her stride, and he did the same. "Where are your brothers? Can we call them in?" She glanced over to gauge his reaction. They would miss work time, but Jericho's life was worth a vast sum more than that.

He looked hesitant. "I guess so." He slowed and turned, raising his hands to cup his mouth.

He loosed a shrill whistle, so loud she nearly clamped her hands to her ears. It's low-high-low sound echoed across the mountainside. The others surely heard it.

He sounded the whistle once more in that same three-note

blast. Then he turned and continued up the path, quickening his step and lengthening his stride. "They'll be coming. Best we get to the house to meet them."

She had to trot to keep up, which left her no breath to ask if his signal was a specific alert of danger or a general call. Just knowing Jericho was ill and receiving that summons would be enough to worry his brothers.

She pressed a hand to the stitch in her side as she and Jude reached the ranch yard. Sean and Gilead were dismounting their horses, and a thunder of hoofbeats sounded from the path the men took to one of the lower pastures.

"What's wrong?" Gilead strode toward them, concern marking his features.

She raised a staying hand. "Nothing. Nothing new, I mean. We need you all to help though."

CHAPTER 18

*B*y the time they all gathered in the main room of the cabin, Dinah had caught her breath enough to speak better.

She scanned each of their gazes. Jericho's five brothers. His niece and nephew. Her own sister.

"The smallpox has hit Jericho hard. He was strong when he succumbed, but the sickness struck with more fierceness than usual. Maybe lack of sleep while we worked in the Salish village weakened him. I've been doing everything I can, including praying for him, but I think we all need to pray. Together." She could quote the Scriptures that told them to, but that might feel condescending.

She reached for Naomi's fingers on her left and Lillian's on her right. One by one, they clasped hands in a wide circle that included Jonah in the bed. "I'll pray first, then we can go around and each pray for what's weighing on our hearts."

Bowing her head, she did her best to settle her mind and focus on what she wanted most from the Lord. "Father. We need Your presence here among us. Your healing hand on Jericho.

You've said where two or more are gathered together in Your name, You would be in our midst." So she did end up quoting the verse, but Jesus Himself prayed using Scripture. "We need You, Lord. Jericho needs You. I need You"—her voice cracked, and she scrambled to keep from revealing to much emotion —"to heal him." She squeezed Lillian's hand to let her know she could pray next.

As the girl spoke a tentative plea for her uncle, a tear slipped through Dinah's defenses. So many people loved him. Though he'd hidden himself away on this mountain, the people he allowed in his inner circle were blessed with the depth of his love. Of his protection and goodness.

It was impossible to keep from returning that love. That fact was one she'd learned too late to protect herself.

~

*J*ericho's body trembled as he lay in darkness that smothered. Like drowning in a pool of misery. Had he died? If this was the lake of fire the reverend used to speak of, why was he so cold?

Voices broke through his haze.

He focused on the sounds, straining to make out words through the murkiness in his mind. That was Jude's voice.

"...bring him back to us. Don't take him. Please. Heal him. Make him well."

Who was he talking to? Dinah?

If his brother was giving Dinah a hard time...

But Jericho could do nothing to help her. He couldn't even pull from this blackness.

Jonah was speaking now. Jericho strained once more.

"Please, God. You know how much Jericho means to us. You can't take him too. We need him here with us. Please. Heal him."

An urgency pressed through Jericho. They were praying. And his brothers needed him. He couldn't die like their parents had. Like Lucy.

He tried to open his eyes, but his lids weighed as much as a tree trunk. He couldn't even get his hand to move. Fear rose up, but then another voice drifted in.

"Lord, I ask that You fill Jericho with Your light." Dinah's sister. His fuzzy mind wouldn't recall her name, but her words soaked through him. "Banish the darkness that's trying to consume him. Let him feel Your presence and know he's not alone."

As she spoke, a warmth spread across his shoulders, chasing away the chill. He tried to move again, and this time his finger shifted.

Then Dinah's voice broke in, her tone sure and strong. "Father, we look to You. You have the power of life. We've known that you are the Holy God. The great Physician. Only You can heal him. Clear away the fever. Make the postules scab over and fall off. Fill his body with strength. Bring him back to us."

Jericho strained once more, forcing away the darkness so he could open his eyes. He managed to crack them, but the light burned, and he squinted against the glare.

As his gaze adjusted, the walls of his bed chamber surrounded him. The voices—his family and Dinah—must be coming from the other room.

He tried to speak, but his parched and aching throat refused to cooperate. He offered a weak groan instead.

The sounds of the others grew silent. Then footsteps. Someone entered his room, and it took all his energy to focus on the person.

Dinah's form took shape, coming near. "Jericho?" Her voice murmured soft and gentle.

He opened his mouth, but still he couldn't push out words. His throat convulsed, and he squeezed his eyes shut against the pain, like glass shards scraping.

"Have a sip of water."

Cold metal touched his lips, and he parted them. The water burned even as it brought relief inside his mouth. He let it sit for a few heartbeats, then prepared himself to swallow.

His throat nearly pushed the liquid back up, and he couldn't keep from groaning with the searing ache. But he finally swallowed.

"The next time won't be so hard."

He wanted to open his eyes again. To see her beautiful face and let it ease this pain. But he didn't have the strength to do that *and* take another drink. So he kept his eyes shut and opened his mouth again.

This second swallow went down a little easier. Then something brushed his brow. A cool, soft touch, stroking his temple. He let himself sink into it. Drawing all the comfort and strength from her touch.

When her hand cupped his cheek, he was strong enough to open his eyes. His gaze took too long to focus, but he gave himself time. Seeing her would be worth the wait.

She was watching him, her eyes gentle. He sank into their softness.

"You're going to be well again, Jericho. God is answering our prayers."

Was she...crying? He wanted to touch her. To reach for her. To wipe away those tears.

But his hand wouldn't move. He didn't have enough strength yet. Maybe he could speak instead. He opened his mouth, tightened his throat, and forced sounds through. "Dinah."

His voice sounded rough. Far too coarse to speak the name of this woman so beautiful.

But a smile bloomed on her face, brightening her eyes like the sun's rays. She pulled her hand away from his cheek, making him want to beg for her to put it back. But then her fingers settled around his hand.

He closed it around hers. Gave a squeeze that was hopefully strong enough that she could feel it.

His eyes wouldn't stay open any longer, so he let them drift shut. As long as he could cling to her hand, he would rest.

~

*T*he muscles in Jericho's face felt like he hadn't used them in weeks as he attempted a smile when Dinah entered his room. "Good morning." Though this was the second morning since he'd awakened, his throat still rasped, especially since he hadn't spoken before today.

Her eyes widened. "Good morning. You're looking bright-eyed."

He'd already sat up, but he kept the blanket pulled to his waist. When Jude came in to help him attend to personal matters, he'd discovered he was only wearing a nightshirt and drawers. Had Dinah been there when he'd been undressed?

Surely not. But every faint memory he had of being sick included her, helping him sip tea, wiping his face with a wet cloth, or simply holding his hand.

"Feeling a lot better. It's time I get up."

Dinah moved to the bedside, her fingers brushing his forehead. "You still feel warm. Maybe you should rest longer."

Jericho reached up, grasping her wrist. He could move quicker now. "I've rested enough. I can't be stuck in this bed any longer."

Dinah's eyes softened. "All right. But only for a minute. Let me help you."

She pulled herself from his hold and reached for his blanket, but he clamped his hand over the cloth. "If you'll bring me my clothes, I can take it from there."

Her cheeks flushed, but she looked uncertain. "I can, but I think trousers might rub against the scabs on your legs and hurt."

The blankets already did that any time he moved, but it was only an irritant. He shook his head. "I can stand it." He wasn't getting out of this bed without being fully dressed, not in front of this woman. He planned to woo her, and he certainly couldn't do that in a nightshirt and drawers.

She acquiesced, turning to reach for something on the floor next to the bedside table. If he'd realized his clothes were that near, he would have put them on sooner. He might not have had the strength though. This was the first dose of energy he'd had, so he would make the most of it.

By the time he'd pulled on pants, his strength was waning again. He didn't try to change shirts, just tucked the nightshirt into his waistband. As he gripped the footboard to gather energy to hobble out into the main room, he rubbed a hand over his jaw.

He could still remember Dinah shaving him. As awful as he'd felt, her hands moving over his face so gently had awakened his senses. Had she felt anything more toward him than what a doctor felt for a patient?

He had to find out exactly what her feelings were.

If there was one thing that had come clear to him through this whole awful sickness, it was that he needed—nay, *wanted*—Dinah Wyatt to stay here permanently. She'd come in like a surprise hurricane at the time they needed her most—though it took him too long to realize that.

No one could deny her beauty, with those intense eyes that sparkled with determination and the blond hair his fingers still craved to touch. But it was all the other ways she showed her passion and caring that had broken through to him. He wanted her by his side. Wanted her here on the ranch, bringing hope to Lillian and Sean. Naomi and the baby were welcome to stay too. As long as they wanted.

But first, he had to convince Dinah to choose him.

His fingers brushed through his hair. Far too long. He'd been meaning to cut it off for a while now. If he asked Dinah to help, would she think it beneath her, or that he was taking advantage of having her around? Maybe he could use the opportunity to win her over. He might not have much talent in matters of the heart, but he could try.

Pushing away from the bed, he started toward the door. With this first step, he stumbled but caught himself on the frame. Every action required thought, as if the sickness had burned away the ability for his limbs to function.

When he stepped out of the room, Dinah strode toward him from the cookstove. She looked worried.

Not how he wanted her to look at him.

He straightened, worked for a smile. That seemed to ease her concern a little. A glance around the room showed Jonah in one of the single beds against the far wall. Naomi sat in a chair nearby, and Lillian nestled cross-legged on the floor. The girl stroked a ball of fur in her lap—a mop of hair with a tongue lolling as it stared at him.

He moved toward them, his step more like a hobble.

Naomi jumped from her chair. "Sit here and visit."

He tried to wave her back down, but she shook her head. "I need to put this sewing away anyhow."

As she disappeared into her bed chamber, Jonah met his gaze, a twinkle in his eyes. "That's us Coulter men. Running the ladies out of their chairs so we can lie around while they work."

Jericho frowned, wanting to remain standing just to prove

those words wrong, even though they were in jest. But his strength was already fading, and standing made it hard for his chest to draw a full breath. He tried to ease into the chair but ended up half-collapsing as his legs gave way. He settled in and looked around.

Lillian was watching him, her expression too somber. Too much like the girl she'd been those first long months after coming to the ranch.

He smiled at her, as much as he could manage. "How's the pup doing?" What was her name again?

Lillian picked up the dog and held her under her chin. "Good." It was almost as though she was trying to hide behind the animal.

Jericho reached out. "Can I hold her?" That would bring Lillian closer.

She rose up on her knees and crawl-walked to him, holding the pup close. When she placed the animal on his lap, she stayed at eye level with her. "Say hello to Uncle Jericho."

As he petted and fussed over the pup, Lillian seemed to lighten a little. Had she feared she'd lose him the way she had her mother and father? She and Sean would still have all the others here—his brothers, at least. But he thought of himself as the children's primary guardian. Maybe they thought of him that way too.

As she stroked the dog, he reached out and placed a hand on her head, ruffling her blond hair, then letting it rest there. She sent a shy smile that warmed through him. "Glad I finally get time with two of my favorite girls." He wanted to look up at Dinah and somehow let her know she was definitely one of those *favorites*, but he didn't want Lillian to feel less.

His gaze caught on the blue his niece wore. "Is that a new dress?" How had he not noticed that at first? He leaned back. "Let me see you."

She jumped to her feet. "Miss Naomi made it up for me. And

we even put ruffles." She held up the skirt to display two rows of flounce.

He nodded. "I like it. You make that fabric look prettier than a hillside of spring flowers."

Her grin widened, but then fell, her chin dipping. "Sean has a shirt to match. Uncle Jonah says it's silly."

Jericho turned a hard glare on his brother.

Jonah spread his hands. "I didn't mean that at all. I was just saying... I mean. The dress is perfect. There's no way a boy's shirt could be half as nice."

His gaze slid up to something behind Jericho, and a flash of panic touched his eyes. "At least that's what I thought. But the way Naomi sewed it, the shirt is something special." He glanced at Lillian a bit nervously. "And so is the dress. Both of them. Special."

Jericho turned back to their niece. "Uncle Jonah's been lying in that bed too long. If he doesn't get back to work soon, he'll have that whole leg stuck in his mouth, broken bone, splint, and all."

Lillian giggled. And this time he couldn't stop himself from glancing up at Dinah, just to see if she'd heard that happy sound.

She stood behind Lillian, back against the wall, watching them. She met his gaze with a softness in her eyes and a curve of her lips that made him want to draw her onto his lap. He should probably squelch thoughts like that until he had a chance of making them happen, but now that he'd freed his mind to think of her in that way, he couldn't seem to rein himself in.

Maybe better to focus on his responsibilities than daydreams. At least for now.

He turned back to Jonah. "How are things with the stock? Did the boys start weaning the calves?" Hopefully they hadn't tried to milk any of the cows yet. He'd planned to bring in their oldest, a dark brown mama with a laid-back temperament.

Jonah shook his head. "I don't think so. They were going to, but when things got bad with you, they held off."

Jericho pinched his mouth. He must have really worried them. "Maybe tomorrow then." With a good meal or two, he would be well enough to ride out in the morning.

Dinah straightened from the wall. "If you think you're going to help tomorrow, you might want to delay that plan. Until next week at least." She looked like a jailor, frowning at him like that.

Maybe he should appease her a little. He could hold off another day before starting back to work—use tomorrow to show her how strong he was. For now, he nodded. "You know best."

He didn't miss the way Jonah's brows rose, and a glance at Dinah showed she didn't look exactly pleased either. Maybe better to move on again.

He turned back to his brother. "How's the rest? Did Jude finish what he was working on?"

Jonah frowned. "Oh, you mean the s—" He caught himself just before saying the wrong word, but he managed to change it into their code word. "...strawberries?"

Jericho's gaze flicked to Dinah before he could stop himself. She was frowning at them, her focus a bit too intense. She'd definitely caught the misstep. But did she have any idea what they were really talking about?

She couldn't. Not unless she'd seen the sapphires somewhere and recognized what they were.

Jonah finally answered. "I think so. He hasn't said much. I think they're making progress on the road down toward the Mullan Road too."

He'd forgotten about the vote and how his brothers were practically inviting danger onto the ranch. He'd had about enough frustrating conversation for one day.

He pushed up to his feet and stood until his head stopped

swimming. Maybe it was best he stay in bed and leave the others to their plans.

But then again, maybe he'd better rest up so he could be ready to protect his family. And the legacy they'd worked so hard to build.

CHAPTER 19

*S*hould she ask Jericho about the stones? Or one of the other brothers instead? Jude might be the one she would have questioned, but he'd said to ask Jericho.

She sat beside Jericho's bed now, peeling potatoes and watching him sleep. He'd worn himself out by spending so much time in the main room.

If asking him about what she'd found in the shed upset him, it might set back his recovery.

The strawberries he and Jonah were talking about must be those stones. Some kind of gemstone most likely. Perhaps several different kinds, since there were so many colors.

But where had they come from? As far as she knew, not even gold had been discovered in this area. Certainly not gemstones either. She would have heard of it, surely.

Did the brothers act as a distributor? Somehow using this ranch as a holding place for gemstones bought in bulk from another country and shipped to jewelers in the States? This seemed an awfully challenging place to work from, with all the mountains that made freighting difficult.

Had the crates in that shed been collected over a lifetime of saving and investing? Maybe even a legacy from their parents or an ancestor farther back?

That seemed the most likely explanation. And asking about a family legacy was impertinent for sure. Still, the brothers were actively doing something with them.

If she asked and he refused to tell her, perhaps there wouldn't be any harm done. At least she could be honest about what she'd discovered. Jude would likely tell him what she'd seen anyway, and she'd rather Jericho hear the news from her.

His regular breathing slowed, and she glanced up in time to see him open his eyes. He gazed ahead first, then eased his focus around. A high fever for long periods could rattle a mind. His seemed to be still working to steady himself.

The very fact that he lived was a miracle. In less than three days, his postules had scabbed, and some scabs were already falling off. Only God could bring about a transformation like that.

When his gaze caught on her, she smiled. "Hello."

He blinked. Not used to awakening to a woman watching him sleep, no doubt.

She added, "I hope you don't mind me sitting in here while I peel potatoes. Naomi's reading a book to Jonah and Lillian, but I wanted thinking time while I work." She could have just as easily taken her task outside, but then she would have missed these quiet moments watching him.

He opened his mouth and started to speak, but his voice rasped so much, he cleared his throat and tried again. "I don't mind." He seemed a more subdued version of himself, probably still lacking strength. And maybe his mind was still struggling.

She focused on the potato in her hands. "We're making potatoes au gratin to celebrate you feeling better."

"That sounds good. Everything you make is good."

She couldn't help looking up at him. He so rarely complimented. Maybe he hadn't meant that the way it sounded.

But his eyes held warmth, his head still resting against the pillow.

"Thank you." Even as she tried to be confident, heat rose up her neck. With him in such a good mood, maybe this was the time to ask him.

She studied the potato again as she cut a long strip of skin, doing her best to sound casual. "I was wondering if I could ask you something."

"Sure." He sounded curious, open. Maybe he had nothing to hide.

"I went for a walk the other day, just to get outside and clear my head." She braved a quick glance up, but his expression was hard to read. She dropped her focus again. "I ended up back in the clearing where Jonah was hurt. There's a shed there, and when I opened the door, I saw all those crates."

She had to look again. His expression tensed, but he didn't speak. Maybe he waited for her to ask a question.

"I thought they were supplies you'd stored for the winter, so I looked in two of them." She met his gaze squarely. Now he *knew* that she knew. "Jude came then and walked me back to the house. I asked what the stones were, but he said I should ask you."

The lines at his eyes tightened, but lying there in bed, he still looked almost frail. Small. She should have waited until he was stronger.

Too late to turn back now. They had to finish this conversation, or neither of them would rest.

At last he said, "They're sapphires."

She blinked. "The blue ones?" She'd seen sapphire broaches, but they'd all been a rich navy.

"All of them. Sapphires come in many colors, but the most common is blue."

She couldn't help staring at him. She'd never imagined he possessed this depth of knowledge about such a topic. They hadn't known each other long, but they'd spent so much time together, part of her felt like she knew everything about him.

"Where did they come from?" Maybe she should apologize for being nosy, but if there was anything underhanded going on, she wanted to know. He might not tell her that straight out, but she would sense if something wasn't right.

Jericho's gaze was fixed on hers.

Let him tell the truth, Lord. She wanted so much to trust him.

He gave an almost imperceptible nod before he spoke. "Here. There's a vein of them down near the creek."

Her mind scrambled to work through all that meant for them. No wonder they didn't want people to come on their land. They wanted to keep the jewels for themselves. "How much are sapphires worth?" She nearly clamped a hand to her mouth. If theirs was an honest business, her question was impertinent. She shook her head. "I didn't mean to ask that."

He gave a weak smile. "Not as much as gold." He seemed to sink farther into the pillow. "We don't protect the mine because of any great fortune. The sapphires provide all we need to live on and then some. We just don't want this place to turn into another Helena or Virginia City. If word got out about the strike, men would come pouring onto our land. Not just threatening our quiet life but putting my family in danger."

That made sense.

He started to push upright, and she set her potato and bowl aside to help him. He'd managed to sit up, and now he focused intently on her. "That's why I need you to keep our secret, Dinah. Does your sister know?"

She shook her head. She'd not wanted to worry Naomi until she knew for sure whether something nefarious was happening here or not. And she'd been so focused on Jericho that the two of them hadn't had time to talk alone. "I don't want to keep it from her though."

Once more, the lines around his eyes deepened, his jaw tightening. "Dinah, I have to protect my family."

Defensiveness flared within her. "Naomi won't spill your secret. Not if we tell her not to. She won't want to endanger anyone here any more than you do."

His tension eased. "All right. If it's important to you." He leaned forward. "No one else can know. Please. No one knows except my brothers, Two Stones, and now you."

She tipped her head. "Not even the children?"

He shook his head. "It's too important to keep secret. That's why we call them strawberries. It's a code word Dat made up." His eyes softened. "The only reason I'm telling you everything is..." He paused, making her want to lean in for the rest. "Well, because..." Once more he stopped. He seemed to struggle for how to say what he meant.

It didn't seem possible he intended what she wanted him to say, that she was becoming important to him. But he looked so tongue-tied, in desperate need of saving. She couldn't help stepping in to rescue him. "Because you knew I'd pester you until you did?"

The embarrassment flooding his face eased, softening to a small smile. "Something like that."

~

"*A*re you sure you're well enough?"

Jericho had to let out a breath as he turned to Dinah. He carried his blankets under one arm so he could move back to the barn, but she'd followed him out like a mother hen. He worked to keep the frustration from his voice. "I'm well. Back to my old self. I promise."

With her looking up at him like that, worry furrowing her brow, the angst in his chest melted away. She was so pretty, there was no way he should spend another night in the house with her.

He dropped his voice, gentling his tone. "It's not proper, me sleeping in there without a chaperone." She held his gaze, and he could only hope the warmth shimmering in her eyes was attraction. He'd progressed way past that himself.

It *seemed* like she felt something for him. But he was no expert in the ways of a woman's heart.

He craved to know something certain. To reach out and feel her receive his touch. Maybe even lean in to it.

The boys should all be out weaning the calves, so no one was here in the yard to see if she refused him. He swallowed, gathered his nerve, and took a small step toward her.

She was tall for a woman. But standing this close, she had to crane to look up at him. He didn't want to tower over her. Didn't want her to feel less than equal to him in any way.

He couldn't change his height, but he could lift her up in other ways. He could tell her what a difference she'd made, even though he wasn't good with words. She was gazing at him with such softness, it made his heart race. "Since you came, you've been...a wonder. Not just your doctoring, though we've sorely needed that. And not just the cooking and cleaning you've managed, even with everything else happening. It's the way you've changed our lives. You reminded me of our family's traditions, which I'd let fall away. You've made Lillian blossom more than I've ever seen. I wasn't sure she'd ever smile again, but now she does every day."

He wanted to touch her as he attempted to put into words this last part. But finding the right words would be hard enough, so he kept his hands at his sides.

"And me. You've helped me see my failings. Helped me want to be a better man. More than that, you've awakened something inside me that I've pressed down for years." He did reach up now, brushing the loose hair from her cheek. "You're beautiful.

You're brave. You care about people. I don't know how you feel about me, but I can't help but be drawn to you."

The way her eyes shimmered with something that looked very much like pleasure, perhaps she felt the same. It gave him the courage to do what he did next. Slip his fingers behind her head and weave them through her hair. He took a final step to close the distance between them.

She lifted her mouth as he lowered his, but he paused with their lips a handbreadth apart. Even this close, she was so beautiful it made his chest ache. And she wasn't turning away. Maybe she even welcomed his kiss.

That last thought drew him down to brush her lips with his own. Heat swept through him as he lingered there, then went back for more.

He'd never kissed a woman before, save for Ethel Lucas behind the Western Hotel when he was twelve. But that didn't count.

Not compared to the taste and flood of sensations Dinah Wyatt's mouth ignited inside him. She deepened the kiss, sparking a new flame within. He pulled her closer, wrapping an arm around her waist, cupping the back of her head. Tasting. Inhaling. He couldn't get enough of this woman.

She gripped his collar, holding him close with one hand, wrapping the other around his neck. Something about her skin touching his, brushing under his jaw and the lobe of his ear, released a stronger sensation within him. He moved from her mouth to her jaw, tasting her sweetness as she tipped her head back to give him access.

When he reached her ear, a shiver went through her. He slowed, taking his time. He would—

"Jericho."

The way she spoke his name, he couldn't tell if she wanted him to stop or go farther. He couldn't go much farther. Not now. He couldn't make the same mistake Lucy had.

He pulled back to see her face. Her eyes were dark and round, a bit dreamy. Her lips so plump and full from his own. She still had her head tipped back a little. Still giving him access.

But she whispered, "We have to stop."

She was right. With everything in him, he wanted more of her. But he couldn't take it.

He moved his hands to her upper arms, where layers of fabric separated them. He took a half step back too, putting air between their bodies. But he let himself lower his forehead to rest on hers. Maybe this touch wouldn't put them in danger.

As he struggled to catch his breath, he could feel the warmth of her own. "Dinah, I'm falling for you. I think I might have already fallen."

The corners of her mouth tipped up. "I know."

Did that mean she was falling for him too? That thought lit another fire in his veins. He wanted to taste her again, to feel her hands on his skin.

But he couldn't. Not yet. Too much was at stake.

With all the strength he had, he pulled back, taking another step away. He let his palms slide down her arms, taking her hands in his as he stared into her eyes. "I...don't really know where to go from here. Do I court you?" He wouldn't be sleeping in the house again, that was for certain.

Her smile turned sweet, a little shy. "That would be nice."

He eased out a breath, giving her fingers a final squeeze. "All right then." He finally let go and reached for the blankets he'd dropped. "I guess I'd better get back to work." Though he couldn't for the life of him remember what he'd been doing.

CHAPTER 20

*D*inah couldn't help peeking through the open front door again as she scrubbed the long wall along the back of the cabin. This was Jericho's first day back out working with the animals, and he might return home early. He would likely be tired, and a little part of her wondered if he would find an excuse to come for another kiss.

They'd not had a second alone since his brothers and nephew rode in with the weaned calves yesterday evening. After the commotion of settling the mournful animals down, it had been time for the evening meal. Then when she'd hoped to sneak out with Jericho for a walk under the wide starry sky, Lillian and Sean begged for everyone to play a round of charades.

Watching all those grown men act out the professions written on cards had been a sight she wouldn't have wanted to miss. And Jericho had sat near her, though not so close they could touch. They were still careful not to do anything that might arouse the others' suspicions. When should she and Jericho tell them?

She should probably speak with Naomi privately. Her sister

had never shown a hint of affection toward Jericho, once they met him and learned of the mistake. But she'd come all the way from Virginia thinking she'd be his bride.

Dinah still hadn't told her about the sapphires either. She and her sister clearly needed a long talk.

She glanced over her shoulder to where Naomi stitched in the chair beside Jonah's bed. Now that she'd finished the clothing for Lillian and Sean, she was spending every spare moment on baby clothing. Perhaps tonight, they could tuck themselves away in the bed chamber for a sleepover like they used to do. The kind where they stayed up late and talked of all the things one doesn't share in passing. Dreams and disappointments. Secrets and secret attractions. Sapphires and kisses.

The sound of hoofbeats outside made her turn, maybe too fast, for the others might realize her eagerness. Jericho had come after all. She tried to keep her step to a walk as she strode to the door.

Naomi was watching her, and even Jonah had awakened from his doze.

She peered outside. Two riders. But they weren't coming from the direction Jericho and the others had ridden out that morning. In the barn, Lillian poked her head through the open door way, and Sampson stepped past her into the sunlight.

One of the riders was definitely native. Something about that fact eased the tension in her chest. She might have had a very different reaction two months ago, before coming to this land and getting to know Two Stones's family and neighbors.

This man looked familiar but she couldn't...

Two Stones's cousin. The one who'd been with the hunting party she and Jericho met on the wagon ride back from Missoula Mills. The one who'd smiled at the puppy.

Sampson met the men in the yard, and she stepped outside to greet them as well. The other fellow was a white man.

"Who is it, Di?" Naomi's voice followed her out, but Dinah

was already several steps from the house, and the men had seen her. Even turning toward her.

Something about the white man looked off. He leaned forward in the saddle, almost sideways. Was he hurt? She scanned both sides of him now that he rode straight toward her. His face was pale, his hair wet like he was sweating.

Two Stones's cousin rode closer, swung to the ground, and grabbed the other man's reins. He turned the horse so she could better see the side the man leaned toward. Her gaze locked on a wad of cloth—maybe a flannel shirt—wrapped around the hand. Blood smeared up his arm.

Dinah's heart kicked into a run and she hurried to his side. "What happened?"

"Bear." The man grunted through his clenched jaw.

He braced his elbow while she unwrapped the cloth. Under the first layer, the blood soaked the flannel. He must have cut an artery.

The man's face was pale as she unrolled more fabric. "Is the bone broken?" That might not be a pleasant thing to bring up, but she needed to know before she peeled off all the fabric that might be supporting it.

He was breathing hard, sweat beading down his face. "I don't know. Flesh is gone."

Better be careful then. She would prefer to wait and examine the wound inside with her supplies, but she might be able to stop the bleeding here, before they moved him again.

One look at the wound made her belly twist. The bear had ripped through muscle, but she couldn't determine about the bone. She had to get him inside. At the very least, she would need to stitch these tendons and muscles back together.

She turned to Two Stones's cousin. "Can you help me get him down and inside?" She'd never heard him speak English, so he might not understand.

He moved forward though, and Sampson came to the horse's

head. Working together, they lowered the man to the ground, and she supported his wrist while they helped him walk into the cabin.

"I have a blanket on the floor. Or do you want him on the bed?" Naomi stood near the door.

"The floor in here. I need lots of light. And clean water."

They guided the man to the wool cloth her sister had spread near Jonah's bed. This room was becoming a hospital ward.

"Lie down and I'll give you something for the pain before I stitch." As she helped him lower onto the quilt, Naomi brought Dinah's case. Dinah glanced up at her sister. "That box of bandages in the corner of our room too."

Naomi nodded. "Sampson's getting water. Do you want it hot or cold?"

"One pot of cold and one boiling." She focused on resting the hand on the floor so she could get laudanum for him. Too bad she hadn't brought chloroform, but this would have to do.

She was in the midst of stitching one of the muscles that had been completely severed when a voice broke through her concentration.

Jericho.

She didn't lift her gaze from her work, but she strained to hear what he was saying, and who he might be speaking to. It wasn't English, so he must be talking with Two Stones's cousin. When this was done, she would have to ask the man's name.

Jericho sounded upset. Maybe even angry. Or just...frustrated. Had something else happened?

Naomi had gone out to check on the children, so Jonah was the only one here with her and her patient. She glanced up at him. "What is Jericho saying?" He probably understood the language too.

His mouth pinched. "He's telling Tall Shadow he shouldn't have brought a stranger here."

She stiffened and turned to the open doorway. She couldn't

see the men, but Jericho would hear if she called to him. Should she stop him? Would he feel she shouldn't interfere?

But she couldn't have him turning away patients in as dire need as this man. She sat back on her heels and called, "Jericho."

A moment later, he stepped into the cabin, his stride long and his expression worried. "What is it?" He reached her side and crouched, scanning the man lying before her.

The laudanum had taken effect, and the stranger lay with his lids half-lowered as he took in Jericho.

"Who are you?" Jericho sounded too brusque toward a man so badly injured.

Her own hands were bloody, so she couldn't touch Jericho's arm, but she leaned her shoulder against him. "He's hurt. He came for help, not to bother us."

Jericho's voice tightened. He dropped his volume. "Tall Shadow said he doesn't know the man, only that he's a miner. Tall Shadow rode up as a bear was mauling him. He shot the bear and thought he should bring this man here. He'd heard about what you did in Two Stones's village. That you're a healer."

She managed an encouraging smile. "I'm glad he brought him." She refocused on her work. "Go scrub your hands well and you can help me."

He would see that kindness and caring went a long way when dealing with strangers. And a doctor didn't decide whether an injured person was worthy of care. If Jesus had done that, the entire world would have been doomed.

～

*A*s he scrubbed his hands in the washbasin, Jericho's mind rebelled at the idea of a stranger—a miner—lying on the floor of his family's home. Dinah's caring ran too deep sometimes. Made her blind to safety. To wisdom.

He would help her...and make sure the man didn't bring harm. Then he would see the fellow on his way. After that, he would somehow get Dinah to see that they couldn't bring strangers into the house. That they had to be careful. That not everyone who came calling should be invited in.

But as he knelt beside her and she talked him through what she'd done and how she would finish stitching the man's arm back together, his belly churned. He wouldn't have been able to turn this fellow away either.

This stranger would have died without Dinah here to care for him. If he didn't bleed out this first day, the wound would have festered, and the blood poisoning would likely take him within the week. Long before he could get to another doctor.

In truth, someone with Dinah's skill was greatly needed in this territory.

But someone *else*.

A man. Who didn't live on the Coulter ranch.

Not the woman Jericho planned to make his wife.

At last, Dinah finished bandaging her work. The patient lay with his eyes closed. His chest still rose and fell, so he lived. It was hard to tell if he'd passed out or was simply exhausted.

The rest of Jericho's brothers and Sean had returned from the herd and had even managed to milk the cow Jericho had chosen. Tall Shadow had ridden on, leaving the miner's horse and belongings in their barn. They still didn't know the man's name.

Dinah pushed up to her feet, and Jericho rose too. "I guess he can stay there for now."

Dinah spun to him, her eyes blazing. "Where else would he go, Jericho? The man is fighting for his life. We can't toss him out like used washwater."

She was right, of course. He hadn't meant that. He'd meant keeping him on the floor there might be better than trying to

169

move him onto a bed. But he wouldn't get defensive, not after the strain she'd just been through during that detailed surgery.

He tried to gentle his voice. "Of course not." He bit back everything else. She didn't need him making her day harder, but he would be watchful and protect his family, no matter what he had to do.

CHAPTER 21

*D*inah gathered the stained bandage and pushed up from Mr. Chalmers's side. "Rest now. When you're ready, you can eat again." After a day, her patient had regained enough awareness to tell them his name and a few details about his plans, but not much more.

She sent a smile to Jonah, who lay in the bed on the other side of Chalmers. "Can I get you anything?"

He smothered a yawn. "Nah, thanks. It's about time for my mid-morning nap."

"Sweet dreams." She turned to carry the bandage to the work counter.

As she scrubbed the blood out of the cloth, Jericho came in with Lillian and the pup. He'd not gone out with his brothers today, to keep an eye on their visitor, no doubt.

Dinah smiled at Lillian. "The cream has separated from the milk, so we can make butter now. Wash your hands and I'll show you how to scrape it off."

While she worked with Lillian, Jericho climbed up to the loft. After a few minutes of rummaging sounds, he descended the ladder. She needed to talk with him, to break the tension that had hung between them since Mr. Chalmers's arrival yesterday.

He stood in the middle of the room, looking a little lost.

"Would you like that haircut now?"

He turned to her. "I guess. Thanks." His manner still felt...distracted.

She touched Lillian's shoulder. "Just keep shaking that jar."

"Can I take it outside to play with Apple?" She lifted pleading eyes.

Dinah nodded. "As long as you don't stop shaking."

While Lillian scampered outside, she turned to Jericho. "Should we take our work outside? It looks like the sun's out."

He shook his head. "A cold wind's blowing."

She motioned to his chair at the table. "Settle in while I get my tools."

When she returned with scissors and her spare shirtwaist to protect his clothes from loose hair, she glanced at Jonah and Mr. Chalmers. It appeared both were sleeping, though sometimes she wondered if Jonah feigned sleep so he could hear what happened around him. Or maybe to make the time pass. He had to be bored out of his mind, in bed so long.

She placed her comb and scissors on the table beside Jericho. "Later this week, we'll get Jonah up and see if the leg hurts when he doesn't put weight on it. He'll need a pair of walking sticks. Do you think you could find two sturdy branches about the same length he could use?"

"I can find you better. Dat made a pair of walking sticks when he broke his leg right after we finished the cabin. I think they're still in the barn."

She grinned as she placed the extra shirtwaist over his shoulders. "That's perfect." She took a moment to rest her hands on his upper arms, relishing the power there, reminding herself of the feel of him.

His strength rippled beneath her hands as he lifted the sleeve of her old shirt to his nose. He sent her a sideways look, his eye twinkling, still keeping the cloth against his face. "It smells like you. Like fruit and lye soap."

Her smile turned sheepish. "I'm not sure that's good."

He leaned back in his chair, turning toward her more as he reached for her hand. "It's very good."

Too much of her wanted to settle into his lap, wrap her hands around his neck, and kiss him the way she had in the yard. But there were others in the room, and even if both men slept, Naomi could step from the bedroom or Lillian in from the yard at any moment.

So she tightened her grip on his hand and moved behind him, pressing their joined hands against his chest. She stroked her free hand through his hair. "I'd better get to work."

He released her with a grumble, but she could feel the warmth of his body as she trimmed his hair. She worked in silence, doing her best to focus on the task, yet far too aware of his every movement. His every breath. She needed something to distract herself.

She'd planned to use this chance to help him feel better about the situation with their guest. "Mr. Chalmers said he'll be heading back to Fort Benton as soon as he can travel again. He has friends waiting for him there."

Jericho's lashes drifted closed while she worked the scissors around his ear. "The sooner the better."

That wasn't quite the response she'd been hoping for, but at least he didn't feel angry. "He tried to pay me all his gold dust for fixing his arm, and for the room and board."

Jericho eased his head around so he could look at her, moving slowly enough that she didn't cut him. "What did you tell him?"

She met his gaze. "I told him I don't have an open clinic, so I couldn't accept payment. But I would check with you about the room and board. He doesn't need to worry about it now though. All his energy should go to recovering."

Jericho turned straight again, but a moment passed before he spoke. "He doesn't need to pay for sleeping on the floor. But you should be compensated for all you did on his arm. He would have died without you."

She swallowed. "That doesn't feel right." She let out a breath. "It was a lot easier to accept payment when I treated patients in Pop's clinic."

He glanced at her from the corner of his eye. "Is that where you learned your skills?"

She couldn't help but smile. "I started working with him when I was five years old. Any time I didn't have to be at school, I spent with him. He let me go on calls, even in the middle of the night."

"Did he serve as a medic in the war?"

She nodded. "That's when I took over his clinic completely."

He tipped his head enough to look at her. "You were only...?"

"Eighteen by the time he left. But I'd been in full apprenticeship for four years. That's more training than many physicians receive."

He turned forward again. "He must have been skilled, for you're a wonder."

Those words felt good, curling inside her and spreading warmth through her chest.

"Where is he now?"

She bit back a sigh. "Back in the clinic. When he returned from the war, he took a sabbatical, but I could tell he needed to work again. We've both seen patients these last two years, but..."

His voice turned wry. "But then your sister found a mail-order bride advertisement, and God said you should head west."

She tried to keep her voice even, but the pain of those weeks hit too hard. "That's not quite the way it happened."

He stilled, his voice softening. "My guess is *you* found the advertisement."

She gripped the hair so tight her fingertips turned white. "It seemed like the perfect opportunity. Naomi was desperate to leave Wayneston. I think Nana and Pop would have let her stay, but she wouldn't tell them."

He reached up and found her hand, gripping it in his strong, sturdy warmth. "I'm glad you came. I'm glad she has a safe place here to have the babe."

Even as she held his hand, letting him cradle her in his strength, she replayed his words in her mind. *She has a safe place here to have the babe.* That sounded like he planned for them to stay through spring. That wouldn't be appropriate unless either Naomi or she were married.

She'd thought that might be what he was leading toward with those glorious things he'd said to her after their kiss. But she hadn't let herself think about it too long. She couldn't get her hopes up.

In truth, she'd never really wanted to marry. But now that she'd met Jericho Coulter...

The door banged open, making her jerk back as Lillian trotted in. "We have butter, Dinah. There's a big glob of butter in the middle."

Dinah smiled at the girl, working to slow her speeding heart. "Wonderful. Let's see how much." She examined the clump that had developed in the center. "Keep shaking. I think we'll get a bit more, then you can drink the buttermilk."

Lillian beamed. "I haven't had buttermilk in ages."

Dinah turned back to Jericho's hair. "Keep shaking."

"C'mon, Apple. We have to keep shaking." The pup raced ahead of her out the door, yapping in the fresh air.

Dinah chuckled. "Those two are the best of friends."

Silence settled again, and she could feel Jericho thinking about something. Maybe preparing to speak.

"I'm glad you suggested a dog." The earnestness in his voice planted hope in her chest. Maybe he would be open to other suggestions.

She moved around in front of him, lay down the scissors and comb, and perched in the chair beside his so she could take his hands. His expression looked amused as he settled his hands in hers.

She leaned in. "I have another suggestion, and I think it will be as helpful for the family as getting the dog."

His gaze turned wary, but he didn't pull his hands back. "What?"

"I know you're worried about allowing strangers on the ranch, but there are probably many good people around. People you could trade with, people who would be happy to lend a helping hand. Neighbors who might want to buy your stock."

She inhaled a breath. "And...people who might need medical care. Not just emergencies like bear attacks and smallpox outbreaks, but regular things, like a festering tooth or the ague. There probably hasn't been anyone in this area to help, but when they learn there's a doctor nearby, people will start showing up."

He sat back in his chair, the strong line of his jaw locking in place. This man was every bit as stubborn as he was handsome.

She pressed on. "We could get ahead of that by establishing a regular day and place where they could come for what they need. It doesn't have to be here at the house, or even on the ranch. But that way, we could help the people in this area *and* have some measure of control over who comes and when."

She finally paused to wait for his answer. She'd said everything she could think of that would appeal to him.

He didn't speak for a dozen heartbeats, maybe more. She gave his hands a little squeeze. He didn't return the pressure.

At last, he said, "I like the idea of keeping people from coming on the ranch, but where would this clinic be?"

Hope surged within her. "I don't know. Near the Mullan Road? That might be too far away. Somewhere on the far edge of your property? You know the area best."

He was quiet again, his brow gathering in deep lines. She'd cut more off his hair than she'd planned to, but this shorter style made her heart swoon with every glance at him.

The door opened again, and Lillian strode in. "I think this is all the butter that's going to come."

Dinah kept her gaze on Jericho. Would he give an answer before she had to turn her focus to the girl?

He met her look, his eyes earnest—though troubled. "Give me time to think on it."

She squeezed his hands and smiled. "Thank you." If his niece hadn't been in the room, she would have leaned forward and brushed his lips with hers. Just a little something to sweeten the idea.

But hopefully they would have a chance for that later.

CHAPTER 22

*D*inah cradled Jericho's face between her palms, relishing his arms around her. "Go do your work. Don't worry about us." He'd stayed near the cabin for two days since Mr. Chalmers came. Surely his brothers needed him with the animals.

He studied her, his face a handsome storm. "I don't like leaving you all here with a stranger." His eyes darkened and he lowered his voice. "I don't like leaving *you* at all."

She grinned and met his kiss. Not a long or deep one, but enough to make her wish he *wasn't* going out to help his brothers in the valley pasture. When he pulled away to rub her nose with his, her chest ached. "Just come back to me."

A growl rumbled in his throat. "You're making it hard to leave."

She giggled, then slipped her hands down to his chest and pushed. "Go then."

He stepped back and mounted his brown-and-white horse with a smooth motion that showed his lithe muscle. He sent her a final grin as he nudged the gelding forward. "I'll be back."

The longing that knotted within her made her insides ache. Why did love have to bring both pain and joy at the same time?

When he disappeared, she turned back toward the house, the sound of her footsteps muffled by the soft dirt. She needed to spend time with her patients, helping Jonah practice on the walking sticks and changing the bandage on Mr. Chalmers's arm.

Inside the cabin, Lillian was cleaning dishes from the morning meal. Naomi must be in their bed chamber. Sometimes she lay down to rest after the men rode out in the mornings.

Dinah turned to the men resting on the left side of the main room. "Are you two ready for the doctor's rounds?" She focused on Jonah. "You first. Let's see how the walking sticks fit after the adjustments I made."

He'd left the bed for the first time yesterday, but the walking sticks his father once used were too short for Jonah's taller frame. He managed a few steps, but he couldn't keep his injured leg from dragging the ground. Hopefully, adding extra layers of cloth had raised the T-supports high enough.

As Jonah sat up, she lifted his splinted leg and helped him turn to rest it on the floor. He gripped the walking sticks to pull himself to standing.

"Let me help." Naomi's voice sounded from behind her as she hurried from the bed chamber.

Dinah sent her raised brows. "I thought you were resting." Naomi had spent a great deal of time with Jonah these past days, enough that they could be forming an attachment.

But in Naomi's condition, that didn't seem wise. Dinah had tried to hint at that the other night when she told her sister about Jericho's affections. Naomi hadn't seemed to catch on.

Now, she positioned herself on Jonah's left side. "You need an extra set of hands for this."

Dinah took up his right, and as Jonah rose to standing, she

gave instructions. "Make sure you keep all your weight on your good leg." She helped position the walking sticks under his arms. "These are a better height, but I might add one more extension. See if you can position them forward, then swing your body to catch up with them."

With his first try, he did what she asked, but the movement jerked. His second step was smoother.

"Look at you, Uncle Jonah. You'll be on a horse again soon." Lillian grinned as she dried plates.

"Plannin' to do that tomorrow." He flashed a cheeky smile.

Dinah stayed by his side as he moved, though he seemed to be gaining good balance. "Two laps around the inside of the cabin, then we'll stop for the day."

"That's not enough. I'm strong now, see?" Jonah sent her a look that was probably supposed to charm her into agreeing.

She shook her head. "I don't want to jostle the bone while it's still healing. You need to spend most of your time in bed."

"Can I at least sit in a chair?"

"You can sit up in bed for one hour, as long as you keep your leg straight. Then we need to attach the traction again."

He grumbled under his breath, but nothing he said would change her decision on this. Too much could go wrong if he didn't adhere to her instructions.

Once she had Jonah back in bed and Naomi fussing to make him comfortable, she turned to Mr. Chalmers. He'd been quiet these past three days he'd laid on the pallet on the floor. She'd asked if he wanted a mattress, but he waved the offer away. Said he was used to bedding down on the ground.

He still slept a lot, and when awake, he lay and watched the happenings within the cabin. The laudanum she'd been giving him might have something to do with his silence, but that would change soon. Now was the time to wean him.

She carried her medical kit to his side and knelt. "How are you feeling today?"

"Fine." He regarded her in his usual quiet manner.

She reached for his arm. "Let's see how you're healing."

Beneath the bandage, the first hints of new flesh were growing in his wound. Relief eased through her. No sign of excessive festering. There was definitely red tinging the edges of the skin, but not more than she would expect from a bear claw. The salve she'd been applying should stop that in time.

He would need to use the cream for several weeks to keep the wound healing correctly. It would be helpful to have extra tins of the stuff that she could send with patients.

She needed a great many supplies actually. She would have to talk to Jericho about how to send an order. Maybe some materials could be purchased in Fort Benton, but most would have to be shipped up the Missouri River.

Once she wrapped a fresh bandage securely around the arm, she gathered the soiled cloth and started to rise.

"What about the medicine?" Mr. Chalmers scowled. "Still hurts a powerful lot."

She crouched down to his level again and gentled her voice. "I can't give you that anymore, but your arm is healing nicely. The pain should get better every day."

He frowned. "It hurts like hades. Do you got spirits or somethin' to take the edge off?"

"I'm sorry, Mr. Chalmers. All we can do is let it heal." She stood again and placed her case against the wall, then carried the used bandage to the wash bucket.

Naomi stepped from the chamber, her cloak in hand. "I need some fresh air. Will you girls take a walk with me?"

"Apple and I will come." Lillian dried her hands on a cloth.

Dinah plunged her hands in the water to scrub the bandage. "I'll stay here and do some cleaning. You girls enjoy the sunshine."

Naomi had made sure the cabin was swept every day, but

Dinah needed to scrub around the table, the kitchen, and the main pathways through the rooms.

She should probably mention to Naomi the need for a braided rug to be placed inside the front door. That way it could pick up the dust and mud from the men's boots before they tracked everything into the house.

After she scrubbed and hung the bandage to dry, she glanced around the kitchen. Sampson had taken over milking the cow until she was fully gentled, but he must have forgotten to bring the milk in that morning. Dinah needed to strain it clean before the cream separated.

She strode to the door. "I'm going to the barn for a minute." The men murmured replies too low to hear, so she slipped outside.

The wind had kicked up stronger than when she'd been out with Jericho, taking on an icy bite that bespoke winter coming soon. Enough leaves had fallen from the trees that she could see a range of mountains in the distance—majestic rocky peaks that made her chest swell every time she stopped to admire them.

When she stepped into the barn, the cow lowed softly to greet her. The animal's stall opened to an outside corral, but she must be taking refuge in the barn from the wind. Sampson had left the bucket of milk hanging on a hook beside the stall, so Dinah picked it up and turned to head back inside.

A man stood in the barn door opening.

Her heart surged into a thundering pace, but then she made out Mr. Chalmers's outline. Especially the way he cradled his injured arm.

She let out a breath. "Mr. Chalmers. You shouldn't be out yet. Is there something you need?" She'd set up a chamber pot for him in the house so he wouldn't need to come outside for that. And certainly not to the barn.

He shifted his weight. "Need to talk to you. About the medicine."

She tensed. "What about it?"

"I need more. Just for today. This pain is awful, too much to endure." His voice was low, almost pleading.

He must have already formed a dependency. Most people didn't have trouble after only three days, but if he'd had previous addictions, his body might be more sensitive.

She kept her voice as calm and firm as she could. "I understand you're in pain. But I can't give you more laudanum. The effects would be far worse for you."

He advanced a step forward. "You don't care how bad I hurt."

She stepped back before she could stop herself. But then she braced her feet, unwilling to let him believe he had power over her. "Of course I care about your pain. That's why I'm making sure your arm heals properly. But I can't give you more medicine. It's not safe."

She glanced sideways. Chalmers was still moving slowly. She could probably get into the cow's stall and out to the corral without him catching her.

He took another step forward, his expression turning menacing. "I think you're lying to me. I think you're keeping that medicine for yourself."

"That's not true." She reached for the pin that locked the gate. "Please, Mr. Chalmers. I need you to go back inside and rest. I'll make willow bark tea to help with your pain."

He took a longer stride toward her, bringing him almost within arm's reach. "You're a pretty thing. Maybe you can help me feel better without your medicine."

The man had become a full lunatic. She jerked the gate open and turned to slide into the stall.

He grabbed at her, gripping her sleeve and a lock of hair the wind had pulled loose.

She scrambled to yank free, but his hold was too strong. He held her in place with an iron fist.

"Let go!" She tried to turn and plant an elbow in his side, but the gate blocked her effort. Her arm slammed the wood, shooting pain up her shoulder to blend with the searing of her scalp where he pulled her hair.

"I've had enough of you..."

Her heart pounded as she struggled against him. He'd lost his mind. She never would have thought he had this much strength left after all the blood he lost.

"I said, let go!" She spun to strike him, this time pushing the gate wider with her body so she could reach him. If she could hit his injured arm, that would stop him. Surely.

His good arm was so long though, he held her too far away to reach the injured limb. He pulled down on her hair, forcing her backward to the ground.

She kicked out with her leg, trying to catch his injured wrist, or maybe strike his groin area. Anything to cripple the power he wielded.

The effort only threw her off balance, and she succumbed to the force of his arm, tumbling backward to the ground. She lay on her back, her right leg twisted beneath her. She scrambled to push up from the dirt.

She had to get free. What would he do to her? *God, save me.*

He loomed over her like an ugly monster. Then he came down hard on her, slamming his knees into her belly as he knelt on her. The air exploded out of her lungs and pain shot through her body.

CHAPTER 23

*D*inah writhed as Chalmers's knees pressed her belly. She fought for breath. Fought to throw him off of her.

Air. She had to find air.

She would give him some laudanum if only he would let her go. But she couldn't draw breath to say so.

A blast sounded in the distance. Or maybe that was the panic of her heartbeat. She sucked in a tiny gasp, but her lungs screamed for more.

Then his knees lifted off her. His body fell sideways, removing the weight from atop her.

She sucked in a gulp and forced herself up, onto her side, then to her hands and knees so she could crawl away. She had to get far from him while she could.

"Dinah, are you hurt?" A man's voice broke through her panic.

She was away from Chalmers now and scrambled to stand, stepping on her skirts and tripping. Once she caught her balance, she spun to see where Chalmers was. To see if she should run farther.

He lay in a heap on the ground. Not moving.

"Dinah."

She finally let herself follow the voice. Jonah?

She squinted to see better with the light from the door behind casting him in shadow. He stood with his walking sticks under each arm, leaning into them with a rifle in his hands.

"I realized he was gone, and he didn't answer when I called for him. I was already out of the bed when I heard you scream."

Bile rose in her throat as reality washed through her. Jonah had shot Chalmers. The man she'd worked so hard to save. A man created and loved by God. His life might well be wiped out with that single blast.

Yet Jonah had done it to save her. She could still feel the weight of the man's knees pressing into her abdomen. The panic to breathe. The desperation.

She drew in a deep breath to keep the churning inside from spewing up her esophagus and out onto the ground. Maybe she could save him somehow.

As she crept toward Chalmers, her chest refused another breath. He lay on his side, his face pressed into the dirt. His bandaged arm rested on the ground, the wrist at an angle that would surely be too painful to stand if he could feel pain. A bright red circle pressed his shirt to his side. The bullet must have struck him hard enough to knock him sideways—off of her.

She knelt quickly, keeping distance between them as she pressed two fingers against his neck. She didn't have to worry about holding her breath to better feel his pulse, since her lungs still wouldn't drag in air.

Not even a tiny flutter moved within him. She needed to try once more though. In a different place. She pushed his shoulder, turning him on his back. His eyes stared upward. Unseeing.

Her chest finally released, allowing the bile to surge upward in her throat. She spun away, dropping her hands to brace against the ground as the contents of her stomach spewed out.

~

*J*ericho pushed Pinto as hard as the horse could run up the rocky slope. When the ranch buildings came into view, he scanned everywhere he could see. Nothing looked out of place.

Yet that shot. It hadn't been one of his brothers bringing down an elk they met on the trail.

Something was wrong, he could feel it in his veins. He should have never left the cabin with that stranger there.

The front door stood open, so he reined Pinto toward the house. Sometimes they left it ajar for fresh air.

But a movement near the barn caught his attention. Lillian. She was motioning him that way.

He turned hard and pulled Pinto to a stop by his niece, jumping to the ground before the animal stopped. He'd ridden with his Hawkins in his lap and now gripped it in one hand. "What's wrong?"

She looked pale. Scared.

His heart hammered as he approached her, gripping her shoulder. But he tried to gentle his voice. "What is it, Lilly?"

She pointed into the barn. "Miss Dinah."

A new round of panic flared through him. He never should have left her.

He turned and grabbed the barn door. But when he jerked it open, he nearly plowed into Jonah, standing with walking sticks by the doorway.

"Jericho." His brother's face held a twist of emotions that flamed the fear inside him even higher.

"What's happened? Where's Dinah?" He looked past Jonah, but the inside of the barn was cast in shadows.

Jonah shifted to the side, his voice shaking a little. "I didn't have a choice. I had to."

A scream built inside Jericho as he plunged into the barn, squinting to force his eyes to adjust to the dim light. If his brother had hurt Dinah...

Naomi knelt on the ground beside...Dinah. With her arm around Dinah's shoulders.

He sprinted to them, moving around in front. Only then did he see the mound on their other side.

His mind took an extra second to understand what his eyes were seeing. Chalmers. Dead. That unseeing gaze forced a shiver through Jericho.

He pulled his focus back to Dinah. She looked as pale as Lillian had. Trembling. And as she met his gaze, she looked stricken. Had she killed this man?

He dropped to his knees in front of her, and she crawled into his arms. He pulled her onto his lap. "Dinah." He murmured into her hair. Her trembling turned to shivers, and he tightened his hold as she curled herself against him.

"Shh." He rocked a little, doing his best to quiet his racing heart.

She was alive. Unhurt, as far as he could tell, but definitely distraught. Were there injuries he hadn't seen?

He glanced at Naomi. She looked calmer than any of them. He raised his brows, doing his best to ask with his eyes what had happened.

She murmured quietly. "Lillian and I were out for a walk. We ran back when we heard the shot. She was kneeling here, casting up her accounts."

He kept rocking, sliding one hand up Dinah's back to smooth her hair that had fallen from its moorings.

What Jonah had said... He looked over at his brother, still positioned at the barn door. Like a sentry.

He held a rifle in his hand...somehow Jericho had missed that before. Jonah must have been the one to shoot.

So why was Dinah so distraught? Something must have happened between Dinah and Chalmers. Of course it had. Jonah wouldn't have killed the man for no reason.

Naomi used her hands to push to her feet. "I'll find out what happened and check on Lillian. I told her to wait outside."

An invisible hand squeezed Jericho's throat. His poor niece. Children shouldn't have to experience so much death. Had she seen this man's lifeless body? Even if she hadn't, she was frightened enough, left alone outside, fearing the worst. Knowing something awful had happened here.

While Naomi stopped to murmur something to Jonah, Dinah stirred in his arms. She straightened, pulling back as she used her sleeves to wipe her eyes. "I'm sorry." She sniffed, looking toward the barn door before glancing up at Jericho. Thankfully, she didn't look at the body.

"It's all right." He moved one hand to rest on her arm, keeping the other loose around her back.

She sniffed once more, then her shoulders rose as she inhaled an audible breath. She seemed stronger as she turned to him. "It was my fault. I told Mr. Chalmers he couldn't have laudanum today. I didn't want him to become dependent on it. I should have weaned him more slowly. I didn't realize how attached he'd become. I mean...I did. He begged for more, and I knew he must have struggled with an addiction before. I shouldn't have cut him off."

He was doing his best to follow her stream of words, but it didn't answer any of his questions. At least, not that he could understand.

"So...did he follow you here to ask for more?" The man had barely stirred from the floor during the four days he'd been here. The few times he'd needed to use the chamber pot, Jericho had to practically lift him to his feet and hold him upright. How had he managed to stumble all the way to the barn?

She nodded as she inhaled another breath. "I came to get the milk. Then all of a sudden he was behind me. I should have run sooner. But he grabbed me. He was so strong. I never would have guessed he'd be so strong..." Her voice trembled near the end.

He reached up to stroke her hair again. "Shh." He wanted to turn and kick the life out of the man who'd attacked her, but he had to stay calm for Dinah right now. And he needed to know if there was more. "Did he... Are you hurt?"

She shook her head. "Jonah came when I was on the ground. I was trying to tell him I would give him laudanum, but I couldn't breathe." Again, her voice gave away her emotions.

He needed to get her to the house. Away from the scene of this awfulness. "Do you think you can walk?"

She nodded and pushed up to her feet. He tucked his arm around her waist. She didn't look very steady, and he wasn't ready to let her go just yet.

Voices sounded outside. The others had probably all ridden back at the shot. He'd left Sean and Sampson behind in the lower pasture, simply jerked Pinto around and plunged his heels into the horse. Pinto had felt the urgency, taking the upward trail faster than ever before.

If only Jericho hadn't left the women alone, then none of this would have happened. He'd known better, but he'd allowed Dinah to talk him out of his convictions.

No more.

The only way he could assure the safety of those he loved was by keeping strangers off their land. She would have to accept that. Surely after what happened here, she would agree with him.

∾

"**W**hen we heard that shot, Dinah, I was so scared. I would have fallen over if Naomi hadn't grabbed my hand and made me run with her."

Dinah reached out for Lillian's hand and gave a gentle squeeze as Naomi slipped an arm around the girl's shoulders. They all three sat on the big double bed. They'd needed a girls' night tonight. A chance to talk through the happenings of the day.

The men played some kind of card game at the table in the other room. The game didn't involve betting, just innocent rivalry, so she didn't question Sean joining the fun. They'd even pushed the table close enough that Jonah could participate from his bed.

Naomi rubbed her hand up and down Lillian's back. "We were all afraid. But you were brave." Naomi turned her focus to Dinah. "*You* were brave too. My goodness, Dinah. You fought back and stood up for yourself."

Dinah shrugged, avoiding eye contact. "I had to get away from him."

Lillian looked up at Dinah with wide eyes. "Did he hurt you?"

Dinah shook her head. "No, sweetie. I'm not hurt." Except for her insides. If only she could go back and make different choices.

Lillian's brow still scrunched in worry, so Dinah squeezed her hand again. "God sent your Uncle Jonah to help me just when I needed him. The Lord always takes care of His children, though it doesn't always happen the way we expect it to. God knows what we need. He's never late."

The girl's mouth pinched, though the worry seemed to have eased from her eyes. "Are you God's children because you help make people better?"

Dinah's heart ached even more. "I'm God's daughter because

I've asked Him to be my Father. To clean away the things I've done wrong and help me live for Him."

"Is that why you're a doctor? Because God wants you to be?" Her gaze was so earnest, Dinah chose her next words carefully.

"I don't have to do anything to earn God's love. He gives it freely. But...I guess I am a doctor because God wants me to be. It's a special work He's given me."

A feather of warmth eased the weight from her chest. She'd needed that reminder.

"He made you really good at helping people get better."

She stroked her thumb over the back of Lillian's hand. "Thank you for saying that."

Her wide blue eyes shimmered. "It's true. I wish you'd been there in Virginia City. You could have kept my mama and pa alive."

The sting of tears sprang before Dinah could stop them, and she swallowed down the knot clogging her throat. "I wish I could have."

A yawn forced Lillian's mouth wide.

"I think it's time for all of us to turn in." Naomi patted Lillian's shoulder, then scooted off the bed.

After the men straggled to the barn, Naomi saw that Sean and Lillian were tucked in their bedding as she usually did. Dinah turned to make sure Jonah was comfortable for the night, with the traction weight in the proper position.

The quiet settled over them like a scratchy wool collar as she worked. She needed to thank him, but it felt wrong to thank him for taking her patient's life. Even if it was to save her own.

Still, Jonah might be wrestling with his actions too. She needed to do this for him.

She turned to face him. He was staring up at her with an expression unreadable in the dim light.

"Jonah." She rested her hand on his foot. "Thank you for what you did today. For saving me."

He didn't answer right away, and she couldn't see his eyes well enough to determine his thoughts. At last, he spoke. "I've never killed a man before. It's not something I ever thought I was capable of."

A fresh pain lanced her chest. New tears burned her eyes. He was barely more than a boy. *Why, Lord. Why bring this pain on this family?*

So much they'd endured. Losing their parents. Their sister. And now a man's life snubbed out because of her. If only she'd handled his first request for laudanum differently.

But all she could do now was pick up the pieces. To help heal as much as she could. "You did what you had to do. Thank you for being brave. For caring about me enough to come and help, even when it was hard for you."

Jonah's voice turned soft. "Jericho might have turned that rifle on *me* if I hadn't. He's the one who left the gun with me. Said I was in charge of protecting you girls and the homestead while he was gone."

A flash of anger seared through her. Jericho and his fear of danger. He was the one to plant the idea in his brother's mind that strangers couldn't be trusted.

Even as the thought made her fists clench, the memory of that man kneeling on her belly rushed in. He'd done far more than she expected he could or would. How might he have hurt her if not for Jonah's intervention?

She turned away. "Good night." Her mind and heart couldn't handle the churning of emotions anymore this night. She could only pray for sleep and its blessed rest.

In the morning, maybe the world wouldn't feel so twisted out of shape.

CHAPTER 24

*J*ericho dumped another armload of logs on the pile with a clatter, wood rolling in all directions. He'd split enough to last weeks, and now he'd just about run out of other things to do in the barn and yard.

This day had stretched endlessly long. He wouldn't leave his family and the house unprotected. Not again. Even if there didn't appear to be a threat on the property.

He'd not foreseen Tall Shadow bringing Chalmers either. They had simply shown up.

He couldn't hang around outside every day, but this was all he could think to do for this first day after the attack. Every time he'd attempted to go inside the cabin, the turmoil in his chest had kept him outside.

He was just so blasted angry still.

Mostly with himself. But he couldn't face any of them yet. Not until he got this anger under control.

He should never have allowed that man on their property. He should have been stern with Tall Shadow. It seemed wrong to send a man away with the kind of injury Chalmers had. But maybe Dinah could have stitched it, bandaged the arm, then they could have loaded him on his horse and let Tall Shadow lead him away.

Not that the man was Tall Shadow's responsibility, but he'd sort of taken that on when he shot the bear and brought Chalmers injured to the Coulter ranch. Hadn't he?

Jericho flung the log in his hand onto the stack and scrubbed his hands through his hair.

He wanted to scream, but if he opened up this pressure of pain boiling inside him, he might never clamp the lid down again. Where did the burden of being a decent human being end and protecting his family begin?

It's up to you, son. I need you to protect our family. Keep your sister and brothers safe and together. His father's words in that weak quavering voice wove through his spirit as they had so many times since the final minutes of Dat's life.

They'd been Jericho's guiding light through all the years since. He'd failed miserably where Lucy was concerned. But up until now, he'd thought he was doing all right with his brothers.

Having Dinah here to help with Lillian and Sean seemed to make up—at least a little—for all the ways he'd let their mother down.

But maybe even allowing Dinah and Naomi to stay had been wrong. That thought gripped his chest so tightly, he couldn't draw breath.

Did it matter at all what *he* wanted? That she made him feel like the man he wanted to be? Like together, they could accomplish his dreams? The thought of losing her. Of losing her light in the cabin. Of never having her in his arms...

He squeezed his eyes shut, still clutching his head. *If there's a God up there looking down now, why are You doing this to me?*

Dat's faith had been so real to him. Mum's too. Jericho had never before questioned whether God existed. Only whether He cared. But it might be easier to believe that no all-powerful

Being watched from a distance than to know He was real and that He'd simply turned his back.

His eyes burned. His body ached. He hated this. Hated the weight of responsibility. Hated knowing that no decision would satisfy everyone he cared about.

He had to do his best. Had to stick with the one command that had never failed him, as long as he followed it completely. No divided loyalties.

Maybe if Dinah and her sister became family, they could stay and be part of the Coulter legacy. But no one else.

From this day forward, no strangers—none at all—would be allowed on Coulter property.

Now he had to tell Dinah.

~

D inah used the back of her wrist to wipe the loose hair from her sweaty temples, then returned to scrubbing a corner of the children's bed chamber. She should have cleaned these nooks and crevices before now, but she'd not had the time or this churning unrest in her spirit that drove her to such deep cleaning.

Jericho had been rumbling around outside all day, like a hungry bear marking its territory. Making her feel too much like a hostage. Lillian had gone out a couple of times to let Apple attend to matters, returning once to report that Uncle Jericho even growled like a bear.

All of them were unsettled after the awful events of yesterday, and she and Jericho hadn't yet talked through everything. That would probably be the first step to resolve the tension and help their entire group move forward in healing.

"Dinah."

His voice sounded behind her, and she turned to see him in

the doorway. Lines etched across his brow as he frowned. "Can I talk to you?"

She straightened and pushed up to her feet. "Of course." She moved toward him to join him in the main room, but he closed the door. The two of them, alone in a bed chamber with the door closed, was the height of impropriety, but by his expression, he certainly didn't look like he planned to take advantage of her.

He seemed to realize what he'd done, and embarrassment shifted his features. "I'm sorry. I didn't want the others to listen in, not yet. We can go outside if you'd rather."

Her reputation could hardly be tarnished out here, and Lillian was tucked away with Naomi on the big bed Dinah and Naomi shared in the other chamber, reading a book. "We can talk here."

He faced her, half the room between them. A world apart. Where had the tenderness from days before gone?

She waited. Maybe she should speak first. Break the tension. But it felt like Jericho needed to decide something within himself first.

At last, he breathed out a long sigh, his shoulders sagging as he scrubbed a hand through his hair. From the way the locks stood nearly on end, he'd done that more than once today. "This is hard, Dinah."

He motioned toward the door behind him, sweeping his arm to encompass the entire cabin they couldn't see from this room. "What happened yesterday. I think it made us all wake up." The earnestness in his eyes pressed in her chest. "It reminded me why we don't allow strangers on the ranch. My father warned me. His last words told me that it's my responsibility to keep the family safe."

His jaw clenched, flexing as he searched for what else he needed to say. She wouldn't let herself speak until he'd said his fill, until she knew everything on his heart.

"I have to protect us. I'd like *you* to be part of *us*. To be a Coulter, and, as such, your sister would be welcome here as long as she wanted. But no one else. I understand you have a gift. A talent for healing. But we can't endanger more lives—your life—to help strangers."

Oh no.

She understood why Jericho felt that way. Were she in his shoes, maybe she would make the same choice. It was his responsibility to protect his family, and this was the only way he'd been successful in that goal before.

Her heart longed to say yes to this man. He hadn't asked her to marry him exactly. Not yet. But that would come soon, he'd made that clear. *If* she could stay here on his terms.

Could she really close herself off from people in need? Turn her back on the gift God had given her to help His people?

She needed time to think and pray. Time to raise this turmoil in her spirit to the Father.

But for now, she had to let Jericho know she understood. He was hurting just as much as any patient she'd treated since she'd come here. And he was doing his best. Making a hard decision for the good of his family.

She stepped forward, steeling herself to give kindness but not succumb to her feelings for this man. She didn't meet his gaze, just stepped into his arms, wrapping her own around him. He pulled her close with an intensity she wasn't prepared for.

As if he needed her for his next breath.

He needs You, Lord. Show Him You are enough.

With that silent prayer, clarity slipped through her. She'd assumed Jericho was a Christian because Two Stones had recounted the impact Jericho's father had on his faith. And the way the brothers prayed before meals and the hymns they'd begun singing on Sundays.

But she and Jericho hadn't talked about faith. Nor had she prayed about whether God blessed this love growing between them. She'd felt the rightness of the way He'd led them here and had assumed He was giving her Jericho.

But she'd not sought the Lord's guiding. Hadn't had the conversations about faith with Jericho she should have. *I'm sorry, Lord.*

This wasn't the time for that, but maybe she could plant a seed to help Jericho trust God for his family's safety.

She eased back from his embrace so she could see his face. A face so handsome her heart ached just to look at him, especially with the worry marking his brow. Now that she knew him so well, she could even see a hint of the fear that drove his actions to protect his family.

Give me the right words, Lord. She swallowed to bring moisture to her mouth. "Jericho, God is stronger than anything you face. Anything that could hurt your family. And He's enough. You can trust Him."

His brows lowered, but he said nothing. Maybe he needed time to think through it all.

So did she. She eased out of his arms, taking his hands in hers so she could give them a final squeeze. "I need time to pray about this, Jericho. I'll let you know as soon as I make a decision."

The warmth of his large, callused grip nearly stole her resolve. How easy it would be to step into his embrace again. Let him wrap his strength around her. She could promise to stay here, secluded from the rest of the world and its pain.

But resolution slipped into her spirit, and she stepped back, releasing his hands. "I guess I should start the evening meal." And then maybe she could slip out for a walk in the cool evening air.

It was time to seek God's will for their next step. Something she'd done far too little of since she and Naomi had come to the Montana Territory.

～

"*I* think we need to leave, Naomi." Dinah sat curled in bed, the covers pulled over her legs against the chilly night.

Beside her, Naomi used her elbows to push herself upright, the roundness of her belly making the act much harder than it once was. "Why? What's happened?"

That now familiar clinch in her chest made it hard to breathe, but she worked to keep her voice even. "I've been praying."

Naomi's eyes softened, and she stroked her fingertips over her belly. " I almost asked to go with you on your walk, but I thought you might need time to think."

Dinah couldn't find a smile, not with the pain of her decision. She'd given in to tears on the trail as she accepted the nudging of God's voice in her spirit. She pressed that memory away before the burn rose into her eyes again. "Jericho feels he needs to close the family away from strangers again so he can protect them. My being here as a doctor will go against that. I can't put him in that position, to feel he has to turn away injured or sick patients who seek my help. And I don't want the strife that would come between us."

Naomi rested a hand on Dinah's arm. "But what about the two of you? You can't leave the man you love. Surely you can work things out. Did you tell him he's being unreasonable? Did you tell him he has to trust God for protection?"

Dinah shifted her arm so Naomi's hand slid into hers. "I did encourage him to look to God, but I can't tell him he's being unreasonable. This is a conviction that's been nurtured in him for years, ever since their parents died. I can't expect to change him. In fact, it's his commitment to his family, his willingness to set aside his own happiness for those he loves, that makes me love him all the more. I can't tell him he should only do that when it suits my purposes."

She squeezed her sister's hand. "I simply have to decide if I can live with his choices or if I need to make my own way. I asked God what our next step should be, and I kept feeling Him say He's given me a talent so I could use it for Him."

Just speaking the words aloud brought a fresh layer of certainty. "I can't do that if Jericho won't allow people who need a doctor to come to me. I understand why he feels the way he does. But...I think it's time for us to leave." She managed the words once more without her voice breaking.

Naomi stared at the footboard. " Did God point you in any particular direction?"

A rush of emotion rose up to sting her nose and eyes. Naomi always put a pleasant face on things. Always pushed aside her disappointment and looked cheerfully toward whatever unpleasant task awaited her.

If only Dinah could have made this work. If only she could have shielded her sister from the slap of yet another disappointment. Now, with the cold of winter coming on, they would have to leave the warm security of the Coulter ranch and these people they'd both come to love.

She swallowed back the tears. She had to focus on the next step. If she let herself linger on their losses, she wouldn't be able to face all that would be required over these next days. "I think we should head to Missoula Mills. It was quieter than Helena. It might be a challenge to find lodging we can afford, especially at first. But God will provide. I have no doubt of it." *Right, Lord?*

Naomi nodded, the movement a little slow, as though she was summoning her resolve. Was her sister also mourning an attachment of the heart she would have to leave behind? Dinah couldn't bring herself to ask. Naomi might not admit special feelings, given her condition. It was better not to speak of it. Better to focus on the future and what their next step should be.

Dinah inhaled a breath. "I suppose there's not much to pack here. Only what we brought with us. We could leave..." She scrambled for a reason to delay, but that would only make things harder. "We'll say our farewells tomorrow night and leave the next morning."

"All right." Naomi's voice lacked its usual strength. She scooted down into the bed and turned her back to Dinah.

It was better not to belabor the conversation. They would both mourn. But God had a plan for them. A plan for good in a place where they could both flourish in the work He'd created them for.

She had to believe that. Cling to that.

Else, this parting would rend her heart in two.

CHAPTER 25

*J*ericho sent a quick glance around the table before dipping his gaze to take another bite of cornbread. They'd all been quiet at yesterday's morning meal, too, but that had been the morning after Chalmers's death. He'd been hoping after he spoke with Dinah yesterday that the tension in the air would ease.

But he'd not seen his brothers this somber since...well, since Lucy left. And he hadn't even told them of his decision to close off the ranch to outsiders. They might try to override him with another vote, but he would make them see the importance of privacy. No matter what he had to do.

Even Sean and Lillian kept their gazes on their food. Sean still shoveled beans and cornbread into his mouth as usual, but Lillian nibbled one bean at a time.

He couldn't bring himself to check Dinah's expression. She'd said so little after he told her his decision.

She'd come to him though. Wrapped her arms around him. Hadn't that been acceptance? And maybe—he could only hope— it meant she'd say yes when he offered an official proposal. He'd certainly made his intentions toward her clear.

But her words. They still rang through his mind. *God is stronger than anything you face. And He's enough. You can trust Him.*

Dinah cleared her throat, and his wayward gaze sprang across the table to her. She looked...pale. And maybe even fragile. Maybe she hadn't slept well.

But then she lifted her chin and spoke. "I, um, wanted to tell you all that Naomi and I will be leaving. Tomorrow."

The words slammed into him like a charging buffalo. He hadn't heard the thundering hooves. Hadn't steeled himself for the pain of sharp horns piercing his heart.

A few of his brothers murmured, but before Jericho could react, Lillian sprang to her feet, knocking her chair backward. "You can't leave. Why would you?" She turned a fierce glare on Dinah, but the pain beneath the anger sliced through him like another ram of horns. How could Dinah hurt his niece like that? Didn't she know how much Lillian adored her? How much she'd come to need her?

Dinah reached out and touched the girl's arm. "It's all right, Lillian. This is what we need to do. I was always planning to set up a clinic in Missoula Mills. We need to proceed with that now, before winter sets in." Her gentle tone only ignited the anger sparking inside him, and apparently it did nothing to soothe his niece either.

Lillian jerked her arm away from Dinah's touch and stepped back from the table. She bumped into her fallen chair, then spun and strode around the table toward the front door. Apple scampered after her, just barely slipping through the doorway before Lillian slammed it shut.

As silence reverberated through the room, he turned back to Dinah. She still wasn't meeting his gaze. What in the land of Goshen was she thinking to make a declaration like that? Surely she didn't actually intend to leave. Not after he'd all but offered for her.

Maybe *that's* what she was about. Pushing for a full proposal.

He could do that, though he certainly didn't like the way she was going about it. Regardless, he had to talk with her.

Gilead looked like he was about to speak, so Jericho pushed to his feet. "Dinah, can we speak outside?"

Even now, she didn't meet his eyes, only nodded and stood.

He started toward the door. They'd have to make sure Lillian wasn't near enough to listen in, but he needed to be outside— needed space and fresh air for this conversation. And he certainly didn't want his brothers looking on as he fumbled with his words and made a cabbage of himself.

After opening the door, he waited for Dinah to reach him and pass through. Then he sent a look to his brothers to make it clear they weren't to follow. The mixture of worry and solemnity reminded him far too much of how they'd all acted after Lucy ran off with Derek. Her sparkling personality was gone from the ranch, and they'd mourned her. Grieved her loss as though she'd died, though they hadn't said it that way at the time.

When she actually did pass away last year, most of the grieving was already done. And they'd needed to keep an upbeat mood for the children.

As he stepped outside, he spotted Lillian by the corner of the barn, her arms crossed tightly over her chest. She looked small and vulnerable, like a little girl who'd just had her favorite toy taken away.

Pain twisted with anger in his gut, but he pressed both down as he turned back to Dinah. They needed a private place to talk.

He started toward the side of the house. "Come with me." He sounded too demanding. Not at all like a fawning suitor about to offer for her hand.

As he walked, he inhaled a deep breath of cold air, then let it out, trying to stream the anger out with his breath. It all clouded in front of him, then flowed behind as he walked. This morning was the coldest yet this autumn. Not a good time for two women to set out on their own with no certain place to go.

His gut clenched at the thought of Dinah and her sister being in that predicament. He couldn't let it happen. Couldn't let her leave him.

When they were safely out of sight and far enough away not to be heard by his niece, Jericho turned to her.

She halted, eyeing him with wariness guarding her expression.

He swallowed. Gathered his nerve. Then met her eye. "Dinah, I didn't explain things very well yesterday. What I should have said...what I meant to say is..." He took in another breath. "Will you marry me?"

Her eyes widened.

He fought to keep from cringing. His words were even less elegant than the ones yesterday. He should have said something leading up to it, not attack her with the question.

But it was out now. And the echo of his words hung in the air between them.

Grooves formed in her forehead. She seemed to be considering something.

He couldn't breathe. Couldn't move. Couldn't speak to soften the way he'd asked it.

Her brows shifted to form a tent over those beautiful eyes. "Does that mean you didn't intend what you said about closing off the ranch from strangers?"

The knot in his belly moved up to his chest. That wasn't the answer he'd been hoping for. It wasn't a *no*, but his response might well bring a refusal. What should he say? He had to be truthful.

Yes, he should tell *everything*. Bare his heart. Let her see how she mattered. It was all he had left.

He started to take a step forward, but the wariness returned to her gaze, so he halted. Squared himself. Took a breath.

"Dinah. I have to protect my family. And keeping us together here at the ranch, away from strangers and the threats they bring, is the only way. But I hope that's not all you'll consider as you answer my question."

If only he had a hat brim in his hands to squeeze. This might be the hardest thing he'd ever had to say. "Before you came, I didn't know how much we needed you. I didn't realize we were missing something here on the ranch. But then you and your sister swept in. Even through all the tumult of Jonah's accident, you were strong. Capable. Beautiful. And you crept into our hearts—into our lives—little by little. You made the children happy again. Lillian especially. "

He swallowed. "You brought me back to life. Made me feel things I didn't know could be felt. Dinah, the thought of you leaving... I can't put into words what that does..." His voice cracked, and he let out a breath.

Then tried once more. He did his best to let her see the truth in his eyes. "I need you. I need you to stay."

~

God, this is too much. You can't expect me to stay strong through this.

Dinah attempted to swallow the tears clogging her throat. She couldn't hold them back much longer though. Not with this pain twisting her insides.

She loved this man. Loved him even more than she'd let herself realize. Her heart craved to say yes. To step into his arms, to take his hand and turn her back on the idea of a clinic and seeing patients. Of bringing relief to sickness and healing to injury.

After all, this man carried his own pain that she could ease. This ranch might possess more of a challenge than even a town full of miners.

But she couldn't heal the broken places inside Jericho. Only God could. She couldn't go into a marriage expecting him to change. If God planned for them to be together someday, she had to step back now and allow the Lord to work. And proceed in the calling He'd given her.

Through eyes blurred with the tears streaming down her cheeks, she took in the face of the man she loved. Those eyes that held such fear and longing. His strong profile, the jaw she'd shaved, praying with every breath that God would spare his life from smallpox.

A sob rose up, but she pressed it down. "I can't, Jericho. I can't stay here and turn my back on the calling God brought me to accomplish. As much as I love you"—her voice broke on that word, but she pressed on—"I have to follow His leading. I want that for you too. More than anything, I want you to open your heart to Him. Trust Him. He can handle your pain. He's the only One strong enough to bear the load. And He can protect your family too. Trust Him."

Anguish twisted through her body so strongly, she could speak no more. There was nothing more she could say anyway. God was the only One who could help him.

She took in a deep breath that shuddered too much. "I need to go talk to Lillian. I'll speak with Sean, too, and do everything I can to make this easier for them. They're welcome to come visit us in Missoula Mills."

He wouldn't bring them though. He'd already made that clear.

She turned from the man she loved, and with the shreds of her heart in tatters, she walked away.

~

"*J*almost wish we'd sneaked away in the middle of the night."

Dinah couldn't answer her sister, not with the way her insides felt like shattered glass. They were riding down the mountain, following the new trail the brothers had cut to lead strangers toward the house, avoiding the mine and stream bed where they gleaned sapphires.

Jericho had been stoic, a bit aloof, as everyone gathered to see them off. It was probably for the best that he hadn't spoken directly to her. She might not have been able to bear it. And certainly not with any form of dignity.

Lillian had cried, and as Dinah hugged her, she whispered that the girl could come visit anytime. Perhaps she shouldn't have made the offer. Jericho certainly wouldn't allow it, and the suggestion might bring friction between uncle and niece. But it seemed Lillian needed hope. Hope that she wasn't losing her friends completely, the way she'd lost her father, then her mother. Even her dog.

This loss didn't have to be forever.

But would that be true? Dinah was being obedient to God's calling, to the direction He'd given her. But so much of her was praying, hoping, longing—maybe even counting on—Jericho's heart changing. Was she going to Missoula Mills simply because it was the nearest town to the Coulter ranch? The place Jericho went for supplies, where she might run in to him occasionally.

Was this really obedience? Or was she feigning submission to God's direction while secretly hoping Jericho would come after her, admit he was wrong, and promise to change so she could escape back to the ranch with him?

The latter settled like an ill-fitting boot, rubbing at the blisters of her aching heart. If she truly intended to follow God's leading, she had to devote herself to the place He put her, not search for the first escape she could find.

If God intended for her and Jericho to be together one day, He would make the way when they were both fully ready. When they'd grown into the son and daughter their Heavenly Father was developing them to be. Only then could they build the strong marriage God planned.

Her chest ached. If that wasn't God's plan, the last thing she wanted was to be faced with the possibility of running into Jericho at any moment.

She needed to put him behind her. Fully immerse herself in the life God called her to. And that meant not turning left when they reached the Mullan Road. Should they go right, back to Helena? *Guide us, Lord.*

By the end of two long hours in the saddle, they reached the Mullan Road, and her heart knew for certain what she had to do. Naomi's eyes held that weary look again as Dinah reined in her gelding. "Let's stop and rest a minute. And I've been thinking about where we should go. I feel God nudging us toward Helena. I think we need a fresh start, and I have no doubt they're in need of a doctor there."

Naomi gave a weary nod. " Wherever you think best."

Maybe her sister was trying to be agreeable, but the words settled a weight on Dinah's shoulders. She had to get this right. Had to succeed. More lives than her own depended on her.

CHAPTER 26

*I*f Jericho had to spend another day at the house, he might break the last fraying thread of his restraint.

He saddled Pinto and rode to the lower valley to work cantankerous colts with Sampson, Sean, and Lillian. Jude, Miles, and Gil were moving cows to the west pasture, but they didn't need his help, and would think it strange if he tagged along with them.

Besides, he was hoping seeing the foals would boost Lillian's spirits. This was the first time he'd required her to come help with the animals since Dinah and Naomi arrived.

She'd so enjoyed working at the house with them. In truth, the place had never looked better, and Lillian...well, her red puffy eyes today showed just how hard this turn of events was on her. She might have done better if he'd let her stay at the cabin with Jonah, but he'd been worried about leaving her alone in such an emotional state. Jonah would have trouble helping her if something went wrong.

Not that Jericho was any good at consoling her.

Especially with this thundercloud nearly smothering him. He needed work. Good hard sweaty labor, like cutting down trees. These foals were just ornery enough to press on his last nerve.

Maybe he should grab the ax they kept here to break the ice on the creek in winter and start felling trees. He could have enough logs cut by nightfall to raise a barn.

The colt he was grooming lifted its head, pulling tight against the lead rope tied to a tree.

"Easy there." Jericho stroked its back to settle the animal.

But whatever the colt sensed still had it on alert, and the small body tensed beneath his hand.

"What's wrong with him, Uncle—"

At Sean's call from behind, the foal jerked backward, flinging itself on its haunches and straining against the rope with all its might.

"Hey, boy. Easy." Jericho braced a hand behind its rump to stop the colt from pulling back.

The animal struggled harder, but the tree held firm. In its panic, the colt threw itself to the ground.

Jericho's heart raced as he pulled out the knife strapped at his side. The knot in the rope would be too tight to untie. He'd have to cut it.

As soon as he sliced through the cord, Sean and Sampson moved in to catch the colt and calm him.

Jericho let them handle the youngster, turning away from the scene. The colt was probably on edge from his own frustrations. He needed to get himself away where he couldn't hurt anyone else. "Make sure he's not injured, then turn him loose," he called over his shoulder, striding to the little shed where they kept the ax.

They'd been talking about adding a lean-to off the back side of the building for the animals to take shelter. This would be a good time to start on that project.

By the time the sun passed its zenith, he was felling his

eighth tree. He'd stripped off his shirt but hadn't let himself stop to rest.

The sound of footsteps tramping through the woods made him pause. He slid a glance backward to see that it was Gilead, then heaved the ax up and swung another blow into the tree.

Another. Then another. Five more swings and this tree would fall. Gil stood several steps behind him so he wasn't in the way of the tree's path.

It took seven more blows to fell the pine. Jericho was getting weak.

He turned to the next tree he'd planned. Eyed the length of it, figuring where it would land. Gauged where the back cut should be placed. And the angle.

"I can't believe you let them leave." Gil's voice broke through his concentration, raising a sour taste in his mouth.

He hoisted the ax and swung. Hard.

Bark chunks flew backward, but he'd not made a very large dent. He raised the ax and swung again. Harder this time. Not as much bark splintered away, but the wedge barely deepened.

"You're working with a dull ax."

He raised the tool again. "The story of my life." Another swing.

Faster now. Up. Swing. Up. Swing. Up. Swing.

All that just for the back cut. He moved around to the other side of the tree and lifted the ax once more.

"You can take your anger out on every tree in the forest, but that won't change the way things are. Not until you do something to fix them. "

A fresh wave of anger surged, and he spun to his brother. "You think I don't know that?" He tightened his grip on the ax. "You think I'm not *trying* to fix things? It's not... It's not that easy."

Gil stepped closer, his expression firm. "No, but you can stop wallowing in self-pity and start owning your mistakes."

Jericho squared his shoulders. "What mistakes? Everything I've done was for the rest of you. If that's wrong, then I guess I don't know what's right."

Gil crossed his arms, his scrutiny itching. "You know, you might be right."

Jericho glared, preparing to turn his back on his brother and raise the ax again. "What's that supposed to mean?" This entire conversation felt like wandering in circles. A waste of time.

"I always thought you were just bitter, thought that explained why you don't like people anymore. Why you keep it like a prison around here. But maybe you really think you're doing the best thing for us."

He could only gape at Gil. "A prison?" He threw a hand out. "Look around you. You're surrounded by the prettiest mountains in the world. No people for miles, just wide open sky, a warm house, plenty of food, and the chance to put in a good day's work on our own land. Not to mention we have the money to order anything we fancy. You call that a prison?"

Gil raised his brows. "When we're not allowed to leave. Not allowed to have friends. Yeah, I do."

Jericho turned back to the tree. "We have friends. Two Stones and his family are the best neighbors a family can have." He'd had enough of Gil's whining on top of everything else.

He swung the ax, the blade barely sinking into the trunk. He yanked it back out of the tree and swung again.

"Why didn't you ask her to stay?"

Jericho wanted to groan, but instead he swung the ax again. When he tried to pull it out, the metal head snagged in a patch of sap. He yanked harder. With a jolt, it tugged free, and he stumbled back a step.

He stood, heaving as the answer tasted like bile in his mouth. Gil deserved to know the truth. They all did. At least they would know he'd tried.

He kept his gaze on the tree. "I did." His breaths came loud in the quiet between them.

"What did you say exactly?"

He lifted his focus to the branches above, anywhere except at his brother. "I asked her to marry me."

Again Gil was quiet a few beats. "And what did she say?"

He shrugged. "She said she couldn't stay here on the ranch. She's a doctor and has to use all that skill somewhere."

"Did you try to work out how she could do both? Be married to you and be a doctor?"

He swung around and glared. "She can't, Gil. I have to keep you all safe. If she's gonna take in every sick good-for-nothin' who walks by, she needs to do that somewhere that doesn't put my family in danger."

He half expected Gil to snap back at him, especially the way he'd been pushing. But his brother's gaze turned thoughtful. Almost gentle. "Do you think this is the way Dat would want things? Us keeping the ranch so secluded?"

Jericho nodded. "It's what he told me to do. Almost his last words to me."

Gil's head tipped. "I thought you said his last words were to keep the family together."

Again he nodded. "By keeping others out."

Gil tipped his head. "He said that?"

Hadn't he? Jericho replayed the scene in his mind. Dat lay in the big bed, his body fading so quickly. After only a couple weeks of sickness, he'd shrunken to a frail old man. *Son, you're the man of the house now. You're strong. Capable. And your Heavenly Father is on your side. Keep the family together.*

Tears had leaked through Jericho's defenses, but he ignored them. Just held his father's weak hand. *I will.*

Dat squeezed his fingers. *Promise me.*

I promise.

The sting of those long-ago tears burned his nose once

more. He hadn't cried in years. He couldn't do it now. Not in front of Gil. He lifted his chin to look up into the branches again, anything to keep his emotions at bay.

But he had to be honest. "I don't think he did. I only remember him saying to keep the family together." He squared his shoulders and glanced at Gil. "But all our problems through the years came from letting strangers onto the land. Especially what happened to Lucy."

He couldn't bring himself to list Dinah as a problem. He wouldn't be hurting now if she'd never come to the Coulter ranch, but he wouldn't have had the chance to know her. Even with his insides twisted and sliced, he wouldn't trade these past weeks with her.

Gil's expression softened, but his words came out earnest. "I think you need to go after her. Find a way to make things work. Even if it means setting up a clinic on the edge of our land." His mouth curved in a wry smile. "And maybe you can open the prison gates every so often. Give us a bit more freedom. You might be surprised to find that we don't actually want to leave. We just don't want to be held prisoner."

Then he stepped forward and gripped Jericho's shoulder, an act that felt like solidarity. Like they would face this together, a thought that relieved him more than he wanted to admit.

As Gil turned back toward the pasture, his final words drifted over his shoulder. "You might want to sharpen your ax too."

He watched his brother step through the fallen branches littering the ground, then slowly disappear through the trunks.

Could he be right?

What Gil said made sense, but Jericho needed time to think.

He turned back to the tree, swinging the ax once more. Too bad he couldn't chop away his confusion with each strike. The sound of each blow echoed through the woods, and soon he found a comfortable rhythm.

One.

Two.

Three.

He counted each time the ax made contact with the tree trunk, letting the rhythm calm his mind.

His thoughts wandered back to Dinah. Her face, her smile, the way she'd look at him across the table. Across the room. His chest ached and his belly churned. Was this the way Mum and Dat had felt about each other? A love that created a physical pain when they were separated? A love that made him rethink all his plans so they could be together? So she could be happy?

But he couldn't turn away from his responsibilities. He had to keep his family safe.

Except... Dinah would want that too. Maybe together, they could find a way to accomplish both goals.

He slammed the ax into the tree a final time, and a crack split the air as the trunk gave way. He stepped back, giving the stub plenty of clearance as the mass of branches worked their way through the trees around them.

He would find Dinah and her sister. He would tell her he'd been a close-minded fool. And together, they would work out a way to move forward.

He spun and started toward the valley where he'd left Pinto. He didn't have a moment to lose.

CHAPTER 27

"*A*re you sure you haven't seen them?" Jericho braced his hands on his hips as he scanned the livery in Missoula Mills for any sign that Dinah or Naomi had been here.

Clip shook his head. "I've had a few women pass through here of late, but none that look like you say. An' I know I've not had a chestnut gelding with four white socks here in weeks."

Of course the man would remember animals better than people. But surely he would recall if he'd seen a woman in the family way within the last day.

Jericho did his best to keep his frustration from showing as he nodded to the livery owner. "Thanks. If you do see them, will you get word to me at the hotel?"

"Will do." Clip's mouth curved in a grin. "How's that girl pup you took with you?"

Jericho almost found a smile himself. "Good. More energy than we know what to do with."

When he stepped back outside the livery, Lillian, Sean, and Gil waited on their horses with hopeful expressions. Maybe Jericho shouldn't have brought them all, getting the children's hopes up. But he'd wanted to prove to Dinah that he was willing to change. Allowing not just one of his brothers to come to town, but also the children, would be solid evidence to back his words.

He'd been sure they'd find her here in Missoula Mills.

He shook his head as he took Pinto's reins from Gil. "They didn't stop at the livery. Let's go to the hotel where we stayed. I'm sure they would have gone there."

He walked while the others rode—he'd had more than enough time in the saddle this morning and yesterday afternoon since they left the ranch. Had they missed the sisters on the road? Maybe Dinah and Naomi camped away from the main route, and his little group had ridden right past them without knowing.

That was probably what happened. The sisters would ride into town any time now.

He would double check at the hotel, then stop in at the trading post to check on his order—and maybe add something special for the woman he hoped to marry. And her sister and the coming niece or nephew. He could do for Naomi what he was never able to for his own sister when she was expecting.

But meeting the disappointed gazes of his niece and nephew after leaving the hotel pecked at his certainty. "They'll ride into town any minute. Don't worry." He nudged Sean's arm. "We'll stop at the trading post and get some penny candy, then find a place to eat real food."

Sean perked up, straightening in his saddle. But Lillian nibbled her lip, her eyes rimming red again.

Jericho's gut tightened. He was no match for all these tears. Dinah always knew just the right word, or gave a hug that made Lillian beam. But his words dried up when she started crying. And his hugs felt awkward. He couldn't even offer *that* now while they rode horseback.

He'd have to settle for a simple encouragement. "We'll find her, Lilly. Don't worry." Lucy had never liked her daughter's name shortened, but Dinah had called her by the nickname and Lillian seemed to appreciate it. Maybe him doing the same would remind her of Dinah.

His niece turned those red eyes to him. "What if they met someone bad on the way? What if he hurt them? Did something unscrup'lus?"

His gut clenched tighter, twisting as his mind conjured all the things that could happen to two women alone. Maybe he should ride out and look for them. He'd already taken a room at the hotel. He could get Gil and the children settled there, then search the Mullan Road until he found Dinah and Naomi.

But he couldn't leave his family in this town without him. Gil didn't know which establishments to avoid after sunset and which to steer clear of at *any* time. Gil's innocence was Jericho's fault, but he couldn't feel too badly about it yet. Part of him was wishing he'd left them all back at the ranch so he could focus on finding the women, who might even now be... He couldn't let himself dwell on the dangers.

Why had he let them leave alone? He was such a selfish bull-headed lout, thinking he had to stay and protect his brothers and the children instead of at least seeing Dinah and Naomi to town.

Jericho decided they'd stop in at the trading post. Maybe get food to eat on the trail, then start back until they found Dinah and Naomi.

Entering the shop filled with so many new things distracted even Lillian, and he let his brother and the children wander the rows while he spoke to Higgins about his order. The only other customers were two men who stood near the cookstove in the middle, tin cups in hand as they talked.

Higgins met him at the counter, wiping a sleeve across his brow. "Sorry, Jericho. We don't have your order yet. I don't expect it for another month, at least."

Jericho nodded. "That's all right. Thought I'd place another while we're here. Also, you haven't seen two women come through here, have you? They're sisters, both blonde. One is in the family way. They might have been together, or maybe not."

The man's forehead wrinkled.

Jericho added. "It would have been within the last day."

The shop owner shook his head, his expression clearing. "I know I haven't seen any new gals today or yesterday." He raised a brow. "If I see 'em, should I mention you asked after 'em?"

Before Jericho could nod, a voice spoke up behind him.

"That sounds like those two I passed on the trail yesterday."

He spun to face the men at the cookstove. The one with the overgrown beard and dirty clothes spoke again. "One of 'em was in the family way, just like you said."

Jericho's heart leaped. "Where did you pass them?"

The bearded man shrugged. "On the road from Helena. Somewhere around midday, I think. They were headed t'other way."

The other way? Had they turned around to go back to the ranch? Hope inched higher in his chest. Maybe Dinah had already changed her mind. They could work things out.

But...midday yesterday. With that timing, he should have passed them on the trail between the ranch and the Mullan Road.

A new thought settled in, one that flared panic like a spark taking hold of paper. Had they decided to go back to Virginia instead of coming to Missoula Mills? Had he ruined things so completely that Dinah wanted to go as far away from him as she could?

He was already striding toward the door. "Gil, Sean, Lilly. Let's go."

He had to catch Dinah before he lost her completely.

~

*D*inah watched the departing wagon. Friendly old freighter, but he'd not stopped to talk. Was he going to Missoula Mills? Part of her wanted to catch up with him and follow along.

Her sister's gasp made her spin forward again. Naomi held her reins with one hand and cradled her bulging belly with the other.

Dinah's own middle clenched as she took in the pallor of her sister's face. "What's wrong? Are you hurting?" They should rest again. There was no need to rush this journey. As uncomfortable as it was sleeping on the rocky ground beside the trail, when they reached Helena, there might be other hardships.

Naomi's mouth pinched. "I keep getting these pains. I can't tell if it's the baby moving around or the way I'm sitting in the saddle."

Her heart picked up speed. With less than two months left till the birth, Naomi would feel a number of pains, but if these were the real kind that produced contractions...

She turned to scan the side of the road ahead of them. They were plodding up a tree-covered slope, and several rotting trunks lay to the side of the path—likely trees that had been cut down when the road was built.

She guided her gelding off the trail between two parallel trunks. "Let's rest here." At a clear patch of ground, she dismounted and turned to help her sister down.

Naomi gripped the saddle with white knuckles as she leaned forward to dismount. When her boots sank onto the ground, she exhaled with a long, slow breath. "There. That's better."

Dinah moved to unfasten one of the blanket rolls. "I'll spread this out so you can lie down."

After Naomi was settled, she looked up with a weary smile. "Thank you. I'll be ready to ride again soon."

Dinah touched her arm. "This might be a good place to camp

for the night." She would have preferred to move farther off the trail, where their campfire wouldn't be noticed by anyone passing. But stopping Naomi's pains was more important than that. She still had two months before the baby should come, so surely these were only preparation pains. Or maybe the babe was moving around, objecting to so many hours in the saddle, as Naomi had said.

But as Dinah stood, her sister wrapped both hands around her belly and grimaced, then rolled onto her side.

Dinah dropped back to her knees and rubbed her back. "Breathe. Take long, slow breaths in, then count to five as you exhale."

She could feel the difference in Naomi's tension with the first breath out, but her second exhale turned choppy. The weight pressing Dinah's chest made her own breathing harder. "What are you feeling?"

Naomi blew the air out. "Pain. Here. It wraps all the way down." She moved her hand from the center of her navel down to the base of her abdomen.

"Does it keep steady or come and go?"

"It hurts for a bit, then eases. Maybe now it'll stop completely." Naomi gave her a hopeful look, but the weary lines under her eyes belied the expression.

Dinah reached for the water flask. "Take another drink." What her sister described could be false pains, or the real thing. Only time would tell for certain. But if this was real labor, by the time they knew for sure, it could be too far along to help. Even now that might be the case.

As far as she knew, no proven medical procedures could halt labor once it began in earnest, but she knew of a few homespun remedies she'd be more than willing to try.

Lord, take the pain away. Stop her body from pushing the baby out too soon. Safeguard them both, Lord. She wouldn't let herself think about what might happen if God *didn't* protect her sister.

If rest didn't help...if water didn't help...was there anything else she could do to stop labor from progressing? She needed to check her books to see if she'd forgotten anything.

After replacing the cork on the flask, she stroked the hair from her sister's face. "Rest now."

Naomi nodded, and her eyes drifted shut. Finally, peace eased her features.

The tightness didn't lessen in Dinah's chest, though. This was her fault. Why had she made Naomi leave the ranch so close to her time? So Dinah could open her own clinic?

Her heart squeezed. God had said to use her gift, the talent and training He'd blessed her with. But couldn't she have waited until Naomi gave birth to a healthy baby?

Though staying there longer, seeing Jericho every day—living in his home—would have been torture, knowing they were at odds in their core beliefs. She might have grown bitter toward him. Watching him close himself off might have smothered this love that burned so sharply inside her.

Yet keeping Naomi and the baby safe would have been worth any amount of heartache she had to endure.

She straightened. It *still* would. Maybe they weren't too late.

If these pains stopped completely, could she get Naomi back to the ranch without causing more trouble for her? That would be better than trying to reach Helena. And she couldn't let her sister have a baby out here on the side of the mountain. *Lord, please.*

Naomi shifted, drawing Dinah from the prayer. Her sister's eyes were open, staring straight ahead.

"Are you hurting again?" She kept her voice gentle.

"Not as bad." Naomi didn't shift, maybe afraid movement would make the pain worse.

Dinah stroked her back. "When it eases, drink more water." *Lord, let them be stopping. Help us make it back to the ranch.*

Maybe in another couple hours, Naomi would be well

enough to ride. They could take an hour at a time, then rest as long as her sister needed before riding another hour. It might take days to reach Jericho, but as long as Naomi and the baby were safe, she would be thankful.

If only they had a wagon where Naomi could lie and rest while Dinah drove.

Jericho had a wagon.

Did she dare leave her sister and ride back to the ranch to borrow it? Jericho would come with her, she had no doubt. But that would mean leaving Naomi alone for at least a day and a half. Maybe two.

She couldn't. What if the babe tried to come while she was gone? The thought wrenched her stomach.

What about the wagon that had passed them just before they'd stopped to rest?

She pushed to her feet. "Naomi. Do you think you'll be all right by yourself for a quarter hour? I'm going to get a wagon to take us to the ranch."

Naomi's eyes fluttered open, and she looked confused for a moment. Then her gaze rounded. "Back to the ranch?" Was that hope in her voice?

Once more, Dinah dropped to her knees by her sister. "Is that all right with you?" Maybe she should have asked what Naomi wanted to do. But this was truly the only good choice.

Her sister nodded, her eyes glimmering. "Yes."

The pressure in Dinah's chest tightened, clogging her throat. "I'm sorry I made you leave."

Naomi reached for her hand, and Dinah gave her a gentle squeeze. Then Naomi lifted her bright gaze again. "I know you want to make a difference. To heal and nurture and care for the sick and injured. But you don't have to open a clinic and dispense medicine to help people. You help and heal everyone around you just by being the person God made you. That's part of the healing gift he's placed inside you."

Her grip tightened, as though a pain was coming on. But she continued speaking. "There might be times you have an actual clinic where people come for medical help. And other times God places people around you who need your care in other ways." Naomi managed a tight smile.

A burn stung Dinah's eyes, but she blinked it back. "Thank you, Na. We'll get you back where you can deliver a strong healthy baby." She released her hand, then stood. "Drink more water, and I'll return soon."

She untied her gelding and mounted. She still had her packs tied on the saddle, including her rifle in the scabbard. The driver had looked like a decent fellow, but she would be facing him alone.

She pressed back the niggle of worry that twisted in her gut and nudged her mount onto the trail. She would use good judgement, but Naomi needed that wagon.

CHAPTER 28

*D*inah pushed her gelding into a trot down the slope but didn't dare canter until the ground leveled off some. As soon as it felt safe, she pushed him faster, leaning lower as she scanned the road ahead. Maybe around that curve she'd see the wagon. Somewhere ahead, the road crossed a creek, then traveled along a valley before climbing up another rocky, tree-covered slope.

Her pulse quickened as she caught sight of the wagon ahead. The vehicle crawled slower than before, as if the mules were tired or the weight of the cargo was too much. But the back had only been half-full, the cargo covered by oilskins.

She urged her mount faster to catch up.

As she approached, the driver glanced back at her, and his eyes widened in surprise. He drew up the reins and called to the team, "Ho, there."

She reined in her gelding beside them.

His long white beard fluttered in the wind as he turned to her. "Ma'am. Something wrong?"

She nodded as she worked to catch her breath from the hurried ride. "My sister. She needs help. She's with child and having trouble. I need a wagon to get her back to the Coulter ranch."

The man frowned. "I'm late delivering these supplies."

Dinah's chest tightened. "Please. It's a matter of life and death. I'll pay whatever you ask." Though she didn't have much left. Jericho would help, though, if it came to that. "Or...I'm a doctor, if there's anything you need help with?"

The man's gaze scanned the length of her, his brows rising. "A doctor, you say?"

Something in his tone pricked unease in her chest. Maybe he disliked the idea of a female doctor.

"Yes, sir. But my sister needs help right now. After we get her to safety, I'll be happy to assist in any way I can." Jericho wouldn't like her bringing a stranger to his property, but surely he would allow it for this reason.

He eyed her another moment, his gaze narrowing as if trying to decide something. Then he nodded. "All right then. You can sit up front with me." He gestured toward the seat next to him.

She turned her gelding. "I can ride."

"You might need to do some doctorin' on your horse if you do."

She frowned. "What do you mean?" Surely he didn't intend to hurt her gelding if she didn't sit with him.

The driver motioned toward her mount's back legs, and she leaned over to look down at them. A deep gash marred the long cannon bone, the skin peeled away and blood running down to cover the hoof.

"Oh, boy." She swung to the ground and bent to examine the wound. The gelding must have cut himself on a rock as she'd made him hurry down the mountain. It's a wonder she hadn't felt him limping. The gash needed to be cleaned and bandaged to keep out dirt, but that would have to wait until she had Naomi settled. Until then, it wouldn't be fair to the horse to add her extra weight when she had another seat available.

She stood and turned to the driver. He seemed kind enough, and her concern from a moment ago had clearly been her nerves overreacting.

He motioned toward the rear. "Just tie him to the ring at the back."

She strode to where a piece of round metal had been fastened to the wood, and tied the gelding quickly. They had to get back to Naomi.

Once she climbed onto the seat, he signaled the mules forward. The grass on the left side of the road allowed him to turn the wagon in an arc, as the wagon creaked and groaned back onto the road, her mind raced with worry. What if Naomi's contractions were getting worse? What if the baby was coming too soon? Why couldn't these mules walk any faster?

The driver shook the reins, but it didn't hurry the animals. "So what brings a pretty gal like you this far west?"

Her middle tightened. He was just a lonely old man making small talk. "My sister and I came so I could start a clinic here." That wasn't the full answer, but it was all she was willing to tell at this point.

The driver nodded. "Reckon back east they weren't wild about a woman doctorin' on men. Round here, we don't get to be picky."

She gripped the wagon bench. Would it be too rude to ask him to keep his comments on her profession to himself?

If Naomi didn't need his wagon so desperately, she would say something. But maybe if she held her tongue, he would stop talking.

As they started up the rocky slope, the driver suddenly jerked the left rein, turning the mules off the road.

Dinah's heart leapt to her throat. "What're you doing?" Why hadn't she thought to bring her rifle with her when she dismounted her horse?

The team entered a narrow opening in the brush—a gap

she'd not even seen. Panic surged through her. "Stop!" She reached for the reins to halt the mules.

The driver threw out his arm, slamming her back against the wagon bench. "You keep yer hands to yerself, doc." His voice came out rough.

She struggled to free herself, but his arm was like an iron bar across her chest. How could an old man possess such strength? "Let me go."

He shook the reins, though this time she was thankful the mules didn't plod any faster. *Lord, help me.*

She could leap off the wagon and make a run for it. She might even be able to untie her gelding before he could climb down and catch her.

As though he read her mind, his hand gripped her, keeping his arm locked over her chest. He slipped the reins in the keeper slot, then pulled out a handgun and aimed it at her.

As she stared down the small barrel, she struggled to make her mind work past the strangeness of it. That tiny little black hole could produce a bullet at a speed quick enough to end her life.

And what would happen to Naomi?

The thought jerked her from the stupor like a pail of ice water, washing away the fog.

"What do you want?"

He sent a glance ahead of them, just quick enough to make sure the mules weren't wandering into a tree. Then he narrowed his gaze at her. "A doctor."

A tiny bit of her panic eased. He had someone sick or injured. She just had to convince him to go to her sister before she tended his friend.

She swallowed but took care not to move any other part of her body. "I'll gladly provide medical care if you have someone in need. I already said that. I can't be away from my sister long though. Can you tell me what the problem is?"

He sent another longer look forward, then turned back to her. "You'll see."

Her insides twisted. Why couldn't he just tell her what was wrong with his patient? Why did they have to sneak off the road and into the woods?

She cast a glance around, taking in the dense trees and rocky terrain. If she had to make a run for it, she could follow the wagon tracks back to the road.

But the wagon lurched to a stop. In front of them stood only trees and brush.

The driver kept the gun pointed at her as he moved his grip to her arm closest to him. "You just get down with me."

He half-dragged her off the bench as he climbed down, and she scrambled to keep her feet beneath her. The iron in his grip helped keep her upright.

The driver shoved her through the dense foliage, the branches scratching her face and arms. This wasn't a trail as far as she could tell.

Suddenly, the trees opened up and they stepped into a small clearing. In the center stood a wood slab building, its walls weathered and leaning a little. The driver led her to the front door and stopped. "Thomas!"

A man's voice called from inside the building. "What d'ya want?"

The driver shoved Dinah forward and pulled open the door. "Got yer doctor."

He pushed her into the building, finally releasing her arm. She stumbled to a stop in a room barely lit by a single lantern. As her eyes adjusted to the dimness, she surveyed the area.

A form lay on a bed in the corner, barely raising the thin blanket. But then the person pushed up on an elbow, revealing wild bushy hair poking out in all directions.

She forced herself to take a step forward, then stopped. "What's wrong?" Though the figure looked emaciated, he might still have the strength to hurt her. The driver had certainly surprised her with the power in his grip.

The driver leaned against the door frame, the gun still in his hand. "He took a bad fall. Broke his leg, I think."

She stayed where she was as she spoke to Thomas. "May I see your leg?"

He glared at her but then slowly lowered himself back onto the bedtick, flipping up the ragged blanket to reveal a swollen limb with a badly infected wound on the side of the calf. A putrid odor filled the air, even stronger than the musty scent of the building.

She stepped forward again. The driver hadn't been lying about the need for medical care. And as bad as that wound looked, the injured one probably had a high fever that weakened him.

She didn't touch the leg, just bent over to peer at the wound. Though the light was too dim to see well, she could make out a protruding bone amidst the puss and swollen, infected flesh. The gash had festered so badly that he might already be suffering from blood poisoning.

Sweat beaded the man's face, matting the edges of his wild hair. His cheeks held bright red circles. She didn't have to touch him to know how high his fever would be. His raspy breathing filled the air between them.

His wary eyes watched her. Though they sank into the shadows of their sockets, she could just see their cloudy pale blue color. Those eyes might have been riveting when he was a younger man, in his prime. She could almost imagine him standing tall in a suit, entertaining at a party or escorting a lady into church.

Regardless the kind of man he'd been, he was still created by God, intricately formed and cherished. Made for a purpose.

Emotion lodged in her throat. Had he fulfilled that purpose? Or did a host of wrong choices send him into a downward spiral that led to this moment. *Show me what I'm to do here, Lord. How do You want me to help him?*

But what about Naomi?

A flash of emotion surged through her. Frustration and worry and fear.

Her sister needed her. The one who'd shared the womb with her. Who'd shared birthdays and every important moment in their lives, whether thrilling or heart-wrenching.

Now, instead of being with Naomi in this terrifying moment, she was forced to help this stranger. A man whose past she didn't know, though it might well be filled with awful deeds.

Love My child.

The thought slipped into her mind, bringing instant remorse. This man was as beloved by the Father as Naomi was. God had brought Dinah to help this son in his time of need. She would have to trust that the Lord would take care of her sister in the same way He was providing for Thomas.

Please, Lord. Help my sister.

With that prayer easing her spirit, she summoned her courage and turned so she could share the hard news with both Thomas and the driver together.

She focused on the man in the bed, gentling her voice and bending to be closer to his level. "The wound has festered so much, the infection might have entered your bloodstream. I can't be certain of that, but the only chance we have of saving your life is to amputate the leg."

What life his eyes had held seemed to leak out of them, and he sank farther into the mattress.

Guilt pressed her chest. She should have been more careful about how she delivered the news.

She moved to his head and crouched, resting her hand on his blanket-covered arm. "I'm sorry. I'm so sorry for the pain you're in. I hope you don't mind me speaking candidly with you. It's possible the infection has already spread too far for us to save your life, even after we remove your leg."

His brows tented as he studied her face, as if memorizing every word she spoke.

He didn't speak, so she pressed on. "I can give you something to sleep through the surgery, but the leg will hurt just as much when you awaken. I have another medicine that will help ease the pain for a while, but I don't have much of it. When it's gone, you'll still have more healing to go. And that's if we can rid your body of the infection. If it's already moved into your blood, removing the leg may not be enough to stop the blood poisoning from consuming your body." She swallowed.

The look in his eyes said she didn't need to finish that statement. He stared at her, but his mind seemed far away. Was he pondering his decision? Or had his thinking already begun to slip away from the fever?

If she had to make a recommendation, which way should she suggest? In general, she always made every possible effort to save a life.

But the only thing she could do in this case was cut off his leg. The pain after that surgery was immense, though perhaps not greater than what he was already enduring.

Steps sounded behind her, and she glanced over as the driver approached to stand beside the bed. He towered over her, but she kept her crouched position. If he wanted to hurt her, he could wield his strength and the pistol he still held.

But she was in God's hands. And she was here to help.

CHAPTER 29

The cry snagged Jericho's attention, and he drew back on Pinto's reins as he scanned the brush on either side of the road.

There. A horse stood tied just inside the trees.

The others slowed with him, and Lillian spoke just as he reined that direction. "Look."

As his horse picked its way over fallen logs, his gaze roamed the saddled animal. That was Naomi's mare. His heart surged. Where was Dinah's gelding?

He scanned the ground around the animal.

"It's Naomi." Again, Lillian was the one to speak, and she kicked her horse past his.

Only then did he catch sight of the woman lying on the blanket in the shadow of the tree. She faced away from him. His pulse hammered as he urged Pinto through the mess of branches and logs that cluttered the ground, Sean and Gil plunging through behind him. Was she dead?

Once more, he scanned the area. Where was Dinah? Only a single saddle pack lay next to Naomi.

Lillian jumped from her horse and raced to Naomi's side as Jericho reined in and did the same.

"Naomi, what's wrong?" His niece dropped to her knees by the woman's head.

The steady heaving of her shoulders made his chest tighten with panic and relief at the same time. She was alive, but something awful had happened.

Was she having the baby? This was too early.

Where is Dinah?

Had something happened to her, and Naomi was lying here distraught? A new wave of terror slammed through him.

He crouched beside Naomi. "What's wrong?"

She looked miserable in the late afternoon light, and her shoulders rose and fell with every heavy breath as her eyes lifted to him. "Pains. Dinah. Went. For wagon."

His gaze dropped to her belly as his mind whirled. She was giving birth.

No.

He looked up at Gil, who'd dismounted and looked as panicked as Jericho felt. Sean still sat on his horse with wide eyes. Clearly, neither knew what to do.

Jericho had no idea.

Dinah.

She would know. She could stop the baby coming if anyone could.

He leaned down to Naomi again. "Where did Dinah go?" She wouldn't leave her sister for long.

Naomi took in a slower breath, then blew it out with a long exhale, her shoulder sagging with the effort. Had the pains stopped?

She turned her gaze to him more fully. "A freighter passed us on the road just before we turned off here. Dinah went back to ask him if he would take me in his wagon."

Jericho frowned. Dinah was going to trust a stranger with

their lives? He started to rise, but crouched again. "He was headed toward Helena?" He still didn't know why Dinah and Naomi had turned toward Helena themselves, but he would have to ask that question later.

Thank God they'd heard Naomi's cry.

" Missoula. She should be back by now." Naomi still sounded out of breath, and her eyes drifted closed. She looked exhausted.

He touched her shoulder. "Rest while I go find her. Hopefully your pains are over now."

Her eyes flew open, wider this time. "Over? They're coming every few minutes."

He squinted. "You mean they come and go?" Was that normal? He had no notion of how childbirth progressed, but he'd assumed it was steady agony until the babe finally...came out. Even the thought of what happened made his ears heat.

Her eyes closed again. "Yes, that's normal. Please find my sister and bring her to me."

She clearly thought him useless as a midwife.

He surged to his feet. Seems they agreed on that fact.

That and the urgent need to find Dinah.

He moved around Naomi to speak quietly with his brother, and Lillian crowded in with them. She would likely play a part here greater than what should be expected of girls her age.

But thank God she was here. She probably wouldn't fumble as much in caring for Naomi as he and Gil would.

He spoke quietly so he didn't disturb Naomi with the details. "I'm going after Dinah. Naomi said she should be back by now, so I hope she's close. We didn't pass a wagon, but they may have pulled off the road for some reason." Though contemplating why they might have left the main thoroughfare made his belly curl.

He met his brother's gaze. "Stay here and do everything you can to make her comfortable."

Gil stiffened. "Wouldn't you rather I go with you?"

Jericho gave him a look. "I think one of us should stay here and catch the babe."

Gil's eyes flared wide like a frightened colt.

Jericho clapped his shoulder and turned for Pinto. "I'll be back soon with Dinah."

~

"*I* want you to do it."

Dinah spun back at Thomas's words. He couldn't really mean he wanted her to cut his leg off. Most people fought that option vehemently.

He still lay against the mattress, but he didn't look as limp as he had. His eyes possessed more life than a moment before.

His hand slipped out of the blanket and reached for her but stopped at the edge of the mattress. "I'm not ready to die. I want you to try to save me."

Her chest squeezed, and she took Thomas's hand, doing her best to ignore the grime and sweat covering his rough palm. "Are you certain? Recovering from surgery is so painful. And your body will still be fighting the infection. You'll still have the fever for a while. You could still die."

He gripped her hand harder, using it to pull himself up to rest on his elbow so they were the same level. His earnest gaze searched hers. "I don't want it said that Thomas Booker gave up at the end. I want folks to tell the story about how I fought for my life 'til the last breath. And if this ain't my last breath, all the better. I've got more livin' to do."

She still needed to give all the details of what he could expect after the surgery, but this determination to live made her twice as determined to help him succeed.

God had placed her here—in this musty ramshackle cabin—for such a time as this.

Just keep my sister safe, Lord. Please.

⁓

"She still hasn't returned?" Jericho fought the panic rising in his chest. He'd gone twice as far down the road toward Missoula as he would have expected Dinah to travel to catch the wagon Naomi spoke of. He'd thought surely he missed her along the way.

She should be back here with her sister.

Gil shook his head, worry furrowing his brow. "We haven't seen her. You want me to come help look?"

Jericho glanced around the little camp they'd made. Sean watched them from the low fire as he fed small branches into the flame. Lillian knelt beside Naomi. His niece looked every bit as worried as Gil, but Naomi's eyes were closed. She must be resting between pains.

Then her eyes flew open, and she rolled onto her side toward Lillian. "Ohhh." The anguished moan as she curled her knees up raised another spurt of panic within him.

He turned Pinto and spoke to Gil. "Stay and help her. I'll search the road toward Helena." Maybe she'd not had success with the wagon they saw before and had turned back the other way in hopes of finding another rig.

If so, he would meet her soon. She wouldn't leave Naomi in this condition long.

He kicked the gelding into a canter and searched the road and into the trees on both sides. The trail climbed a slope, and soon the trees fell away as the ground turned steeper and rockier. He had to pull his mount back to a trot, the animal's breath coming in heaves. When he tried to rein down to a walk, Pinto pressed forward. *I know, boy. I want to find her too.*

He *had* to find her.

As much as Jericho worked to press away the images of what might have happened to Dinah, the awful possibilities crowded in. A beautiful woman, alone on a remote road in the mountain wilderness... He would almost rather her be faced with a wild animal. Yet what that bear had done to Chalmers's arm...and he'd seen even worse from a grizzly attack.

Pinto stumbled, tearing Jericho's focus back to the present as he pulled hard on the reins to keep the animal's head up. The gelding regained his feet, then slowed to a walk as they neared the top of the slope.

Jericho scanned the area around them, searching every nook in the rock, every shrubby tree for sign of movement behind it. He even turned to study the terrain behind them. The trees were so thick that he couldn't see much except the road.

But in what he *could* see, there was no sign of movement. No beautiful blonde hurrying back to a sister in the midst of childbirth.

Panic flared through him. *God, not for me, but for Dinah. And Naomi and that tiny life she's struggling to birth. It's too early. Help. Please.*

At the peak, he reined in Pinto. The opposite side of the mountain didn't contain nearly as many trees, and he could see the road winding down into the valley beyond. It would take an hour to travel that distance, even if they rode at a fast clip.

And there was no sign of anyone, as far as he could see.

He turned Pinto to stare at the route they'd just traveled. *What now, God? Where is she?*

Something had happened to Dinah. Something awful, but he was powerless to know where she was or how to get to her.

He plunged his heels into Pinto's sides, maybe harder than he should have, for the horse charged down the slope, back toward Missoula Mills. Jericho sat back, steadying the gelding.

He needed to search both sides of the road carefully. Should he call for her? He hadn't done that yet. If a man had taken her, alerting the scoundrel that Jericho was searching for them might put Dinah in even more danger. Or at least make it harder to find her.

But he had to try something different, so he raised his voice. "Dinah!"

The word echoed across the open area around him. Only the sound of his horse's hooves filled the air, pounding against the hard-packed dirt and rock.

He called again, louder this time. "Dinah!"

Still no answer.

He scanned the trees and brush for any sign of her. Through the areas where thicker growth lined the path, he reined Pinto slower.

As he passed the place where Gil and the children stayed with Naomi, he called out to ask if Dinah had returned there yet.

"No." Gil's voice sounded through the branches. "We haven't seen her."

A cry of pain echoed after his words, gripping Jericho's chest. "Do you need me to come help?" Though what could he do? He had no way to bring relief to the woman or the babe determined to come into this world.

"Find Dinah." Gil's tone sounded resigned but held an edge of panic.

Jericho pushed Pinto forward again as he scanned from one side of the road to another. He couldn't miss hoofprints where she'd turned off the trail.

The slope eased the farther he went, and he'd nearly reached level ground when a patch of bare ground grabbed his notice.

There.

How had he missed the gap in the trees ? Wagon tracks and hoofprints pressed into the ground, but without dismounting, Jericho couldn't tell how many animals had come through.

He couldn't waste a second though. Someone had forced

Dinah to come this way—every instinct within him confirmed that as fact. What had they already done to her?

Bile rose up to his throat, but he swallowed it down as he guided Pinto over the trail. He had to focus on following the tracks.

CHAPTER 30

*A*s Jericho turned into the opening, the path leveled out. The grass had grown high, but no trees obstructed the trail. Maybe this had once been a narrow wagon road. He scanned both sides, watching for motion among the trees or a sign that a person had split off from the path.

He didn't spot the wagon and mule team ahead until the entire rig was fully visible. A familiar horse stood tied to the rear.

Dinah's gelding.

He jerked hard on his reins and raised the rifle to his shoulder. His gut twisted as he scanned the wagon and the trees beyond. No sign of movement except the animals.

He nudged Pinto forward but kept the gelding slow. Every one of his senses strained for a hint of threat.

Nothing moved, save the stamp of the gelding's hoof. The mules raised their heads to watch his approach, and when one of them released a high-pitched bray, he swung the rifle and nearly fired at the poor beast.

Steady, Coulter. Keep your head.

When he reached the gelding, he scanned the horse and

saddle for a sign Dinah had struggled. None that he could see except a gash on one of the gelding's rear legs. Blood had run down to cover the hoof, then dried into a crust. That probably meant the animal had been waiting here several hours at least.

It also meant Dinah had been forced to leave her horse against her will. She never would have abandoned him when he was injured.

He peered over the wagon's side. The bed was half empty with an oilcloth over the contents. Did it hide a body? His gut clenched at the possibility, and once more, bile rose up to burn his chest.

God, you can't take her away. I know I was wrong—about so many things. Keep her alive. Show me where she is. Help me rescue her from whatever her attackers have done. Help me make things right. With her. And with You.

The prayer infused a bit of strength in him, and he leaned over the wagon to lift the oilcloth enough to peer under. Only crates and a couple barrels.

He guided Pinto around to check the other side. If someone lay in wait for him, the scoundrel would have most likely attacked by now.

No one there either.

He shifted his focus to the forest. This seemed to be the end of the road, which meant Dinah's captors had taken her through the woods on foot. Or maybe they rode other horses and had transferred her onto those animals.

Within less than a minute, he spotted footprints. Dinah's delicate boot heel left a distinct impression in a section of soft ground. There was at least one other man's tracks, maybe two. No horses, as far as he could tell. Unless they'd entered the trees in a different spot.

He guided Pinto through the woods, following alongside the path Dinah and her captors had taken. After only a few minutes, the trees ahead thinned, like maybe the woods opened up to a clearing.

He slowed Pinto. Maybe he should dismount and move forward to see what lay beyond the trees. It might only be a gap before the forest continued, but surely he was closing in on the blackguard who'd taken Dinah.

And surprise might be his best weapon.

He dismounted and tied the gelding to a branch, then crept on with his rifle at the ready. The closer he came to the opening in the trees, the better he saw the structure.

A cabin.

But when he peered from behind a trunk at the edge of the clearing, his unhindered view showed it was really just a tiny shack, the boards ill-fitting and some nearly rotten.

A surge of anger swept through him. Dinah must be in there. And what were they doing to her?

He scanned the distance to the building. They wouldn't expect him. Dinah herself wouldn't even expect him.

A check of his rifle showed it was ready to fire the instant he pulled the trigger. He sprinted forward, staying low. Trying to keep his steps from pounding the ground as he neared the cabin.

When he reached the building, he halted, doing his best to breathe quietly so he didn't alert anyone inside.

A sound drifted through the wall. Something like a grunt. Then a scraping.

A man's voice spoke. "Are you sure—?" His words cut off. Then a gasp.

Jericho ducked to see in through one of the larger cracks between boards. It took a moment for his eyes to make out the two forms standing in the middle of the cabin. The outline of one showed she wore a dress.

Dinah.

It had to be her, though he couldn't see more than a vague

form with so little light inside. The other figure stood beside her, and they seemed to be bending over something.

He had to see better. And he had to get in to save her.

He stepped toward the door. It wasn't latched, just pulled to. Maybe the latch didn't work, as dilapidated as this shack was.

Or maybe this was a trap.

He pulled the door open a crack to peer in. From this angle, he couldn't see much more other than the fact that Dinah's arm moved back and forth. What was she doing, bent over like that?

Keeping the door cracked open with his foot, he prepared his rifle. He'd go in quietly until he knew what was happening, but he'd be prepared to shoot if necessary.

As he slipped inside, the man standing beside Dinah cried out.

Jericho's pulse slammed in his neck, and he aimed at the stranger. "Get away from her or I'll shoot."

~

*D*inah had to get this artery closed. She pressed hard on the binding she'd secured, but blood still leaked through. At least it wasn't the full flow.

This was how Pop had stopped the bleeding the time she'd helped him with the amputation. Wasn't it? Had she missed a step?

A voice buzzed behind her, and it wasn't until the man at her side turned and spoke to the newcomer that she registered what was happening.

Was that Jericho?

Keeping steady pressure on the bandage, she glanced over her shoulder. Her heart raced at the sight of him holding a rifle. He must think she needed saving. At one time she did, but now she was willingly performing this surgery. How had he found her?

He wasn't looking at her though. His steely glare focused on Mr. Ishmael, the driver who'd brought her here. "Get away from her or I'll shoot."

Mr. Ishmael sidled away. She had to turn back and focus on slowing this artery enough that she could stitch it closed. But she could talk as she adjusted the pressure. "Jericho, he's not dangerous."

"Are you hurt?"

There. The flow had slowed enough that she could stitch the artery closed. She reached for the suture she'd already prepared. "I'm not hurt. He brought me here to doctor this man's broken leg. The only way to help him was to remove the limb. I have to move quickly so he doesn't lose too much blood."

She nodded toward Ishmael, whom she'd made scrub his hands and arms clean before they began the surgery. "Hold this steady for me."

He'd been an unwilling participant from the start, but she couldn't manage this operation without an extra set of hands. He didn't approach to do her bidding, so she glanced up at him. His leathered face had turned impossibly pale, and he stared at the wash of blood before her.

She used a stern voice to pull him from the stupor. "I need you to hold this. Now. He'll bleed out if I don't hurry."

"I'll do it." Jericho's quiet tone came from behind as his footsteps approached.

He placed himself between her and Ishmael, keeping his rifle in one hand.

"You'll have to put down the gun. He won't hurt us. He just wanted help for his friend here." She shifted to allow Jericho room to take the bandaged artery from her. "Hold it just like this. Firm and steady pressure while I stitch."

He leaned the gun against his leg and did as she directed. Thank the Lord Jericho wasn't squeamish around blood.

With a capable assistant, she was able to focus fully on

closing up the new end of the limb. By the time she finished the job, washed her hands, and applied a clean bandage to the site, the strain had tensed every part of her. Especially her neck and shoulders.

Her back ached when she attempted to straighten.

Jericho was packing the last of her supplies in her case as he glanced at her. "I'm sure you're exhausted, but we need to get back to your sister. I think she's having the baby."

Panic jolted through her. "She is?" In her focus on Thomas's leg, she'd lost sight of everything else. "What's happened?" She nearly grabbed Jericho's arm to shake the answer from him.

He closed her bag. "Gil and the children are with her. The pains are coming off and on. She said she thinks it's time."

Dinah spun to Ishmael. "I have to help my sister. Can we take your wagon?"

The man frowned, then nodded toward Thomas. "What about 'im?"

She blinked, trying to think of what instructions he'd need. "I just removed the chloroform, so he'll wake soon. Give him the dose I've poured of this medicine as soon as he's alert enough to swallow it. " She glanced at Jericho. Was it safe to come back here? She couldn't abandon a patient after such a life-threatening surgery.

A thought slipped in. Naomi and the babe—if either survived the birthing—wouldn't be able to travel all the way to the ranch yet. They could come here for shelter while they recovered.

She threw a glance around the ramshackle building. It would be better than nothing. And she'd have all her patients in one place.

She turned back to Mr. Ishmael. "As soon as my sister is through the birthing, I'll bring her and the babe here so I can care for them all. Keep Thomas comfortable until I return. If I'm away long, I'll send more medicine for his pain."

She didn't wait for agreement, just spun for the door and took Jericho's waiting hand. He already held her bag and his rifle and was propping the door with his foot.

As soon as she cleared the stoop, she charged into a run. He matched her, stride for stride, tugging her faster at times. They paused in the woods long enough to retrieve his horse. In the clearing, he tied the animal to the back of the wagon beside her gelding. She climbed onto the seat and freed the team's reins, then released the brake as Jericho joined her there.

He took the reins and urged the mules forward to turn the rig around. The animals moved impossibly slowly. She tried to use the time to question Jericho about how close Naomi's contractions were coming, but he seemed to know almost nothing.

Despite his urging, the mules kept a steady walk. Dinah gripped the seat to keep from yelling at them to hurry. Naomi might be hemorrhaging at this very moment.

She straightened. "I'm going to ride. Bring the wagon behind me."

He frowned at her and reined in, but she didn't have time to wait. As she jumped from the bench, his voice called behind her. "Take Pinto. Your gelding looks injured."

She'd forgotten. "Thank you." She yelled the words as she jogged back to the animals. Her gelding would get the care he needed as soon as she made sure her sister and the babe came through the birth alive and well.

Please, Lord. Keep my sister safe. The baby too. Childbirth could be deadly even under healthy conditions. But giving birth so early. And on the side of a mountain...

Jericho's bay and white gelding barely flicked an ear as she fumbled to untie the reins and leaped onto his back. But when she turned his head and dug in her heels, the horse plunged forward.

No wonder Jericho loved this horse. Pinto handled easily,

turning with the slightest bit of pressure. His powerful stride covered far more ground than her own horse's. She had no doubt if she asked him for more speed, he would deliver abundantly.

When they reached the Mullan Road, she turned the horse up the slope and urged him faster. *Protect us from a fall, Lord.* The last thing she wanted was to injure Jericho's mount the way her own gelding was hurt, but every second might make the difference for Naomi's life.

How much farther?

She strained to find the section of fallen trees where they'd turned off the road. Would she recognize it? Especially at this speed?

She shouldn't have worried. Or perhaps she should have worried more.

Naomi's anguished cry alerted her to her sister's location long before she reached the turn-off.

Panic flared through her. *God, help Naomi.* At least Naomi still lived.

She pulled hard on Pinto's reins when they reached the edge of the road where other horses stood. After leaping to the ground, she reached for her medical case. But she'd left it in the wagon. No matter. Jericho would bring it.

She spun and jumped over the logs that blocked the way to her sister. When Naomi and the others came into sight, she slowed so she didn't disturb a contraction.

Naomi lay curled on her side, in almost the same position Dinah had left her. But the guttural cries tearing from her throat showed exactly which part of childbirth she'd reached.

The final stretch.

She must be pushing. Or perhaps fighting not to push.

Gilead and Lillian knelt in front of Naomi, and even little Sean sat behind her. The boy jumped up at Dinah's approach, and all three looked like she'd just arrived to pull them from a nest of rattlesnakes.

If only she had such a magic ability to fix this situation.

Gil and Lilly scrambled back as she drew near, and she dropped to her knees by Naomi's side. "I'm here. Tell me what's happened. Are you feeling the need to push?"

Naomi gulped in air frantically. Breathing far too quickly as she fought through the pain.

"Take deep, long breaths. We have to slow your inhales." As she spoke, Dinah moved her hands over Naomi's belly to check the position of the babe. "Breathe in slow... Now out slow..." She used her voice to show the speed she meant.

The babe was definitely in the birth canal, maybe even already showing.

The moment Dinah stopped talking, Naomi's breaths came hard again. She helped her count through each breath as she shifted Naomi's skirts to see if the babe had already entered the world. Gil had backed away with both children, giving them privacy.

Dinah glanced up at them. "Jericho's coming with the wagon. You might want to meet him. Lilly, can you stay in case I need help?" The girl didn't look as frightened as the fellows. Her determined nod proved her courage.

While Gilead and Sean made a wide half-circle around them, Dinah focused on her sister again. This contraction had finally subsided, and Naomi lay limp, though still breathing heavily.

Dinah kept her voice soft and encouraging. "That's right. Keep steady deep breaths while you rest. Let me know when you start to feel the next pain."

She focused on what she was seeing amidst the mass of blood and fluid, and the tangle of dark hair made her heart surge. The babe's head had nearly emerged.

CHAPTER 31

*P*anic flared through Dinah once more, mixing with the wonder of seeing her niece or nephew for the first time. "The babe is coming, Naomi. You should see how dark her hair is." She should try to temper the excitement in her voice, but she couldn't. Not with so many emotions churning inside her.

"It's a girl? Is she alive?" Naomi sounded weak, yet hopeful.

Tears rushed through Dinah's defenses, but so did a laugh. "I don't know. I can't tell yet. There's only a mop of dark hair."

"Oh." Naomi's cry came as her face twisted with another pain.

Dinah focused on talking her sister through each step, guiding the tiny babe out into the cold, uncomfortable world. The child still hadn't breathed by the time Naomi pushed the last of her out, but Dinah tried to remind herself that wasn't unusual.

She was so small, barely larger than Dinah's hand as she scooped up the delicate fully-formed baby girl and turned her face down in her palm. "Come on, sweet one. Let's wake you up."

She couldn't tell if the pulse thrumming through her hand was her own or the child's, but she gave a few hard thumps to the child's back to urge a cough and clear the lungs. *Lord, please.*

She turned the babe a little to see her face. The tiny mouth was open, the lips feathering in an O as they searched for air.

Hope rose within Dinah. "That's the way." She repeated the steps, massaging the child's tiny back afterward to stimulate her lungs. "Let's clear the passage so you can breathe."

She still couldn't feel the lungs expand, but as she started to turn the babe again, a tiny cough pressed through her little body. "Oh." Dinah's own breath whooshed out with the strength of her relief.

"Is she alive?" The fearful hope in Naomi's voice pressed in Dinah's chest.

"She's breathing now." She didn't want to give too much encouragement yet. There were still so many obstacles for this precious new life to overcome before her survival would feel secure.

She wrapped the babe in the blanket Lillian handed over. The child's lungs did seem to be working well. Dinah needed to do a full inspection, but maybe a minute for mother and child to meet would do them both good.

The wonder on Naomi's face as she took her daughter and tucked her close made all the fear, all the effort, all the hardship insignificant.

Soft footsteps sounded behind her, and she glanced back. Jericho stood behind her. Naomi looked like she wasn't ready to hand over her daughter yet, and the babe was making sweet cooing noises—a good sign.

For her own part, Dinah wanted so much to sink into Jericho's strength for just a moment. From the instant he'd found her in the shack amputating Thomas's leg, his steady presence and unwavering help had been a relief.

More than that. A gift from above, as though God had brought him to her at the very second she needed him.

Certainty filled her spirit. She'd felt from the beginning, when she first laid eyes on that duplicitous advertisement, that the Lord was guiding them. So many times along this winding path, she'd questioned whether she'd heard wrong. Or if she'd missed a direction the Father tried to give them.

But God was faithful. Even when she didn't listen well, He could still use her mistakes to accomplish His will. And when she yielded to Him fully, He could bring her to this Promised Land more wonderful than she'd ever imagined.

She wiped her hands on the cloth she'd been using as a towel, then pushed to her feet. She had so much dried blood on her skin and clothing, she might need a full day to get clean.

But when she turned to face Jericho, he wasn't looking at the stains beneath her fingernails. His eyes searched her face, meeting her gaze with a longing that made her own spirit respond.

"I'm sorry I let you leave." His voice rasped with intensity. "I'm sorry I was bull-headed and blind and..." He paused as his throat worked. "...and afraid. None of this would have happened if I had listened to you." He motioned toward Gilead. "And my brothers." Once more, the nob at his throat bobbed. "And to God. He's been trying to get my attention a while, but I was stubborn."

Again, the tears flowed freely down her face. Could this really be happening? Had Jericho chosen to yield to the Father, to trust instead of letting fear control him?

He looked hesitant. "I'm sorry my actions brought all this pain." He nodded toward Naomi, then met her gaze again. "Can you forgive me?"

She swallowed and used a sleeve to wipe her eyes.

His brows tented in concern, a worry she could ease with a single action.

She took that step, moving forward into his arms.

His hands wrapped around her, drawing her close, clinging to her with the strength she'd been craving for days. New tears welled inside her. A rightness settled within, cloaking her flurry of emotions with peace that could only come from the Heavenly Father Himself.

Thank You, Lord. Maybe God had needed to take her and Naomi away from the ranch so He could work in Jericho's heart. Or maybe He had another reason for bringing them here.

An image slipped in of Thomas the way she'd left him, just beginning to wake from the chloroform. Perhaps God brought her to help him. Likely, Thomas and Ishmael both wanted her to return posthaste.

She pulled back from Jericho and soaked in his handsome face. "Of course I forgive you. And I'm so thankful God brought me to you. And you to me."

He kept his hands at her waist, and she hated to leave the warm security of their hold. He read her mind though, for he gave a little squeeze. "You have patients to care for, I know. We can talk more later. Show me what to do to help."

The joy that surged through her as she took his hand and turned to her sister didn't leave during the next hour. Not as she performed a full check on little Mary Ellen's body. The child was so tiny, it seemed a wonder she could be fully formed. But her heart sounded strong, if a little fast. Her belly made enough sounds that it might be developed enough to process food.

The child seemed hungry as her coos turned to cries and she rooted in Dinah's hand. "All right, sweet one. Let's give you to your mama." Mary Ellen's mouth might be too small to nurse properly.

But when her cries grew louder, her mouth proved capable of expanding as much as needed, and finally sounds of relief murmured from the hungry babe.

Dinah sank back onto her heels and studied her sister and

niece. Naomi met her gaze, exhaustion clear in every feature. Soon, they could move her to the wagon, and then they would all retreat to the shack where Thomas waited.

Lord willing, they could all rest. Recover. Then finally return to the ranch.

Her gaze lifted to Jericho where he stood with the animals, far enough away to give Naomi privacy. As though he could feel her attention, he turned to her, meeting her look across the distance.

His gaze felt like home. Like he understood all she'd been thinking. Like he would be there at her side. Helping. Protecting. Loving.

I love you too.

She would have the chance to tell him that soon. And hopefully every day after, for the rest of the lifetime God gave them together.

~

"You did everything you could." Jericho willed Dinah to believe him as he cupped her face between his hands.

They'd just buried Thomas despite Dinah's valiant fight to save him. The man seemed at peace near the end, but with the way she cared so deeply, she would feel the loss of this patient strongly.

She met Jericho's gaze, sorrow turning her eyes glassy. "I know. Before we took off the leg, I told him the infection might have already reached his bloodstream. That the amputation might not save him. That a surgery that intense might be too much for his ill body." But her eyes told him the fact that she'd warned him of the possible consequences didn't matter. She would mourn this man's death as deeply as if he'd been a long-time friend.

Jericho ran his hands down her arms and pulled her to him. He couldn't make her care less about those she devoted herself to. And in truth, he didn't want to. This was a part of what made Dinah so special. He could only walk this path with her. Be at her side for anything she needed—whether that be as a surgical assistant or as someone to hold her while she grieved.

Her shoulders didn't shake with tears as she clung to him, but the way she held on, she needed this touch as much as he did.

She also needed sleep. In a comfortable bed, away from the side of a patient whose rasping breaths woke her every few minutes.

He rubbed one hand up her back and murmured into her hair. "Will you and Naomi and Mary Ellen come back to the ranch with us?"

She looked up at his face. "Yes." But something in her voice hesitated. What did she need from him? He wasn't good at reading a woman's mind. Dinah often spoke plainly, so he didn't have to guess with her. But this time, she seemed to be waiting for him to set her mind at ease.

Maybe she needed assurance of what he'd said before, after her sister's babe had just been born. They'd been rushed, and she might not have understood everything he intended. "I meant what I said the other day. I was wrong about forcing others to stay away from the ranch. It's going to be hard for me, and I'll need you and my brothers to keep me in line, but I'm determined to seek God's help with protecting us all. To not lock us down completely."

A smile curved her mouth. "I'm glad. So thankful." But still, her voice held a catch. A hesitation. What was he missing?

He squeezed her waist. "Your sister and the babe are welcome to stay as long as they want. Forever if that's what the two of you decide. We can build a bunk house for my brothers, and she can have her own little cabin when she's ready."

Dinah's brows rose, and something a little playful touched her eyes. "That's nice of you. And where do you intend for me to sleep?"

Like a waterfall crashing over him, realization slammed in. He'd not made clear that his proposal from before still stood, a lantern in a snowstorm, begging her to come near and say yes.

This he could remedy.

He dropped to one knee, the way Mum always told the story of how Dat proposed. "Dinah Wallace. From the day I met you and tried to run you off the ranch, you've taken me by surprise. Swept in and saved me and my family. Not always in the way I wanted, but always how I needed. Your caring. Your passion. Your strength. They drew me in from the beginning. Though I'm a troublesome creature, will you marry me and make me the happiest of men?"

Once more, a sheen made her eyes glimmer, but this time the light inside them shone with joy. She didn't answer right away, and a smile tickled the corners of her mouth. That was good, right? Was she too full of emotion to speak? Surely she wasn't still trying to decide. *Lord, I know I've been asking for a lot lately, but...*

Finally, she cleared her throat. "My answer to that will depend on how you respond to what I asked a moment ago."

He hesitated. What she'd asked...about sleeping arrangements? The teasing glint that crept back into her gaze showed he'd hit on it.

Keeping hold of her hands, he rose to his feet with a playful growl and pulled her tight against him. "With me, woman. Always with me. You can plant our bed in whatever house you wish, as long as you're there by my side."

Then he lowered his mouth to hers. After the first brush of his lips, she pulled back enough to let out a few breathy words. "I guess my answer is yes then."

Joy swept through him as he closed in to celebrate.

EPILOGUE

"*L*ook how fast she's growing. I wish I'd brought a scale to weigh her." Dinah wrapped the blanket back around Mary Ellen to warm the babe after her examination.

"Add it to the list. Jude said he'll ride to Missoula next week." Jericho spoke from the bench near the fire where he carved a new pair of walking sticks for Jonah. A better fitting pair.

Her heart stirred as she studied him. He'd worked so hard this past fortnight to prove he'd changed. That he was willing to trust those he cared about into God's hands. How could she not love him more and more each day?

He must have felt her gaze, for he looked up. The warmth in his eyes stirred more than her heart, heating her insides. She snuggled the babe against her shoulder and turned purposeful strides toward Jericho.

Jonah sat up in bed, his nose in a book, and Naomi was taking a much-needed nap. With Lillian working in the barn and the others out with the stock, she and Jericho could have a few minutes mostly to themselves. If she didn't count Jonah and the babe, of course. Perhaps if the two of them whispered, they wouldn't garner Jonah's attention.

She snuggled in against Jericho's side on the bench as he wrapped an arm around her, pressing a kiss against her temple. Her eyes drifted shut as his mouth lingered there, his breath caressing. Every touch from this man brought her nerves to life.

"Two Stones should be here any day now," he murmured against her hair. "But you can be sure I'm not letting anyone leave until he comes. No chance I'll risk a delay in marrying you."

She allowed a smile. The moment they'd all returned to the ranch, he sent Jude to the Salish village to find Two Stones. Then he'd tasked his friend to seek out a minister he knew in Helena and bring him here to the ranch posthaste.

She could have offered to go with Jericho to the town to find the man. But she didn't dare leave Naomi and the baby yet. And they both wanted their family around for the nuptials.

Mary Ellen stirred on her shoulder, bouncing her head as she searched for milk. Dinah rubbed her tiny back. "Are you hungry again, sweet one? You need lots of food to grow big and strong, don't you?"

As hard as it was to leave Jericho's side, she pushed to her feet and started toward the bedchamber where Naomi slept. Her sister hadn't left the room much these past days. Mary Ellen needed to nurse so often, and when Naomi wasn't caring for the babe, she seemed exhausted.

Was it more than the weariness of new motherhood? Dinah had attended many births and checked in with each mother and child frequently after. But this was the first time she'd overseen the daily care of a new mother.

Naomi didn't answer her soft knock, but when Dinah pushed open the door, her sister's eyes flicked open. They held a red-tinged sheen that might be exhaustion...or could be the result of tears.

Dinah padded to the bedside and settled onto the edge of the mattress.

Her sister pushed up in bed. "Is she hungry again?"

A glance at the babe rooting in the curve of Dinah's neck gave the answer well enough. Dinah eased her away so she could place her in Naomi's arms. "She's determined to grow."

As Naomi took her daughter, the smile sweetening her expression eased the worry in Dinah's chest. Being a new mother was hard, both physically and mentally. But Naomi had been created for this exact role.

Give her strength, Lord. Help this sweet child grow in wisdom and stature and favor, just as Jesus did.

When suckling sounds filled the air, Naomi lay her head back against the headboard. "Thank you."

That seemed to be a dismissal, and likely the two would appreciate privacy.

Dinah rested a hand on her sister's arm. "I'll come check on you in a little while to see if you want me to take her."

Naomi shook her head. "She'll probably sleep when she's full."

After standing, Dinah pressed a kiss to her sister's brow. "I love you, Na. I'm here for anything you need."

When she pulled back, Naomi met her gaze with a weary smile. "Thank you." Once more, her eyes glistened. Emotions could be abundant after enduring all her sister had.

She gave Naomi's arm a light squeeze, then turned and made her way back to the main room. As she latched Naomi's door behind her, Jericho laid aside the stick he'd been working on and stood.

He slid a silent glance toward Jonah, still hidden behind his book, and motioned her toward the front door. She followed him past his brother and stepped out before him.

The gust of wind made her turn back for her coat that hung on a peg inside, but Jericho had already picked it up with his own. He held hers out for her first, then slipped into his.

When his hands were free, he pulled her close, brushing his lips over hers once, then resting his forehead against her brow so his breath warmed her nose. She let her eyes sink closed to relish the tenderness in his touch. He was strong, virile, and protective to the core, yet it was that very protectiveness that made him treat those he loved—her especially—with a gentleness that made her feel fully treasured.

"What's wrong?" His voice called her from that place of peace, back to the niggle of worry that pressed in her chest.

She opened her eyes to his earnest gaze searching her face. No need to hold anything back from him. "I don't know if I should be worried about Naomi or not. She's sleeping more than I would expect, though she *is* up with the babe throughout the night. She seems sad though. Maybe it's just weariness. Caring for a babe is hard work. Exhausting, especially as her body is still healing."

Maybe she shouldn't be so frank with a man, especially one who wasn't yet her husband.

Lines furrowed his brow. "Your instincts aren't usually wrong. What can we do to help her? Is there something we can bring from Missoula that would make things easier? Can the rest of us help more?"

A fresh wave of love warmed through her, and she cradled his cheek. "I don't think there's anything more than what I'm already doing. Mary Ellen seems to be thriving. Far more than I would have thought with her born so early." She worked for a smile. "I'm just being a worried sister, but she'll feel better as the babe grows larger and they both get more sleep."

He shifted his hands from her back, sliding them down her arms to cup her fingers within his. His eyes closed, and it took her a second to realize what he intended.

"Father in Heaven, You call us to cast our worries on You, for

You care for us." As he lifted his voice in prayer, she closed her eyes and sank into the peace of knowing the weight of her sister's happiness didn't rest on her shoulders alone. Jericho would walk this journey with her.

And even more, the Father would guide them, shelter them, and bring them all to the fullness of the life He had planned for them.

With this man beside her, she couldn't wait to see where each adventurous twist would lead them.

∼

I pray you loved Jericho and Dinah's story!
Would you like to receive a **free bonus epilogue of their wedding and a peek at their happily ever after?**
Get the bonus epilogue and sign-up for insider email updates at https://mistymbeller.com/HTMMH-bonus-epilogue

∼

*N*ow are you ready for Jude's story?

Turn the page for a sneak peek of *Protecting the Mountain Man's Treasure*, book 2 in the Brothers of Sapphire Mountain Ranch series!

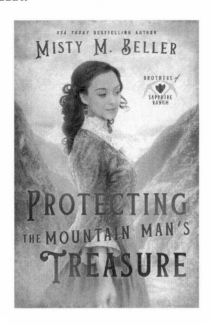

CHAPTER ONE

The sun hung low in the sky, casting a golden glow over the bustling streets of New York City as Jude Coulter stepped out of the ornate office building. The marble and opulence felt foreign compared to the rugged mountains of his family ranch in the Montana Territory he knew so well.

"Have an excellent day, Mr. Coulter." The uniformed man who'd opened the door for him gave a half bow before closing it behind him.

Jude nodded his thanks, though the fellow had already disappeared. He tightened his grip on the carpet bags in each hand and started down the cascade of steps to the street.

It now seemed foolish to carry so many gold coins with him instead of having them sent to the train station by delivery wagon—in padded unmarked crates of course, the same way he'd brought the sapphires from their ranch all the way to the city.

He'd been worried about traveling with so much money though. It seemed safer to always have it with him. Especially since it wasn't too much for him to carry himself.

Yet perhaps these two bags made him stand out from others.

The cab he'd ridden in from the train station still waited for him on the street, as he'd instructed. When he reached the rig, he climbed in. Did the driver wonder what was in the bags? Jude hadn't had them when he first hired the man back at the train station, so their presence now would surely raise a question in his mind.

"The station, sir?" The wiry man on the bench looked back at Jude, brows raised.

"Yes. Thank you." He should have thought to give the direction, not expect the fellow to read his mind. He was out of his element here, no question.

The driver called to the horse, and the cab lurched forward, weaving into the flow of traffic.

Flow might be a generous word. More like a swirl.

Hordes of people and vehicles moved in every direction, their sounds melding into a discordant chorus. Shouts. Calls from street vendors. Horses snorting and shod hooves clopping against cement and stone. Wagon wheels, the creaking of so many harnesses. Too many sounds to dissect, and the effort tightened his body until his head pounded.

He closed his eyes and brought up a memory of the creek on their ranch, the peaceful murmur as it flowed over rocks. That's where they'd first found the sapphires. Blue and pink stones lying visible among the many brown and gold-flecked pebbles.

The gold wasn't real, of course. Just pretty mica. Which is why the place wasn't overrun with miners like other parts of the Montana Territory. But Dat had realized the significance of the other colored stones.

Jude had loved working with him back then. Then when Dat and Mum passed on, he'd spent long days by himself at the creek, searching for more sapphires. Digging in the areas where they'd found the most.

Mining the gems that Dat had treasured became Jude's special role. His contribution to the family. His responsibility.

"Here we are." The driver's words sounded just as the cab jolted to a stop. The vehicle rocked as the horse found its footing.

Jude straightened and scanned the busy station. Even more people packed in here than on the street. He gripped his bags and stepped from the cart.

He had to set down one of the satchels to pull out payment for the driver. "Thank you. Will that suffice?" He'd added another dollar to the amount the man had quoted for the round trip.

The cabby's teeth flashed as he nodded. "That'll do."

Jude re-secured his grip on both bags, and turned toward the end of the station where he'd left his other piece of luggage in locked storage.

The porter who'd helped him before was speaking to a dark-haired woman, so Jude waited his turn. As the man gathered her luggage, she was asking about trains heading west, and the porter was explaining the different options available.

Though she didn't say so exactly, her words sounded like she was traveling by herself. That seemed odd, but maybe things were done differently in the city.

She was a pretty thing. Not bigger than a minute, with dark hair pulled back in a tight knot. Though she was asking questions, she seemed to know exactly what answers she needed. As though the man was simply filling in gaps of her knowledge.

"Thank you, sir. Good day." Her final words held a light accent that hadn't showed in her earlier questions. Not strong, but...different.

When she turned to walk past Jude, she offered a polite smile. Her dark eyes held just a hint of a slant, a look that made her beauty even more striking than he'd first thought.

He tipped his chin in greeting. Should he also say hello?

She passed before he could decide, so he turned to the porter.

"How can I help you, sir?" The man looked like he was forcing pleasantness he didn't feel. Dealing with strangers all day couldn't be easy.

"I have a bag in holding." Jericho nodded toward his piece. "That one. Coulter is the name."

The porter nodded and pulled the carpet bag out of the fenced area. "May I see your ticket, please?"

Jude set down his load and pulled the stub from his pocket, then handed it over.

The porter nodded. "Very good." He handed over the bag, then pointed to a large number suspended from the metal rafters by the train tracks. "You'll be leaving from platform number three."

After thanking the man, Jude meandered toward the spot. A crowd had already gathered, but he worked his way around the edge until he reached a place to stand and wait on the platform.

It would be a quarter hour before the train arrived, but he'd wait here. The sooner he boarded the train, the sooner he would get to the Montana Territory.

And home.

He'd never realized how important the peace and quiet of the mountain wilderness had become to him.

Angela Larkin watched the man from a distance, doing her best to keep a bored look that showed neither the target of her gaze, nor the way her heart pounded louder than the incoming train. She would likely have a long journey, unless she could learn what she needed during one of the early legs. If she had to travel all the way to the western territories, she was prepared to do so.

She carried a significant responsibility with this assignment, and she would fulfill her part no matter what it required. She took a deep breath and smoothed the folds in her dress. She was more than capable.

Lord, guide me. This would be a delicate dance of deception and trust, and she had every intention of leading.

The arriving passengers had finished disembarking, and the porter began calling for boarding to begin. She followed the surge of people moving toward the cars. One thing she'd learned early on in this city was to go with the flow when possible. You could weave your way through as you needed to, but you'd reach your goal much faster by working with people than trying to outsmart them. That motto generally proved accurate both in traffic, and in accomplishing each mission she was assigned by the central office.

As she boarded and made her way into one of the passenger cars, she did her best to keep the target in view. She stopped in the same car he did, and slid into a seat three rows behind him. His back was to her, but that was fine. He wouldn't see how often she watched him.

When all had been loaded, the train shuddered, then started forward with an unsteady rocking motion. An older man still standing in the aisle stumbled. Her target started to jump up to help the man, but he grunted and sank onto his bench before Coulter could act.

As the train picked up speed and the view through the windows changed from city streets to rolling countryside, the rocking of the car eased into a smoother rhythm.

She reached for the book in her bag, but she'd barely opened to her marker when a movement ahead caught her notice.

Coulter rose to his feet and stepped into the aisle. He paused for a moment, gripping his seat back as he found his balance with the movement of the train.

She kept her focus on the page before her, watching him from the edge of her gaze. Should she look up and smile? Sometimes it was better for the target to be aware of her, seeing her as just another passenger. Especially if she had a convincing backstory. More often though, she succeeded best when she could fade into the background.

So she kept her gaze down, reading the same line over and over as he moved slowly down the aisle toward her. The outside platform was through the door behind her, and he probably wanted air.

As he passed beside her, a violent jerk shook the train.

Gasps filled the air, and Jude grabbed onto her seat back to keep from tumbling. A scraping sounded above her, and she spun to see its source.

"Watch out." Jude lunged behind her, diving for a box that slid off the upper shelf. A woman screamed.

Angela lost sight of him as he pulled the box sideways, away from the elderly woman on the bench behind Angela.

A crash sounded, and she leaped from her seat to make sure Jude hadn't hurt himself.

The woman screamed again, the one he'd just saved with his quick actions.

But Jude himself lay on the floor, his head slumped against the side of the crate. Eyes closed.

"Mr. Coulter!" Angela sprang to his side, dropping to her knees.

Lord, don't let him be dead. His chest rose with a breath, so she called again, daring to touch his shoulder for a gentle shake. "Mr. Coulter."

He didn't blink. No sign of alertness.

His head was pushed forward by the box, his chin pushed into his neck. With one hand under his head, she pulled the crate out and laid him flat on the train floor.

He still didn't open his eyes.

Her mind scrambled for what to do next. She needed help. She was skilled at many things, but her medical knowledge wasn't nearly strong enough for this situation.

She looked up at the worried faces gathered around them. "Is anyone a doctor?"

No matter what, she couldn't let anything happen to Jude Coulter until he led her back to the source of the sapphires he'd just delivered.

A great deal more than her job depended on her succeeding in this mission.

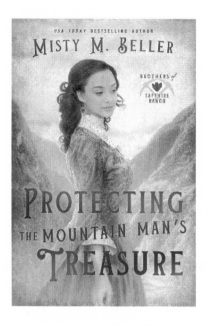

Get PROTECTING THE MOUNTAIN MAN'S TREA-SURE, book 2 in the Brothers of Sapphire Ranch series, at your favorite retailer!

Did you enjoy Jericho and Dinah's story? I hope so!
Would you take a quick minute to leave a review where you purchased the book?
It doesn't have to be long. Just a sentence or two telling what you liked about the story!

To receive a free book and get updates when new Misty M. Beller books release, go to https://mistymbeller.com/freebook

ALSO BY MISTY M. BELLER

Freedom in the Mountain Wind

Hope in the Mountain River

Light in the Mountain Sky

Courage in the Mountain Wilderness

Faith in the Mountain Valley

Honor in the Mountain Refuge

Peace in the Mountain Haven

Grace on the Mountain Trail

Calm in the Mountain Storm

Joy on the Mountain Peak

Brides of Laurent

A Warrior's Heart

A Healer's Promise

A Daughter's Courage

Hearts of Montana

Hope's Highest Mountain

Love's Mountain Quest

Faith's Mountain Home

Honor's Mountain Promise

Texas Rancher Trilogy

The Rancher Takes a Cook

The Ranger Takes a Bride

The Rancher Takes a Cowgirl

Wyoming Mountain Tales

A Pony Express Romance

A Rocky Mountain Romance

A Sweetwater River Romance

A Mountain Christmas Romance

ABOUT THE AUTHOR

 **Misty M. Beller** is a *USA Today* best-selling author of romantic mountain stories, set on the 1800s frontier and woven with the truth of God's love.

Raised on a farm and surrounded by family, Misty developed her love for horses, history, and adventure. These days, her husband and children provide fresh adventure every day, keeping her both grounded and crazy.

Misty's passion is to create inspiring Christian fiction infused with the grandeur of the mountains, writing historical romance that displays God's abundant love through the twists and turns in the lives of her characters.

Sharing her stories with readers is a dream come true for Misty. She writes from her country home in South Carolina and escapes to the mountains any chance she gets.

Connect with Misty at <u>www.MistyMBeller.com</u>

Made in United States
Troutdale, OR
08/14/2023

12083814R00174